Moonlight
&
Ashes

Also by Sophie Masson

(Random House Australia)

Written as Isabelle Merlin

Three Wishes
Pop Princess
Cupid's Arrow
Bright Angel

The Chronicles of El Jisal series

Snow, Fire, Sword
The Curse of Zohreh
The Tyrant's Nephew
The Maharajah's Ghost

Edited by Sophie Masson

The Road to Camelot

Moonlight
&
Ashes

Sophie Masson

RANDOM HOUSE AUSTRALIA

A Random House book
Published by Random House Australia Pty Ltd
Level 3, 100 Pacific Highway, North Sydney NSW 2060
www.randomhouse.com.au

First published by Random House Australia in 2012

Addresses for companies within the Random House Group can be found at
www.randomhouse.com.au/offices.

National Library of Australia
Cataloguing-in-Publication Entry

Author: Masson, Sophie, 1959–
Title: Moonlight & ashes / Sophie Masson.
ISBN: 978 1 74275 379 9 (pbk.)
Target Audience: For secondary school age.
Subjects: Fairy tales.
Dewey Number: A823.3

Cover illustration by Tammara Markegard
Cover design by Christabella Designs
Typeset by Midland Typesetters, Australia
Printed in Australia by Griffin Press, an accredited ISO AS/NZS 14001:2004
Environmental Management System printer

Random House Australia uses papers that are natural, renewable and recyclable
products and made from wood grown in sustainable forests. The logging and
manufacturing processes are expected to conform to the environmental regulations
of the country of origin.

One

Once upon a time, I would have walked in through the beautiful carved doors of the Angel Patisserie and Tea Salon. Once, and not so long ago either, my feet would have glided across the soft carpet in smart shoes, my long skirts swishing behind my mother's as we headed to our favourite table looking out across St Hilda's Square at the bustling morning crowds. Once, we would have sat on the plush velvet chairs while the waiter brought us plates of cream puffs, chocolate hazelnut tart or cream-layered honey sponge served on delicate china plates edged with gilt. We'd have eaten our cakes and sipped fragrant tea from fine cups as the owner of the Angel, Monsieur Thomas, resplendent in a blue silk waistcoat and white tail coat, would have made sure to stop by our table and wish us good day. He'd have told Mama how fine she was looking, and me how much of a young lady I was becoming. Mama and I would giggle about it afterwards because, although Monsieur Thomas always said the same thing, it was always in such a hushed tone as if he was telling us a secret instead of a rather tedious politeness.

That was then. If I tried to go in through the front door of the Angel now, Monsieur Thomas would have me thrown out. And no wonder for my feet, now clad in old shoes that let in the rain, are not fit to tread on the soft carpets. My skirts, patched and old, no longer swish but flop limply around me. And the taste of those cakes is nothing more than a sweet, distant memory. These days I have to go around the back of the Angel and wait in the dingy little courtyard no proper customer ever sees. I am handed the box of cakes my stepmother and stepsisters have ordered, and am warned that if I so much as think of opening it I will have the police set on me. I am told to 'Begone!' by people who once would have bowed to me as the daughter of Sir Claus dez Mestmor, a rich and important nobleman from one of the oldest families in Ashberg. They all know I have become a servant in my own father's house and that has made all the difference. I used to think people were nice to me because they liked me. Now I know better.

But not everyone is like that. Even at the Angel, where faces are hard as overcooked pastry and tongues bitter as wormwood. There's Maria, the scullery maid, who has never stopped being nice to me even though it would cost her her job if anyone were to find out. When she can, Maria slips me bits and pieces she's kept from the kitchens, and always with a kind word or two which is almost as comforting. This day, she had a surprise for me. As I stood in the courtyard waiting for a box of cakes, trying to avoid the drips from the clearing rain, she crept out and handed me a little parcel done up in brown paper and string. 'Happy birthday, Selena,' she whispered, giving me a quick smile before scuttling back in just as Rudi, a waiter who never misses an opportunity to laugh at me, came out. He's got his eye on my stepsister Babette, and thinks that will get in her good books, though if he thinks Babette will even look once, let alone twice, at a waiter, no matter how fine his waistcoat, he's in for a great disappointment. To her and Odette, waiters may as well not exist, or at least no more than as some kind of useful machine.

That morning, as usual, I put up with his heavy attempts at wit at my expense to avoid a quarrel I could not afford to have. Not if I am to keep the promise I made to my dear mother two years ago on her deathbed, whose loss I still feel like an arrow to the heart. I promised her that I would not abandon my father, no matter what was to happen. Papa is not a man who can cope with illness, and my poor mother had been sick for a year or more. She had lost the good looks that had made him forget her humble origins and fall in love with her. I think she knew he could not stay alone for long, and so it proved – for within a few months he had married Grizelda, a rich widow from the imperial capital, Faustina. She had brought her daughters, Babette and Odette, home to Ashberg and had set about removing all reminders of my mother, throwing out her pictures and books, of which I could save but a few. And so my ordeal began.

Of course, there are moments when rage and sorrow boil within me like scalding pitch. When I think of my weak and indifferent father who seems to have almost forgotten my existence altogether. When I remember the day my stepmother summoned me to triumphantly announce the annulment of my parents' marriage and, in turn, my social demotion in the eyes of the law to a mere 'natural daughter' of my father, dependent entirely on his goodwill. When my mother's portrait was burned and her books thrown out, except for the few I managed to hide. When my stepsisters taunt me with a cruel nickname, Ashes, and delight in tormenting me with tales of the parties they've been to, the young men who shower them with compliments, the fine dresses they've ordered from the best seamstresses in the city, and the exciting trips they'll go on while I have to stay in my kitchen.

In those moments the promise I made to Mama seems like a cross that's much too hard to bear. But, always, I master myself; I cannot break my promise to her for fear of losing my honour. They have taken everything else – I will not let them take my word as well. Alone in my room at night I take out one of Mama's books and, though I've read each many times over the years, cover to cover, I take comfort in it. I remember Mama's voice as she read to me, her smile as she read to herself, and it brings her close to me once again. I whisper to the empty room as though she were there. I whisper how I feel – how I really feel – deep inside. It helps me to be patient, to try and hold fast to the hope that my mother would never have bound me to such a promise if she did not think that one day things would get better for me.

Maria's kindness touched me. Sixteen. I turned sixteen today. I didn't expect anyone to remember. My father's away, like he is nearly all the time these days, and his new family would rather think I had sprung from an amoeba. Anyway, who ever heard of a servant having a birthday? Squelching home through the wet streets, carefully holding the box of cakes, I thought of the pleasure I'd have in opening her little parcel later that night. It would mark the day that someone other than myself had remembered. Sixteen – the coming of age, when you are no longer a girl but a woman. I remember Mama saying how this important birthday was marked in her own forest village, far away. How on your sixteenth birthday you'd be given a dish of honey and cream, a crown of roses and a hazel twig. It seemed a strange combination to me and I always asked why, *why*. But she would only smile and say that on my sixteenth birthday, she would tell me.

I was so absorbed in my thoughts and bittersweet memories that I didn't notice the carriage heading down the street behind me. It was only as it was almost upon me that I suddenly heard the rumbling of wheels and the coachman's shout, and tried to jump aside. Instead, I tripped and fell sprawling in the gutter, the cakes flying out of my hands as the carriage squeezed past me with just inches to spare. As I looked after it, breathless from the fright, I saw it was completely closed with black blinds drawn down across the windows. And my heart skipped a beat as I recognised the crest on the side of the door to be the sinister snake and two wands of the Mancers.

Two

☽

By the time I'd gathered my wits together, the carriage had hurtled around the corner and disappeared. I knew I'd be in trouble for the ruined cakes but just at that moment I didn't much care. I was only relieved that whoever was in that carriage had paid me no attention. Not that it much mattered which of the Mancers it was, or even of what rank or seniority – the mere fact it was one of them was enough. My mother had made sure I knew that much.

Because that was the other thing she'd said to me as she lay there on her deathbed, patiently waiting for my father to finally make an appearance before she passed to the next world. She'd told me to come close and whispered in my ear, her dying breath as mustily sweet as a withering rose, 'My darling Selena, you must know the truth. But you must keep it to yourself as tightly as your promise not to desert your father. For if you do not and the Mancers get to hear of it . . .'

A look of terror had passed over her face then – a look that haunts me to this day. I whispered, my voice thick with tears I could hardly hold back, 'Mama, what is it? What have the Mancers to do with *us*?'

'Nothing,' she had said, her voice trembling. 'Nothing, for I have tried with all my might and main to keep it that way and you must do so too, my darling, or else everything will have been in vain and the sacrifice I made to be with your father will have turned to dust and ashes.'

Dust and ashes! That is what my life has become since Mama's death, I thought as I trudged up the street towards the house that felt like prison rather than home. I thought of the look in Mama's eyes as she had clasped my hand tightly with the desperate strength of the dying, and as she told me the truth of what I was – of what she had been.

A moon-sister. I'd heard of them, of course. Who hadn't? They were legendary. They lived in whispered stories, and glared menacingly from the pages of history books. Once, they had been as important as the Mancers; the two co-existing peacefully. But theirs is a forbidden knowledge now. The kind that's been outlawed for more than a hundred years, since the time of Lady Serafina. Better known as the Grey Widow, she was the most powerful of all moon-sisters at the time and perhaps the most powerful ever. In history books, she is depicted as a grim hag with crooked teeth and stringy hair. It doesn't quite fit, however, with the legend that she somehow bewitched the Emperor of the time, Karl the Great. The story goes that when she had gained the Emperor's confidence – and, some say, even his love – Lady Serafina treacherously plotted a rebellion against him, planning to lay waste to the Empire and to cast a terrible spell that would have killed half its inhabitants and turned the remainder into mindless slaves. Or so we are told.

But her plans failed because the Chief Mancer had a good network of spies all over the Empire. The result was the capture, confession and execution of the Grey Widow and hundreds, even thousands, of her followers, including a motley crew of shapeshifters, village wizards and fortune-tellers. As to the remaining moon-sisters, even those who had taken no part in the rebellion, they were hunted down and slaughtered along with their families, and that is how, according to the history books, 'this evil, tainted blood' vanished completely off the face of the earth. Any mention of the moon-sisters other than as evil traitors has been forbidden.

What's more, all kinds of magic except that which is practised by the Mancers has been strictly forbidden within the borders of the Faustine Empire. No more fortune-telling, spell-making, potion-brewing, card-reading or ghost-raising. Shapeshifters are now extinct in the Empire, and village wizards only a distant memory. The Mancers are not only the sole practitioners of magic of any kind, they also police everything to do with it. I'd never questioned it. Like everyone else, I feared the Mancers and their powers. But they were remote from my concerns; they did not intervene in ordinary lives. They were like black shadows hovering at the edge of our ordinary sunlit existence. I'd never imagined that, one day, that shadow might blot out the sun, as it did when I learned the truth about my mother's heritage.

The history books had been wrong. The moon-sisters hadn't all been killed. A few had escaped, vanishing into the deepest parts of the deepest forests. They had brought up children who inherited their gifts; and their secrets, bound in unbreakable oaths, were passed down in utter silence. For there was not to be a hint, a whisper, nor the slightest chance of a sign to the Mancers that there was any kind of surviving legacy of the moon-sisters.

My own mother had learned the truth from her mother and so it had gone, through the ages. But she'd had to turn her back on the knowledge when she fell in love with my father. He never knew the truth. He'd never have married her if he had – he is not a brave man. He had been bold enough marrying a forest girl so far below him in station. That was quite enough courage for him, no matter how beautiful and sweet she was. It had meant that for the rest of her life Mama had to hide her own potential. She could not practise any form of magic at all, not even a harmless fidelity potion when my father's attention began to wander. She couldn't even brew herbs to help her through her sickness. Nothing that could remotely be interpreted as magic was allowed to happen. *Nothing*. She took an oath to that effect. They all did, to protect the others. How many of them were there, hiding, unable to do a thing but pass on a seemingly useless knowledge that could never ever be applied?

I couldn't tell Mama, of course. I couldn't tell her how the secret she'd passed on to me was one I wished I'd never known. Not because it put me in danger, although it did do that, but because it was useless. Being a moon-sister hadn't helped her. In fact, it had made her life more difficult. What is the good of having magic in your bones – in your blood – if you can never use it? It's worse than useless, because it's a constant frustration. And I felt that frustration had eaten away at my mother's very heart, that the 'tainted blood' had slowly killed her every bit as much as her illness and my father's indifference. So can you blame me for rejecting the knowledge? Mama had said that until the right time came, I had to keep it tight inside me like the promise I'd made not to abandon my father. I hadn't asked her what she meant by 'the right time'; I hadn't wanted to talk about it. But I have done as she asked. I have kept the knowledge of my heritage locked and bound inside and secured with chains, and not because I was afraid but because I hated it.

Normally, I can avoid thinking about it. Days and weeks can go past before I remember that in my veins runs the blood of the fabled, notorious enchantresses. But what I cannot forget is that I have gone from being Selena, cherished daughter of the house, to 'Ashes', the servant girl crouching in the cinders of the kitchen fireplace. All the moon-sister magic in the world can do nothing about that because I cannot ever admit to a living soul what my mother told me, for if I did, I would be in an even worse position than I am now. If Grizelda and her daughters had even an inkling of my secret, I would not put it past them to denounce me to the Mancers. They would do so anonymously, of course, as they wouldn't want even a breath of the scandal to jeopardise their standing in Ashberg. But even if they didn't denounce me, the mere fact they'd know would give them a whip hand over me for ever and ever. So I have been very careful to avoid even a stray thought about it in case I betray myself in some way.

It is rare to see a Mancer in the streets, at least it is in Ashberg. Of course, the ones here are only a provincial branch of the Mancer headquarters in Faustina. Their Ashberg quarters are located within a part of the castle on top of the hill, just over the river; quarters that no-one can enter except with special licence. It's said that there are sights there that would make your hair stand on end. But they are only rumours, for it would be more than your life's worth to tell of what you'd seen if you were one of the few people who've actually been there, such as tradesmen and officials. It is said they make outsiders sign a document that spells out the dire consequences of blabbing and, so far as I know, no-one has ever dared to go against it.

Not that Mancers are much in evidence usually. They couldn't care less about the ordinary populace and most people think that if you don't give them a reason to take an interest in you – that is, if you do not break the law on magic – then they will leave you alone. After the Emperor, they are the greatest power in the empire, certainly much greater than the Ashberg city authorities, and are a law unto themselves. And if by accident or design you fall into their clutches – then God help you, because no-one else will.

I'd known I would pay for the ruined cakes, and so I did. They had been specially ordered for an afternoon tea my stepmother was to host the next day and she would now have to make do with whichever ordinary pastries the Angel might be able to supply. All the guests would know they were just the sort anyone could buy in the shop, that they'd not been specially made for her, and the Lady Grizelda's standing would suffer mildly as a result, which was an unspeakable crime to her and, of course, entirely my fault.

My stepmother never hits me. She knows better than to do that, aware that even my weak and cowardly father might rebel if she lifted a hand against me. Besides, violence isn't her style. Cruelty and the refinements of humiliation are her weapons of choice as well as the more blunt instruments of hunger and exhaustion. So I went without supper that night, not even the leftovers I am usually allowed. The housekeeper Mrs Jager, who has always disliked me on principle – she came with my step-mother from Faustina along with the current staff who replaced our previous servants – made me polish every scrap of silver in the place, scrub the kitchen floor twice over and iron the already-ironed tablecloths. And when I was so tired I thought I might faint, after the rest of the staff had long gone to bed, she told me sharply that I'd have to get up an hour earlier the next morning to darn my stepsisters' stockings and mend their clothes.

It was no good protesting that I had done it all that very morning; there was no doubt in my mind that Babette and Odette were quite capable of deliberately making new holes in their stockings and ripping ribbons off their dresses in order to join in their mother's petty games. Although Babette and Odette each have their own personal maid, it is always up to me to perform these menial tasks. Mrs Jager says it is kindly intended, that it is to improve my sewing skills and hence my future employability. But I know better. It is intended, as everything that my stepmother and her daughters do, to try and break my spirit.

I was so tired, I was beyond rage and hatred. Or maybe it was still the shock of seeing that black carriage. Whatever it was, by the time I was back in my poky little room that backed onto the kitchen fireplace (Mrs Jager kept saying how lucky I was to live there and not in the attic) I didn't even have the strength to change into my nightdress but just fell fully clothed onto the narrow bed. It was only when I turned on my side that I felt a sharp bump in my pocket and remembered Maria's gift and that today I had turned sixteen. I don't cry – not usually – for there is no point, but at that moment, as I opened the little parcel to reveal a small, heart-shaped locket on a cheap chain, tears welled in my eyes. Made of green enamel, it was the sort of thing you can buy at fairs – the only kind of gift poor Maria could afford. The locket had a little catch so you could open it and put something inside – though the space was so small and thin it was hard to know what one could put in there. Gently, I unhooked the clasp of the chain and fastened the locket around my neck, hiding it under my clothes where it would not be seen. Once, I'd owned beautiful, costly jewellery, brought back by my father from his trips abroad – jewels which have long vanished into my stepsisters' keep. But not one of those glittering necklaces or bracelets or rings had touched me half as much as this humble trinket on its tawdry chain. Somehow this calmed me so that instead of lying there, overtired, I fell instantly into a deep sleep.

Three

)

I am in a forest. It is green and gold with sunlight filtering through leaves. The grass is lush and there are flowers growing at the foot of trees whose leaves, bathed in the golden light, look like they're made of the finest silk. It is a beautiful place, peaceful and quiet but for the rustling of leaves and water nearby. Drawn to the sound, I walk towards it and find a waterfall gushing out over a shelf of ebony-coloured rocks into a pool that sparkles like diamonds.

The water is so irresistible I cup my hands to drink, and as I do so, I feel a tap on my shoulder. I turn around – and there is my mother. She looks not like the last time I saw her when her face was shadowed by illness and etched with lines of suffering. She looks like she used to long ago, when I was a child. She is young and beautiful; her hair jet-black, her lips red, her radiant skin has a peachy bloom and her eyes are bright with the glorious, clear green that I remember – as green as the sunlit leaves of this forest.

'Oh Mama,' I cry as I am folded in her arms. I can smell her sweet flowery scent and I do not weep because I know that everything will be all right. Each time I have dreamed of her it has been at times of great strain. Times when sorrow and despair have crushed my heart, when I have thought I could no longer go on. Always then would she come to me in dreams and I would be folded in her arms. And somehow she passes on the strength for me to carry on. But this time it is different. For though I feel that everything will be all right, just like the other times, it is only for a moment and then everything I have tried to repress every day boils up inside me and I wrench myself from her grasp and shout, 'No! It is not enough, not any more! Not any more, do you hear?'

She just stands and looks at me, saying nothing, and I cannot bear it. It tears my soul to speak to her like this but I have to. 'I cannot take this any longer, do you understand? You can't expect me to.'

'You are sixteen today, my daughter,' my mother says, quietly.

'Yes,' I say furiously, 'and what of it?'

'Things will change, my daughter. Listen well. Your father will ask you what you want for your birthday.'

I laughed. 'Father? He has forgotten I exist let alone that it is my birthday. He is never home if he can help it. And when he is at home, he never does anything to –'

'He visited my resting place,' she says gently and I am silenced. He has not been to Mama's grave since the day of her funeral. Never. While Mama's grave is a long way from the house, on the other side of the city, I have managed to go there when I can without Grizelda's knowledge – I do not want her anywhere near my feelings for my mother. But I have always gone alone, and never with my father.

'Last night when he came,' said my mother, 'the moon was reaching fullness. A twig from a nearby hazel tree dropped at his feet while he was there. He picked it up and put it in his pocket. That is what you must ask for when he wants to know what you would like for your birthday.'

I stare at her, confused, the back of my neck prickling. I suddenly remember – back in her home village, on their sixteenth birthday, girls were given a crown of roses, a dish of honey and cream, and a hazel twig.

'It is only this you must ask for, no matter what he offers,' she goes on, softly. 'But you must not tell him why.'

'Which will be easy as I do not know why myself.'

'My darling daughter, my sweet Selena, you must trust me. I promise that if you do this, everything will change.'

I whisper, 'Mama, of course I trust you and I will do as you ask.' She clasps my hands, kisses me on the forehead, and vanishes leaving me all alone. Seconds later I wake up with my last cry still on my lips, 'Come back, Mama, please come back.'

There are tears running down my face and my hands are trembling. My forehead still feels warm from her kiss, the warm breath of enduring love. For a moment I feel like I cannot bear it, like my heart has been wrenched out of my body. Then, quite suddenly, like the first time I held Maria's locket in my hand, hope grows inside me. A tiny little shoot of hope, green and bright. This dream was not a mere comforting dream but a real guiding vision. Never before had Mama been so clear and so close. Never before had she told me to do anything apart from endure. Never

16

before had she promised things would change. And so they would.

It wasn't easy to hold on to my new-found hope as the day wore on and I was back on the treadmill of my daily round. In the hours before dawn, with only a mug of black tea and some stale toast, I started with a pile of mending. I sat there pricking my cold fingers on the sharp needle, my teeth chattering and my lap full of billows of tulle and organza and silk and velvet – the kinds of pretty things I would never wear again! It was hard to believe that I'd once had a new dress every few weeks, even more often, sometimes. I used to go with Mama to Madame Paulina, the best dressmaker in Ashberg, and together we would choose colours and fabrics and our favourite styles. Mama had always said it was much more fun to go there than for Madame Paulina to come to us, and she'd been right. That shop was a perfect marvel of mirrors and chandeliers, of soft carpets from far-off lands and wooden mannequins draped in swathes of material. Pretty assistants in pink and white gowns would wait on us while we leafed through huge books featuring designs of glorious dresses that had graced a ball in the court of the Emperor. As a child, I used to dream of going to just such a ball when I was grown up, dressed in one of Madame Paulina's creations. She used to smile fondly at me with my mother and assure me that one day I would. I now know it was not something she meant, of course. It was something she said at the edge of her lips, as Mama would say, and not from the heart. Like the other people who had once been so nice to me, I was just a bundle of position and fortune, that's all, and once that was over, why, so was their interest in me. These days, it is my stepmother and stepsisters who wear Madame Paulina's creations, while the dresses I once owned now rest in dusty trunks in the attic, for they are no longer suitable for my station in life. In any case, I've grown out of them. I used to sneak up to the attic when everyone was asleep and take out my dresses to remember old times, but I haven't done that for a long time for what is the point of turning the knife in my own wound when there are so many others eager to do it for me?

Madame Paulina comes to the house these days; my stepmother thinks that is the right way to deal with trades-people – to have them come to you rather than the other way around. But I never see her. Oh, no, I did see her once and I know she saw me but she made as if she hadn't.

After the mending came many other chores. And all this time there was no sign that my father was to return from his trip and nobody else in the house seemed to expect his arrival. Afternoon came, and with it the ladies Grizelda had invited to her 'collation'. Though I was allowed nowhere near the salon where they all fluttered and laughed and gossiped like a flock of bright malicious birds, I overheard snatches of their conversation as reported by the footmen while on their break. All the ladies, it appeared, had quite ignored the fact that the cakes weren't of the special kind, for they were agog with the news that Prince Leopold, the only child and heir of the ailing Emperor, would soon be visiting Ashberg. He had reportedly just returned from his studies at the famous University of Klugheitfurt, in the neighbouring Kingdom of Almain. He had been away from home for four years and there were big celebrations planned for his return, including a tour of the entire empire to reintroduce him to the people – hence the upcoming visit to Ashberg.

It wasn't just the ladies upstairs twittering over this news, for everyone downstairs was also filled with excitement. While Ashberg did get the occasional visit from minor members of the imperial family, there were rarely visits from those higher up. Leopold had come to Ashberg once before but only as a child long ago. And now, he was a grown man recently returned from university and ready to take on his duties as Crown Prince. Some even said he was looking for a bride. However you saw it, his coming would be a major event in Ashberg, and that thrilled everybody – from those like Grizelda and her friends, who envisaged being invited to glittering functions in his honour, to those like the servants who claimed a public holiday would surely be declared. It even infected me, for I thought that the Prince's visit might give me a few precious hours away from drudgery as my stepmother and stepsisters would probably spend a lot of time away from home and, thus, would forget about thinking up new ways of tormenting me. And so the little seed of hope planted by my dream didn't wither away but kept me going till the moment long after the visiting ladies had all fluttered, or rather lumbered, back home like low-flying pelicans, their stomachs filled with cream cakes, hot chocolate and tea. I'd only just got through the massive pile of washing-up when I received a sudden summons to come up at once to the study, where I found my father waiting for me.

He was sitting at a little desk, scratching away at some document when I came in. He lifted his head, not looking at me but at a point beside me. I was used to him doing that. I don't like looking my father in the eye – not because I hate him, on the contrary, it is because *I don't*. I don't want to see the cowardice and guilt in his eyes, I don't want to hear the pathetic self-justifying excuses that would make me despise and, yes, even hate him. It is not the same with my stepmother and her daughters, who I am free to hate even if I am helpless to act on it. Mama loved *him*. He is my father and whether I like it or not he is a part of me. And though after the annulment of my parents' marriage, Grizelda wanted him to completely disown me and turn me out – he would not. It is poor consolation but it *is* something. So on the very rare occasions we do meet, I do not look at him, and he does not look at me. It is easier that way.

This evening was a very rare occasion indeed, for Grizelda was not present as she usually is for our encounters. I do not know how he managed to get the courage to speak to me without her permission, or maybe he had asked her. Anyway, I was standing in front of him with my eyes looking anywhere but his face and his own glance seemingly fascinated by the very ordinary landscape painting which hung on the wall beside me. He told me that he'd finished his business earlier than he'd thought he would but had to leave again the next day. He told me he'd remembered my sixteenth birthday and went on to say that it was an important birthday for any young woman (I noted his choice of words – '*any* young woman' – and nearly lost my resolve not to hate him). When I still did not speak, he said, a little nervously, 'I'd like to give you a present. What do you want? A new dress? Jewellery? Books?' He knew I liked reading when I had the time. 'Or whatever you want, Selena.'

I felt a pang for the things that I would have loved to own but couldn't, remembering my promise to my mother. I said, quietly, 'I want the twig from my mother's grave.'

His head jerked up, his eyes finally meeting mine. He had gone quite pale. 'The . . . the . . . what?'

'The hazel twig, Father,' I said distinctly. 'The one you put in your pocket.'

Yes, it really *was* fear in his eyes – close to terror, actually. I felt an ignoble little spurt of pleasure at the realisation. But all he said was, 'You . . . are you sure that's what you –'

'Quite sure,' I said.

I saw him swallow. 'Very well.' He reached over to the armchair where he'd flung his coat and pulled something out of the pocket. Just as Mama had told me in the dream, it was a hazel twig. He handed it to me and said, with a pleading in his eyes, 'Selena, I only wish that –'

I couldn't let him finish. My throat dry, I managed to say, firmly, 'Thank you, and goodnight, Father.'

He just nodded, looking miserable and shamefaced and afraid. Part of me, the childish side, wished he would do something – anything – that would break this wall of ice between us. The greater part of me – proud and strong – was glad to turn away and leave him without another word or look, to leave him with that fearful question in his heart as to how I could possibly have known. I knew he would tell nobody. I had seen it in his eyes. And I had seen something else: that from now on he would avoid me even more than before.

Four

I was just leaving when I was stopped by Grizelda popping out of her room like a sinister jack-in-the-box. Although my stepmother is a hard, strong woman without the slightest trace of compassion or tenderness for anyone beyond her daughters, she has an ethereal and fragile beauty, with her cloud of silver-blonde hair, her alabaster skin and her dark blue eyes. But there is nothing in the least that is fragile about my stepmother in reality. Of course, when my father first married her, she was all sweetness and light – even to me – but it took very little time for her to change or, rather, to reveal her real self. And by then it was too late. He was in thrall to her, body and soul, and I – well, I was just the price that had to be paid.

'What did Sir Claus want with you?' she barked. She'd never refer to him as 'your father' to me.

'None of your business,' I flashed. Though I have submitted to her rule in so many ways, and I know from long experience what a show of defiance costs, I cannot stop myself sometimes. She had thought to have me broken by now and the fact I'm not is something she can neither abide nor understand. If I had been more cowed, who knows, she might have shown me, if not kindness, at least a condescending tolerance. As it was, I was a challenge to her – a constant reminder that no matter how much she had done to me, no matter what she'd won, the victory still wasn't complete, and that she could not forgive.

She advanced on me, her eyes sparking with anger, her black velvet dressing gown swirling around her like a storm cloud. 'How dare you!'

I looked at her and said nothing. 'You will answer me,' she hissed. *Or else* hung in the air. I knew what she could do to me but even then I might have continued to stonewall her if I hadn't had the twig in my pocket. She mustn't know about it. I knew my father wouldn't willingly tell her but I could not risk her questioning him. So I bit my tongue and swallowed my pride, excusing myself in the most humble tones. I told her my father had brought back a gift for my birthday and showed her Maria's locket.

She looked at it. I could see she was annoyed that my father had bought me a gift at all but was mostly glad that it was a cheap little thing. She must have thought it showed just what value he placed on me compared to her daughters. After all, for their birthdays, hadn't he given Odette an emerald bracelet, and Babette a ruby one? With a smirk, she said, 'Not good enough for you, is that it? You ought to be grateful he remembered your birthday at all.'

She thought I'd been rude because I was angry over receiving such a poor gift! It was an unexpected blessing.

I played up to it and whined, 'Of course. I'm sorry, Lady Grizelda. Please forgive me. I don't know what came over me. And, please, don't tell my father.'

'You hardly deserve forgiveness, you wicked, ungrateful girl,' said my stepmother, sharply. She thought I was suffering, and she liked that. 'But I don't want to worry Sir Claus with such trivial matters. So get on with you back to your room and if ever you talk to me like that again, I'll –'

But I did not wait to hear the rest. With a browbeaten duck of the head, I scuttled off downstairs, leaving her to look after me with a self-satisfied smile. She'd probably tell her daughters about my father's supposed gift, which would mean that I'd have to put up with their sneers and slights. It was a small price to pay and my heart was light as I returned to my room. The twig was safe and, with it, the story of how I'd come to get it. I also didn't have to hide the locket any more either.

But what was I supposed to do now? Safely back in my room, I looked at the twig. It looked so ordinary – just a hazel twig with a closed bud or two. But there must be something special about it . . . why else would Mama have told me to ask for it? Feeling a little silly, I held it tight, closed my eyes and made a wish. Nothing happened. The twig remained unchanged.

I had a look through Mama's old books which I keep in my rickety old cupboard, hoping I might find a clue. I found one book about the lore of the woods, with a small section on an old legend which said that 'at the right time and place, at new moon, the hazel may become touched with wild magic'. But there was not a word about how it worked. Of course, if it had had anything to do with moon-sister magic, it would have been forbidden knowledge and Mama would hardly have kept a book that might betray her own secret. In the end I gave up, put the twig under my pillow and went to bed, hoping that my mother would tell me what I was meant to do with it in another dream.

But though the same green-lit forest was in my dreams again that night, Mama was not. All I could see were the trees and the grass; all I could hear were the rustling leaves and the sighing wind. No guiding vision, no understanding to take back to the waking world. So when I woke early the next morning, everything was as it had been with the twig still under my pillow, unchanged.

No, wait . . . not quite unchanged. The buds had begun to unfurl; a frilly hem of green now showed at the edge of the buds. But the stem looked like it was withering, drying out, and suddenly I was filled with panic. Whatever else it might be, the hazel twig was a link to my mother. I couldn't let it die!

I had to do something quickly. The kitchen was dark and quiet, but the bustle of the day would soon begin. I went outside and drew some water into a small jug that wouldn't be missed. I put the twig in it and then hid it in the cupboard in my room. I'd think of how best to keep the twig alive more permanently later but for the moment it would have to do.

I was right about Grizelda telling my stepsisters about my locket. Later that day, I was summoned to bring up the mended clothes to Odette's room and when I arrived I found both sisters there trying on new hats in front of the big mirror. When I came in they pretended not to see me at first, then Odette feigned a yelp of surprise.

'Good heavens, Ashes! What do you mean by creeping in here like a thief?'

'Your mending,' I said curtly, dumping it on the bed.

'Ooh, Babette, do you hear how she speaks to us?'

'We should box her ears,' said Babette distractedly, admiring herself in the mirror, the delicate lace and feather concoction she was trying on emphasising the pale beauty so like her mother's. Odette is darker and shorter by comparison and altogether less striking, though she's a long way from being ugly. If they'd been characters in one of those old tales Mama used to read to me when I was little, my stepmother and stepsisters' real selves would show on their faces, twisting them into gargoyles. But most people consider Babette and Odette to be perfect models of young womanhood: pretty, gracious, elegant, nicely spoken. And *charitable*, for with their mother they occasionally grace the 'deserving poor' of the district with their perfumed presence, bearing baskets of leftover food and pious platitudes. News of these occasions is, of course, always discreetly released in plenty of time to the social correspondent of Ashberg's most fashionable magazine so that a touching photograph or drawing can be published for the edification of readers.

Oh, I am turning into a veritable cat – an alley cat, that is – all claws and teeth and bitter heart. But that is better than becoming a mouse, which is what they'd like. I ignored Babette's comment and turned to go when

Odette called me back. 'Show us what *our* dearest father so kindly gave you,' she said silkily.

Her soft brown eyes were aglow with an unpleasant gleam. I knew what she intended by saying 'our father'. She meant to suggest he was hers and Babette's, and not mine at all, while at the same time reminding me of the fact I was indeed his disregarded daughter. Babette may look most like her mother but it is Odette who most shares her scheming, spiteful heart. Most of Babette's thoughts revolve around herself, while Odette also thinks of others — only not in a nice way. And more than once she has caught me out with a clever shot, straight to the heart.

But this time it was I who had the advantage over her. I made a great show of reluctance over showing them the locket and pretended to be embarrassed as they commented on 'how kind', 'how generous' my father had been and 'how well he'd chosen the gift, it's just perfect for *you*'. It took a good deal for me to keep a still tongue but I managed it, knowing they'd tire of their game soon enough if I didn't respond. As I was leaving, Odette took one final shot: 'I suppose you might even wear it next week at the Prince's ball.' I stopped, stunned. 'Oh dear, didn't our father tell you?' she added, her hand flying to her mouth in mock surprise.

'Don't be silly, of course *she* can't go,' said Babette petulantly. 'She's a nobody.'

'That must be why our father didn't say anything,' said Odette in a hushed tone. 'Me and my big mouth! I really *must* learn to control it.'

I looked at her and in that moment I resolved to do two things: first, I would no longer submit to this torture; and second, one day I would be revenged on the lot of them. Tonight, promise or no promise, I would pack my things and go.

But that night, as I finally staggered back to my room, exhausted after another long day, my resolve had dimmed and reality set in once again. I had hardly any money, aside from a few coins I'd managed to hoard. I could swipe some food from the kitchen, but once it ran out I would starve unless I found work, and the only work I knew was that of a servant. If I tried to get a job in any other big house in Ashberg, I'd be found out and brought back in disgrace – for though my stepmother would no doubt love to get rid of me, she would be furious if my flight brought gossip onto the family. Indeed, no matter where I went to in Ashberg, I would be likely to be found out. Which meant I'd have to head into the countryside, where there was the occasional large house with a staff of servants. But I'm a city girl through and through – I've only been to the country once and only for a few hours, and that was when I was little and had gone to stay with a cousin of Father's in a large estate about an hour's carriage ride from Ashberg; I could hardly go there. As to Mama's home village, it was much further, more like two or three days away, deep in the forest lands. And though she talked about it some-times, Mama had never gone back there. Even supposing I might get there, who knew what I'd find? I'd heard that the forest villages were practically empty these days. There would certainly be no work there as a servant, especially considering there were no big houses there as far as I knew. And I had no relatives that I knew about who might look after me.

Coward, I told myself bitterly, as I changed into my nightgown. You are a mouse indeed. Suddenly I heard a rustling, scratching sound coming from inside the cupboard. Talk of the devil and he shows his tail, Mama used to say. It sounded like there was a mouse in there, gnawing on my hazel twig!

I don't mind mice, not usually. There was one friendly one who kept coming to my room last year and who became a bit of a pet. I would feed it crumbs I'd kept back from my meals and it would eat them out of my hand. And then my stepmother found out. Horrified that I would 'encourage vermin', she ordered a trap be set, and every night I'd disable it. So, one day, she set out poison without telling anyone and, because I didn't learn of it in time, the mouse died. It was my fault. If I'd not shown it kindness, the mouse might have escaped Grizelda's notice – my foolish attachment had put it in greater danger than it would have been in. I would not make the same mistake twice.

I wanted this mouse gone. I did not want it to think it was safe here and I also didn't want it to nibble on my hazel twig. Carefully, I crept to the cupboard. I slowly opened the door and stared in amazement, for it wasn't a mouse that had made the sound at all!

Five

Inside my cupboard was a tree – a miniature hazel tree no higher than the length of my hand from wrist to fingertips, but still a tree, perfect in every way. It grew out from the jug, its roots suspended in the water, its tiny but vigorous branches covered in beautiful soft, green leaves that were touched with living gold where the light from my candle fell on them. And as I stared, I saw a slight movement amongst the leaves, a rustle carried by a wind I couldn't feel, a wind that came from – I knew not where.

I can hardly describe my feelings. To say I was astonished would be too slight; to say I was stunned would be too blunt. I felt awe fill me, and delight, and gladness. I felt as if my heart was unfurling like the hazel leaves that had unfurled from the bud. I got down on my knees and put my face close to the little tree, breathing in its scent of green. As I did so, I could hear my mother's whisper and feel her fingers in my hair.

I don't know how long I stayed there in a marvellous peace but after a while I whispered, 'Hazel . . . Oh beautiful hazel, tell me what I must do.'

I waited but nothing happened. A single leaf detached itself from a branch and came floating down to my feet. I picked it up and held it in my hand. 'Oh,' I said, stroking the leaf, 'you are soft as silk, light as a lace handkerchief!'

The words were no sooner out of my mouth than I no longer held a leaf in my hand – but an exquisite handkerchief of pale green silk and lace, with a curly 'S' embroidered in the corner. It was the most beautiful handkerchief I'd ever seen; finer by far than anything my stepsisters or stepmother had in their drawers, finer than anything I'd ever owned or had seen in the finest shops of Ashberg. Why, not even the Empress herself could have something as fine as this!

After the wonder came excitement. The tree's magic was unlocked by *my words* as I touched the leaf! I could make others turn into anything I liked – anything I needed! Trembling with anticipation, I picked a leaf off the tree. I said, 'Oh, you are warm as a coin in the purse, light as a banknote.' I waited but nothing happened. I tried again – and to my dismay the leaf began to curl up, its edges blackening as though it were being burned, and in less time than it takes to write, it had crumbled to ash in my hand.

What had I done wrong? I picked another leaf and whispered, 'You are green as spinach soup and good as fresh bread,' but though my mouth watered at my own words, the leaf did not change. Instead, it melted into sludge, like algae in a pond. Not discouraged, I thought I'd try to conjure another handkerchief, so I picked one more leaf and repeated my first words. But this time, all I ended up with was a skeleton of a leaf that drifted off my hand like thistledown and disappeared as soon as it hit the floor.

'Oh hazel tree,' I said in despair, 'what is it that I must do?' As I spoke an image came into my head of the first leaf detaching itself from the branch before floating down to the floor at my feet. It wasn't me who decided – it was the tree! And until it decided to loose another leaf, there was nothing I could do.

'But I need you to help me now,' I told the tree, 'because I want to leave – I *need* to leave – you must understand . . .' My appeal went unanswered.

'What is the good of you then?' I said sadly. 'What good is a silly handkerchief to me when I need a lifeline? What is the good of granting me a wish I didn't even realise I was making? You gave me hope and then took it away and now it is worse than ever.' I closed the cupboard, unable to look at it. I left the handkerchief on the chair by my bed. It was an exquisite thing, and to glance at it made the gladness return just a little. Pretty as it was, though, it was of no use. It was a frivolous magic of no importance and it could not help me at all.

I woke the next morning to find the handkerchief had vanished and in its place lay a dry leaf. So the magic had only lasted a few hours . . . It was hardly a surprise, in my low state of mind. And my low state of health. For I felt sick. I had a bad headache and churning stomach. Indeed

I felt so bad that it was all I could do to drag myself up and start my chores. But I knew that if I tried to get a sick day, it would be taken from any free time I was due – and in two days' time, on Sunday afternoon, I was due for a half-day off, after, of course, going to church. Time which would be my own, which was precious to me. So I tried to carry on till, by the end of the evening, I could no longer take it and fainted while trying to finish the mopping. I was brought to by one of the cooks, who bathed my forehead in cold water and gave me a steaming bowl of chicken broth. For once Mrs Jager didn't object because, as she told us, tomorrow was a big day and all hands were needed on deck. The Mayor of Ashberg, his wife and half the City Council were coming for dinner to discuss plans for the Prince's ball. There would be massive preparations all day and on no account was I or anyone else to be sick tomorrow.

I must admit it made me feel a lot better – the chicken broth, I mean. It wasn't only disappointment and despair that had made me sick but simple hunger. I'd had supper but it had been as meagre as always. The broth was thick and rich with bits of roast chicken and herbs; and with the slice of bread I had managed to swipe when no-one was looking, it made the finest meal I'd eaten in weeks – months, even.

Back in my room, I opened the cupboard door to see how the hazel tree was faring. It had grown a little more – it was now the length of half my forearm plus that of my hand, and the roots had now reached the bottom of the jug. If it kept growing at this rate, it would soon outgrow the jug and it would either die or be discovered.

I had to put it somewhere else – somewhere it wouldn't be noticed.

If you want to hide a tree, you plant it in a forest. I didn't have ready access to a forest, but just beyond the kitchen's garden wall at the back of the house was a patch of parkland that had been planted by one of Father's ancestors long ago. Neglected and forgotten as of late, it was in rather a state with the gardeners concentrating on the showier flower gardens and vegetable beds. I headed out there in the dead of night, carrying the tree and a trowel, and soon had the hazel planted in amongst the long grass, near a little pond half-choked by weeds.

It looked as though it was meant to be there – at least, that's what I hoped. I would try to visit it when I could but I'd have to be careful. I hoped it wouldn't keep growing, drawing attention to itself and spreading the faint scent of magic that would eventually attract the Mancers, who would descend like wolves on the fold.

At that exact moment a wolf howled somewhere far away. I shivered. No, surely not a wolf. There were no wolves in the city; it must be a dog howling at the full moon. But I couldn't help my skin prickling and my heart thumping as I raced back to the safety of my room with that long, sinister howl echoing in my ears.

Six

I am standing in bright moonlight as I look up at the hazel tree. It is of only mild surprise to me that the tree has grown so much that the topmost branches are above my head. It must have been raining earlier because there are sparkles of raindrops on the leaves and along the branches and, in the pale light, they make the hazel glitter with an unearthly beauty. The little pond gleams too, the weeds have moved away from its surface and I can see myself and the hazel reflected there beside the moon. It's very still and I hold my breath, waiting.

There's a whisper in the branches – a thread of sweet sound like a distant song. And all at once fluttering down from the tree come dozens – no, hundreds – of leaves, falling silent as snow over me, all over my hair, my face and my cold, bare feet.

No, they are not bare any more but shod in thin, soft slippers the colour of moonlight, while my nightdress has become the finest of lace petticoats overlaid with a glorious dress of green silk and silver brocade and an exquisite velvet cloak the colour of night. As I look wonderstruck into the mirrored surface of the pond, I see that around my neck is a glittering necklace of clear gems with the liquid shine of rain-drops, a heart-shaped emerald pendant set in the middle. At my ears glint studs of emerald and silver, and on my right hand is a ring of pearl and white gold. My chestnut hair has a golden sheen and is done up with a silver net as fine and light as cobwebs, my hazel eyes sparkle with an emerald light and my lips are washed with the palest pink, like the faint beginnings of dawn. Happiness blooms in me like a flower and I laugh out loud. In the moonlight, all alone with a song in my heart, I begin to dance, remembering the steps Mama had taught me long ago.

Dance, my darling, dance, for dawn is coming, a whisper says deep in my heart, and everything has changed, and the dark night in which you have been living will be behind you for ever and you will be alone no longer. It is my mother's voice and I know she speaks the truth, for my heart is full of a delight such as I have never known.

Suddenly there is a pebble in my path. I trip. I wake. For a moment I do not understand what has happened. There is no hazel, no moonlight. The night is black as pitch at my little window. I have no jewels, no beautiful dress, no silver slippers – only my old nightdress that's so worn it is thin as a sheet of rice paper and about as warm. It was only a dream. I put my head in my hands and as I do so I feel something caught in my hair. I pull it out and stare at a leaf – a damp hazel leaf!

My heart beats wildly and I close my eyes. When I open them again, I half-expect I've dreamed this too. But *the leaf is still there: small, not fully grown but absolutely real as it rests snugly in the hollow of my palm. I look at it for a moment longer then, reaching up to my necklace, I open the locket and slide the tiny leaf inside. Its soft, damp green seems to glow with the light of magic, the promise of dawn.*

That was this morning. I've had hardly any time to think about it all day as I have been kept busy, busier than I have ever been with the whole house in a frenzy to get things ready for the distinguished guests. The importance of the dinner was highlighted by the presence of Grizelda in the kitchen not once but *twice*, as she hardly ever condescends to descend those stairs, preferring to summon Mrs Jager instead. She was clearly anxious, and I soon learned why: that very morning, she had learned it wasn't just the city dignitaries who would be there in force, but also Count Otto von Gildenstein, a court official sent on ahead of the Prince to oversee the Ashberg celebrations.

Count Otto was a very important man. A senior adviser to the Emperor, he also sat on the Mancer Council, which was made up not only of the most senior Mancers but also of powerful and trusted political figures. His only son, Maximilian, was Prince Leopold's best friend and had only just returned from Klugheitfurt University himself where he had studied alongside the Prince. Although Count Otto owned a hunting estate just outside the city, he only occasionally came to Ashberg and when he did he came alone to hunt, refusing all social invitations. So his presence at dinner tonight in my father's house would be a real honour and it meant that everything must run even more perfectly than usual. I was sent to clean the sculleries from top to bottom – as if Count Otto would put one booted foot anywhere near them! Taking advantage of the whirlwind of activity downstairs, I sneaked out to check the tree.

Still covered in leaves, it was nowhere near as big as it had been in my dream but I was certain it had grown. It hadn't shed any leaves either, and the pond was still choked with weeds, with not a hint of that shining, mirrored surface. It had been a dream and yet the leaf from my dream was in my locket – still fresh and green, still unmistakeably real. None the wiser, I slipped back to the sculleries, just in time before the head scullery maid poked her head around the door to inspect my work.

If downstairs was a perfect ant-heap of busyness, upstairs was no less frantic, according to the footmen and maids. Madame Paulina and several of her assistants spent hours closeted with my stepmother and stepsisters, performing emergency alterations to dresses that had been considered fine enough for a dinner with city authorities but not quite fine enough for a senior adviser to the Emperor. While hairdressers, perfumers and beauticians attended to the women, a tailor came for my father's needs and, no doubt under Grizelda's instructions, Ashberg's finest perruquier arrived to fit a fashionable wig on Father's bald head. The upstairs staff did not much like the house filled with these strangers, and even less that Grizelda had given instructions that they were to run errands for them, but there was nothing they could do except grumble at the servants' table about 'upstart trades-men' who didn't know 'the family' like they did.

Of course, nobody seemed to remember that I was part of that family. And why should they? The real power in the house had decided I was to be disregarded and brought low and, as my father had not objected except in the weakest of terms, that was what counted. And it had not brought me any friends – far from it. I was not one of them downstairs; but I was not one of them upstairs, either. Babette was right – I was a nobody, a creature everyone could safely despise.

Night came, and with it the rumble of carriages and the loud, confident voices of the guests. Word filtered down to the kitchen of the splendid gowns and jewels of the women, and the men's dress uniforms clanking with medals. Even our fat, old mayor, Baron Tomas, looked splendid, apparently, in his magnificent dark red, velvet robes of office and the white, fox-fur-trimmed ceremonial helmet that has always reminded me of the headgear worn by a Ruvenyan warrior depicted in one of Mama's old books. To me, it seemed to touch a pompous and tedious old man with the glamour of exotic legend, as Ruvenya was a vast kingdom to our east, but I don't suppose the mayor would be glad to hear it for, like many people here-abouts, he would consider Ruvenya to be a dangerous and barbarous land. Though, he might not say so in a court official's company, for our Empress herself had been born a Ruvenyan princess.

Count Otto did not arrive for more than an hour after the other guests, and the footmen relayed news of the growing tension upstairs. 'They're afraid he might not turn up at all,' said one of the footmen. 'He's done that before, apparently.' The cooks were also in hysterics at the thought that their vast, carefully planned meal would spoil if it was delayed for much longer, and everyone downstairs looked glum at the prospect that a furious Lady Grizelda would visit her disappointment on us.

But thankfully he did turn up and all was forgiven. Despite having 'a face like a bulldog and the build of a prize-fighter' (a footman's cheeky words), he knew exactly what to say to everyone and charmed the whole assembly with his flattering description of the Province of Ashbergia as 'one of His Imperial Majesty's most loyal' and of Ashberg as 'one of the jewels of the Empire' which the Prince, whose many official titles included Duke of Ashbergia, was looking forward to visiting with immense pleasure and anticipation.

'He said that the Prince is keen to make glad as many citizens of Ashberg as possible, from the high to the low,' the same footman went on, 'and so as well as the ball for the toffs there's to be a big night-fair for us common folk that same night and, later on in the week, the Prince might address the crowds in St Hilda's Square.'

'Must feel different to his father then,' someone muttered.

'Nobody's ever taken a pot shot at him, that's why,' chimed in another. Despite all that stuff about Ashbergia being 'one of the most loyal' provinces, long ago, many years before I was born, someone had actually taken a shot at the Emperor while he was on a visit to Ashberg. The hopeful assassin had been a madman who thought he was a reincarnation of the Grey Widow. It was soon proved there was no wider plot and the assassin was executed, but the fear of lone dealers of death suddenly appearing from within cheering crowds had haunted the Emperor ever since.

'I've heard the Prince is handsome,' sighed one of the maids. 'Hair like gold and eyes like cornflowers, a manly bearing and a gift with words.'

'Bah! That's what those perfumed papers tell you,' scoffed a footman, 'but anyone can look good when they have an army of skivvies to attend to them.'

'I've heard he's not like that at all,' persisted the maid. 'I read that while he was at university, he shared an ordinary apartment with his friend Maximilian von Gildenstein and they just had one of those college servants and that the Prince was like any other young man who —'

'You'll rot your mind reading that rubbish, my girl,' said Mrs Jager, coming into the kitchen just in time to overhear. 'The Prince is not just any young man, he is the heir to the throne and a very great man indeed and the likes of us have absolutely no business discussing him as if he were a mere dandy from the social pages. While I am in charge down here, there will be no more disrespectful remarks, is that clear? From anyone,' she went on, glaring at the footman, who shrugged sulkily but said nothing more.

Seven

I woke from a dreamless sleep to a bright morning, with the delicious thought that it was Sunday. After my early chores and Mass, the rest of the day was mine and I decided to visit my mother's grave on the other side of the city, setting off with a basket filled with sandwiches, a bottle of cold tea and a bunch of flowers from the garden.

Sunday may be a day of rest but, at certain times of the day, the city is more busy than usual. In the morning, crowds in their colourful Sunday best pour out of the cathedral and various small churches and later spill out of their houses after lunch to promenade up and down St Hilda's Square. I had set out in between those times so there weren't many people in the streets. But I didn't mind for it gave me the feeling that I owned the city, that I could look – and look at what I wanted without attracting the suspicion of those who always think that a poorly dressed person is likely to be a thief or up to some sort of mischief. Ashberg is a charming city and St Hilda's Square is splendid, wide and elegant, with the tall tower housing the ancient clock that is one of the wonders of the world and always a great drawcard for tourists. At that moment it was solely mine – with nobody brusquely pushing me aside to let my betters see – and as the clock struck twelve, I watched with delight as the miniature court parade passed out of the palace gates: first came the trumpeters in red and blue, followed by the magnificent king and queen and then all their courtiers, who passed them by in the finest regalia, solemnly bowing before proceeding on to a grand tune.

But it wasn't just St Hilda's Square that I loved. I could dream in front of shop windows filled with beautiful things without braving the basilisk-glare of shopkeepers. I could dawdle in front of my favourite houses, decorated with the delicate colours and carvings that make them look like the most beautiful gilt gingerbread, without attract-ing the attention of the city police, for they too had their Sunday lunch back in their barracks. Clearly, criminals were expected to keep the Sunday peace too, and by and large they did. Even a thief must rest sometime, I suppose, and besides, if there is no-one out and about whose pocket you can pick or watch you can lift, then what's the point of cruising the streets looking for prey? It would all change once the clocks struck three.

Halfway through my journey I stopped in my favourite parkland and, apart from a few strays like me, it was empty too. Finch Park is small and simple, without the statues and fountains and gravel paths that make the bigger ones fashionable, but I have always loved it. Amongst the unmanicured grass are riots of little flowers; there are unruly, fragrant bushes and old but comfortable wooden benches. Best of all, the park is home to lots of little birds – especially its namesake – that dart around in busy groups, their bright movements and chirruping voices surely capable of lifting the spirit of even the most miserable soul. In those moments, sitting on the bench in the sun, eating my sandwiches and scattering the crumbs for the birds, I felt truly happy, without a thought for the past or the future.

By the time I got to my feet again to walk the rest of the way to the cemetery, I felt more refreshed than I had in days. The feeling persisted right to Mama's grave, which was a grassy plot tucked away near a patch of trees at the far end of the graveyard. At her request, it had simply been marked with a plain stone cross, engraved with her name and the single word 'Beloved'. I knelt at her grave, tears in my eyes. 'Oh, Mama,' I whispered, 'I miss you so, so much . . .'

There was a movement in the patch of trees nearby. I stiffened and caught a glimpse of a shadowy figure wrapped in a cloak. In the next instant I heard rapid footsteps behind me and, rather than turn around, I put my head in my hands and made as if I was weeping and unaware of them. The footsteps passed by me without hesitating and when I sneaked a look between my fingers at the patch of trees I saw that the newcomer had joined the figure in the shadows. I couldn't see much of him either, for he was dressed in a long, dark overcoat and wore a hat, but he carried himself in such a way that I had the impression that this was not someone to tangle with. I knew that on no account must I draw attention to myself.

Sunday might be a day of rest for criminals generally but clearly these two were taking advantage of the quietness of both the place and the day. I knew they must be criminals up to something for why else would they meet in such secrecy? They had moved further into the trees so it was impossible for me to even try to see their faces. I just wanted to be away from there should they emerge again and decide I was in their way. 'I have to go, Mama,' I whispered, 'but I'll be back, I promise. I love you and always will,' and then I got quietly to my feet, taking care to keep my back to them, and walked away as slowly as I could bear to, my heart in my mouth, the back of my neck tingling. But nobody shouted after me, nobody came running, and I reached the gate of the cemetery without incident.

Once outside, I quickened my steps till I was almost running down the street. Turning the corner, I had my second shock of the afternoon. Drawn up at the end of the street outside a tall gabled house was a Mancer carriage. Its occupant was obviously inside the house as the coachman had climbed down off his seat and was now leaning against the vehicle smoking. He hadn't seen me yet so I quickly doubled back and went blindly down another street, my heart pounding, fit to burst. The sight of that sinister vehicle – the second I'd seen in just a few days – drove out the earlier fear that had sent me fleeing the graveyard. Malefactors planning a crime were one thing; Mancers on the prowl were quite another. What was going on?

Perhaps, I thought as I made my way back through a tortuous route, it's because of the Prince's visit. They are keeping a closer eye than usual, that's all, checking every stray waft of perhaps-magic that comes their way and making sure the heir to the throne will be safe not only from assassins but from illegal spells. They'd be busy weaving protective spells of their own, of course, but they could never be too careful when it came to the safety of our ailing Emperor's only son. And that meant they would be on the lookout for anything even slightly unusual, however innocent or harmless. It was not a reassuring thought.

I climbed over the back wall and hurried through the parkland, not wanting to run the risk of being seen by anyone in the house. Thoughts of the Mancers on the prowl had made me terribly nervous about the hazel tree and whether, if by some stroke of bad luck they found it, they'd know it was magic. I had a horrible feeling they would know at once and then I'd be doomed.

Oh dear God, it had grown! It was now waist-high – twice the size it had been in my cupboard. If it kept growing at this rate, in no time at all it would be as tall as it had been in my dream and then who knew when it would stop? What if it kept growing till the top of it reached above the walls and higher, maybe even reaching as high as the cathedral spire? And that could mean that it would only be a matter of days – not weeks – before the Mancers came knocking at my door!

Panic-stricken, I flung myself at the tree, pulling at it, heaving as if I would pull it out of the ground. But it stayed fast and all I got for my pains were scratches from the branches whipping at me, as if the tree had been fighting back. Panting, I fell to the ground, sobbing, 'Hazel tree, dear hazel tree, please understand you will be my doom if you don't stay small. What do you want? What must I do?'

Silence. Of course, I could hardly expect the tree to answer me. Feeling stupid and small and helpless, I began to get up when all at once there came a rustle from above and a little yellow finch swooped down and alighted on a branch just near me. Head cocked, it looked at me with its bright beady eyes.

'I know, little one, I'm an idiot,' I said sadly. Chirruping in a scolding sort of way, the finch hopped down the branch. Before I knew what was happening, it broke off a leaf at the stalk and, darting down, dropped the leaf at my feet. Then it flew back to the tree and sat looking at me as if to say, 'Well, do you understand now?'

'I don't know what I . . .' I began, but the words died in my throat as I saw that it was no longer a leaf at my feet but a small picture – a miniature exquisitely painted on a canvas of stretched pale silk. Such miniatures were a renowned speciality of my mother's region and, indeed, we had one in the house, framed under glass. But I'd never seen one as beautiful, as perfect, as this one.

It depicted a ballroom scene with couples dancing on polished floors under crystal chandeliers in a room lined with painted, floral panels. I knew that room, though I had not set foot in it for years. It was the grand ballroom of Ashberg Castle, which was used not only for balls but for other special occasions. As a child, I had gone there every year with my parents for the mayor's Christmas party, to which all the great Ashberg families were invited. There was always a huge, decorated Christmas tree in the corner of the room with the panels draped in holly and mistletoe and gilt paper chains. There'd been tables laden with food and gifts wrapped in coloured paper for every child.

Those days were long gone for me and best not thought of. But what was the meaning of the miniature before me now? I looked up at the finch, then back at the picture – and saw what I had missed the first time. First, the panels were draped in banners bearing the arms of Prince Leopold. And, second, the first couple in the room, the ones who set the tone for all the others, were not the fat old mayor and his skinny wife, but were young. The man was tall and broad-shouldered in an elegant sky-blue dress uniform, and the young woman, dressed in a magnificent white ball gown, had chestnut hair with a golden sheen. I stared, my heart beating so fast I thought it would jump out of my chest, and I murmured, 'No. You can't mean that I should go to the Prince's ball!'

The finch chirruped loudly, and its meaning was so clear it might as well have spoken human words. I looked up at it and whispered, 'But it's not possible . . . It can't be . . . I can't go . . .'

And yet in my mind I knew that I must.

Eight

I can hardly describe how I got through the next few days. It was as though I had walked on air and hot coals at one and the same time. The house had been a hive of activity as my stepmother and stepsisters went through an endless parade of dresses and shoes and jewels. There were constant tantrums with angry tears and feet stamped and hair pulled as the girls fought over who would wear what while my father simply never poked his nose out of his study. Fortunately I only got to *hear* about those tantrums, for both my stepsisters and their mother had forgotten all about me in their excitement.

It was bedlam downstairs, too. The girls' maids had sniped at each other over which of their charges would catch the Prince's eye. The footmen had sniggered about the harassed dressmakers and shoemakers who came in and out of the house like badly wound clockwork toys. The under-maids had been sighing over the social pages of magazines when Mrs Jager wasn't looking, which wasn't often, because in the days leading up to the ball there were fine dinners every night at our house for this bigwig and that. Count Otto came to one of them, which of course meant even more work for everyone, especially the kitchen staff which included me as the lowliest member.

But none of it worried me; I was in the strangest state. Somehow, I would go to the Prince's ball. For what reason, I had no idea. I've never been the sort of girl to moon over a picture of a handsome stranger, prince or no prince. I didn't care if I never met him. I did of course fancy the idea of a pretty dress and dancing, and music and good food and the chance for just a few hours to be in the world where I should have been. Mother would have loved to plan this with me. We'd have pored over patterns, colours and styles together. But I was sure she hadn't reached out from beyond the grave just to give me a night's fancy. Something was going to happen at the Prince's ball – something that would change my life.

I'd hoped every night for a guiding vision but I did not dream at all in those nights before the Prince's ball. And though I managed to sneak out a couple of times to the hazel tree, the finch was never there. No leaves fell and transformed, no whisper spoke in my mind, nothing happened to suggest the tree was anything other than, well, a tree. There was one comforting thing though – the tree had stopped growing, almost as if it had taken my plea to heart.

But even the thought of the Mancers had ceased to scare me . . . at least for the moment.

The great day came early for me. I had had to get up before dawn to iron a mountain of my stepsisters' knickers, petticoats and camisoles. They had demanded a pile of freshly pressed underthings, more than any reasonable person would need for a twenty-four-hour period. But reason and my stepsisters are not friends, unless it is their own particular variety that owes nothing to clarity and everything to spite and self-centredness. Not that it mattered much to me today. As I pressed the warm iron over the delicate garments and sprayed them with a mixture of violet and lavender water, I dreamed of that ball. I dreamed all day through all my chores – through the harried shouting of Mrs Jager and the bad temper of the cooks, through a poor lunch of bread and cheese and an afternoon spent running last-minute errands to this ribbon shop and that perfumery, to fetch special headgear for the carriage horses and to place an order at the Angel. Grizelda was already planning ahead. I had been sent to order a boxful of one of the Angel's specialities, blue and white sugared almonds in silver nets. She reasoned that once the Prince had seen her daughters and fallen in love with one of them, he'd surely accept an invitation to a smaller, more intimate affair at the house.

Or, that was the gossip in the kitchens. And at the Angel, too, according to Maria. She and I laughed at how every mother of an unmarried young woman was thinking exactly the same thing, causing the Angel to be overwhelmed with orders for their sugared almonds. Then she grew serious and said it was a disgrace that I wasn't going to the ball, that I had as much of a right – or more – to be there as those two spoiled girls, and I nearly blurted out my secret but restrained myself in time. I said it didn't matter to me and I had nothing to wear anyway.

'I can lend you something – a dress I've made for my daughter's wedding later this year,' she said. 'I would be happy – honoured – to lend it to you.' I tried to protest. 'No, Maria, you've already been so kind to me – you don't need to do that.' But she said, 'Why don't you come and try it on, anyway, just to oblige me?'

So I followed Maria to her room at the back of the bakery. A widow, Maria lives at the Angel during the week when she works, while her daughter lives with Maria's mother in the country, the two only able to see each other on Sundays. She opened the trunk she kept in the corner. From it she took out a long parcel covered with rose petals and, unwrapping the tissue paper, she revealed a lovely muslin dress with a full skirt of cream and honey-coloured stripes, a cream bodice set with panels of fine lace dyed a delicate green, a hem embroidered with honey-coloured rosebuds, and elbow-length sleeves finished with ribbons of the same colour as the lace.

'Oh, it's *so* beautiful!' Shame on me, I hadn't expected anything quite as lovely. 'You are a wonderful needle-woman, Maria.'

'You think so? I'm glad,' she said, flushing a little. 'It is my hobby when I have time. Once, I dreamed I might ... Never mind, life gave me what it did and I don't regret a thing. But I wanted to give my daughter the most beautiful dress I could afford – and that meant I had to make it. I was lucky – the people at the draper's were very kind and allowed me to have bits of this and bits of that and for not very much. The lace is from a couple of handkerchiefs from my mother's own wedding day, which I dyed to look more modern. And rosebuds for my daughter's name – Rosa, as you know. So you think it does look all right? It doesn't look like it is too much bits of this and that?'

'Not at all,' I said warmly. 'It is most charming and original – no other bride will have anything like it, I am sure of that. Rosa will be the prettiest bride in all the empire!'

Maria's face grew beautiful with her smile. 'You are a sweet girl, Selena.' Then her eyes took on an impish gleam. 'But now, will you try it on – just to show you mean what you say?'

'Maria . . .' I protested, but she insisted, and so I slipped out of my old patched dress and stood in my shabby petticoat as Maria carefully slid the dress over my head.

It fell around me in whisper-soft folds, giving off a faint fragrance of roses, and Maria breathed, 'Oh, it fits perfectly! And you look lovely! Wait, let me show you.'

She took a hand mirror from the table by her bed and held it up to me. The mirror was old, the polished surface a bit tarnished, but I could see myself and the sight gripped at my heart. 'You must take it, Selena, you must, and you must go to the ball, no matter what those ones want.'

'No – I can't – and it's your daughter's dress –' I stammered.

'Rosa would think exactly the same as me,' said Maria firmly.

'But it's her wedding gown –'

'She will wear it just as happily at her wedding,' said Maria, briskly, 'and no harm done.' Suddenly, there were tears in her eyes. 'Your poor, dear mother would have wanted this for you, I know she would.'

'Yes,' I said, without thinking, 'it *is* what she wants.' Then, seeing Maria's puzzlement, I added hastily, 'I had a dream the other night in which she spoke to me . . .'

'You see,' said Maria, returning to briskness. 'If your own mother spoke to you in a dream, then you must listen. If she wants you to go to the ball, then you must go. And how else are you going to go, if not with this dress?'

I would have told her about the hazel tree's magic there and then but something stopped me. It was better Maria didn't know, for her sake if not mine, just in case it ever got to the ears of the Mancers. But it did leave me with a dilemma – how was I going to explain I didn't *need* to take the dress to go to the ball? And then quite suddenly it struck me, as I remembered what the girls in my mother's village received on their sixteenth birthday aside from the hazel twig: honey, cream and roses – all of them on this dress! I had assumed the hazel tree would gift me a ball gown transformed from leaves, as it had done in my dream, but what if that was not what was meant to happen? What if this was intended instead?

But in the magic miniature (which had long since faded and disappeared like the handkerchief) the girl had been wearing a court dress, not a charming muslin frock made for a country wedding. I looked at myself in the mirror, at the way the cream and honey and pale green set off not only the colour of my hair, but also my skin, which isn't as pale as a lady's should be but is touched with a hint of sun. I saw the way the gown flattered my too-thin figure, making it look slim rather than skinny, and I made up my mind. 'Then I'll borrow it, dear Maria,' I said, and hugged her, 'but only if you let me give you something in return.'

'I'll tell you what you can give me,' she said with a bright smile, hugging me back. 'You can give me the pleasure of showing off my dress at such a glittering occasion and you can also give me the pleasure of hearing all about the ball, the dresses and whether the Prince is really as handsome as his pictures – that would be more than enough.'

'Oh, Maria!' I said, and hugged her again.

'There are some underthings that go with it . . .' she said and, after rummaging in the trunk, she brought out a ribbon-trimmed petticoat of fine, white cotton, and a camisole and knickers to match. She put them into the parcel too, and turned to me, her eyes shining. 'Now you'll have to do your hair nicely, perhaps put in some flowers – and some ribbon, too. Wait a moment, I'll see if I can find some –'

'No, no, it's all right,' I said hastily, thinking she might give everything away. 'I'll find some ribbons at the house – my stepsisters have discarded so many. And there are flowers in the garden and the greenhouse. I'll wear your locket, too, just as I am now. See how pretty it looks against the dress?'

'No, no,' said Maria, shaking her head decisively. 'The locket is pretty but it is not suitable for such an occasion. I remember your mother had a lovely pearl necklace that would do very well.'

It would. But it was locked away in Grizelda's jewellery box and there wasn't even the ghost of a chance she'd lend it to me. As to trying to get it out of there without asking her, I didn't fancy my chances at all. Seeing the look on my face, Maria said gently, 'But it would equally work with something very simple, say a single rose at the breast – pale yellow or white.'

'Yes,' I said, 'there are early roses in the greenhouse.'

'The very thing, then. Flowers on a young and pretty woman can look just as effective as jewels and can be much more charming,' said Maria, firmly. I nearly laughed, because to look at the pair of us, you wouldn't think we were kitchen servant and scullery maid, but society ladies discussing the latest fashion. Instead, I said, 'You are wonderful, Maria, and I am so grateful and so honoured that you are my friend.'

'Get on with you, girl,' she said, a little shyly, 'and get yourself back to that house before they begin to miss you.'

'Miss *me*? *Them*? Never,' I said, gaily. 'If I vanished in a puff of smoke I daresay they'd all be glad.'

Maria shook her head sadly and said, 'It's a disgrace, that's what I say, and it's time it was stopped. I'd bet a week's wages that once that Prince sets eyes on you, everything will change.'

I didn't say that I couldn't give two hoots about the Prince to a romantic like Maria – who was I to pour cold water on that? Then she said, worriedly, 'Oh dear, I've just had a thought – shoes. What are we going to do about shoes?'

'I'll swipe a pair from Babette's shoe cupboard,' I said. 'She's the same size as me and has dozens of pairs – she probably doesn't even remember them all.'

'Very well. But try and get something that matches the dress, nothing too showy,' said my new fashion adviser, pursing her lips.

'No, I won't, I promise.' I took the dress off and Maria wrapped it in tissue then brown paper and wedged it firmly in my basket under the cloth I had carried to cover the box of sugared almonds.

'Thank you so much, dear Maria,' I said and then I kissed her on both cheeks and left with her last-minute advice to dab a little rose-based perfume or, failing that, a little rose water behind my ears and at my wrists and neck.

Nine

I only just had time to sneak into my room and hide the dress under my bed before I was summoned by Mrs Jager. She told me that my stepmother had sent for me and I was to get up there at once. When I went into Grizelda's room I found her alone, seated at her dressing table, wearing a velvet wrap, her hair up in curling papers and her face thickly painted with a white clay mask. 'Yes, Lady Grizelda?' I said meekly.

'I was thinking about you,' my stepmother said, rubbing cream into her hands, her eyes on me in the mirror.

I swallowed. What was coming couldn't be good. Before I could reply, she stunned me by going on, 'I was thinking you might want to come to the ball, too.'

I couldn't speak.

'Well, Selena? Speak up, girl.'

'I . . . I –'

'Do you or don't you?'

My heart was thudding and, my head spinning, I murmured, 'I . . . yes. Yes, I do.'

'I see.' My stepmother smiled. 'Then of course, my dear, you must go.'

I stared at her. I could not believe my ears. 'Do you . . . mean it?'

'Of course I do, Selena.'

My legs felt like jelly. 'What does Father say?'

'Nothing, for the present. This is just between you and me.'

'Babette and Odette . . .'

'Between you and me,' she repeated, with a touch of temper.

'Oh, I . . .'

'There is a problem, though,' she said as she spun around to look at me. 'If you'd told me before that you wanted to go, we could have had a dress made for you.'

'If I had told you?' I stammered.

'Don't be Little Miss Echo, Selena. If you had told me, there'd have been time. But now it's going to be a problem, isn't it? You have no dress suitable for the occasion. Don't tell me those old dresses of yours in the attic would do, because they wouldn't. And you can't wear one of Babette's or Odette's dresses because what would people say?' She smiled. 'Really, my dear, you have been very flighty in this matter.'

I looked at her, a nasty feeling beginning in the pit of my stomach. This was just another of her cruel games. 'I . . . I'm sorry . . .' I whispered.

'A bit late, don't you think? Such a pity. We would have

been glad to have you along with us if you had thought ahead.'

I tried to speak calmly. 'I . . . I . . . think there might be something I can wear that –'

'What? Do you think you can conjure a ball gown out of thin air?' She laughed. 'Imagine what the Mancers would say.'

I felt a little sick. There was a light in her eyes that scared me. She couldn't possibly know about the hazel . . . couldn't possibly . . . Frantically, I said, 'It's just that someone . . . I was lent a dress that might –'

Shock invaded her face for an instant, and then her features went very still. 'Whatever do you mean? Who lent you a dress?'

'I . . . someone . . . it's very pretty – I think it might . . .'

'Then you'd better show it to me, my dear,' she said silkily, 'hadn't you? Let me judge whether or not it will do.'

With all my heart, I wished I didn't have to. But there was no turning back now. Sadly, I went down to my room and, leaving the underthings behind, took Maria's dress upstairs.

My stepsisters were now in Grizelda's room. They too wore velvet wraps and curling papers but, instead of a face mask, they wore spiteful expressions. As soon as I stepped into the room Odette said, 'What kind of rag have you been squirrelling away, then?'

'I bet it's ugly as sin, and old-fashioned to boot,' said Babette.

'Now, now, girls,' said Grizelda, the softness in her voice belied by the hardness in her eyes. 'Come on, show us then, Selena.'

Oh Maria, I'm so sorry, I thought miserably as I unwrapped her daughter's wedding dress.

'Hold it up so we can see,' ordered Grizelda.

I shook the dress out and held it up to the three pairs of eyes. There was a silence, then Grizelda said, sharply, 'Where did you get it?'

'A friend.'

'You don't have friends,' said Babette.

'You must have stolen it,' said Odette.

'I did not! A friend lent it to me. She made it.'

'She *made* it! Then your friend is a common person, a dressmaker. Who is she?' said Grizelda in a dangerous tone. 'You will tell me, Selena.'

'No, I will not! It is none of your business.' I was beside myself now with rage. 'She is my friend. She lent me this dress so I could go to the ball. Whatever you think, whatever you do to me, you cannot change the fact I am my father's daughter and have a right to go to the Prince's ball. And I *am* going – in this dress.'

'Really?' said Grizelda, and in two long strides she was upon me, ripping the dress out of my hands. I gave a cry of horror and tried to throw myself at her but Babette and Odette were too quick for me, tripping me up and holding me back, my arms twisted painfully behind me, while Grizelda methodically went about the business of destroying Rosa's wedding dress. She ripped at the lace panels, tore off the ribbons and, taking a pair of golden nail scissors from her dressing table, cut the muslin to shreds. When it was in ruins, she threw what was left of the dress at me, saying, 'Such a fine gown for the ball, don't you think, girls?'

My stepsisters laughed and made nasty remarks but I hardly heard them for my ears were filled with a roaring sound. My throat was clenched so tight I felt as though I couldn't breathe. But all the fight – all the defiance – had gone out of me. All I could think was that through my stupidity I was responsible for the destruction of that lovely dress and of Maria's hopes for her daughter's wedding. If only I'd kept my mouth shut! How could I possibly have been so naive? Oh, if only I hadn't been persuaded to accept Maria's generous offer! I should have been stronger. I should have realised. I'd had enough experience of how hard life could be. But I'd let myself think things could be different. And now everything was ruined.

Grizelda rang the bell and one of the maids appeared. 'Tell Mrs Jager this girl is to be locked in her room tonight,' she said. The maid nodded impassively. Grizelda looked at me, still hunched on the floor. 'Get up, girl. Take those rags with you and get out of my sight.'

Locked in my room, I sat numbly on the bed still clutching the remains of poor Maria's creation. There was too much pain in me for tears; all I could do was stare at the ruined muslin, the torn lace, the shredded ribbons, and wish that I had never been born.

I don't know how long I sat there. When I emerged from my stupor, the room was dark. Soon, the others would be off to the ball. I didn't care about that, not any more. But I did care very much about Maria. How could

I possibly make it up to her? I had no money to buy new materials and I was all thumbs with needle and thread. I could darn and mend but the quality of Maria's work was great art that made a mockery of my poor little skills. Somehow, I thought, I must try and throw myself on the mercy of a dressmaker and beg them to help me. I could try Madame Paulina. But it was unlikely she would help – she does not even meet my eye or say good morning any more.

I had been right to spurn the knowledge of my moon-sister heritage. What good had the hazel tree done me? If I had not hoped things would change, I would not be in this situation. Oh, how I wished I could put things back!

Suddenly there was a rush of wings behind me and I turned to see the little yellow finch perched on my narrow windowsill. And in its beak it carried a green hazel leaf.

The finch looked at me, then flew down and dropped the leaf on the dress. It flew out again but was back in a flash with another leaf, which it also laid on the dress. It did this another ten times but nothing happened until it brought in the final leaf, laid it on the dress and perched on my bedside table, looking at me.

Then came a rush of wind that threw all the leaves up in a spiral and, when they fell back down, the dress was not only as good as new but even better than before with an extraordinary fairy glamour that quite outshone anything I had ever seen – even in my dreams. The cream and honey and pale green had a sheen of unearthly beauty, and the faint scent of roses was stronger than before.

Now my heart was full, not with darkness but a sweet delight, an awestruck wonder that reached deep inside me.

And still I looked at the finch with bright eyes and I whispered, 'Thank you.'

But it wasn't finished, not yet. Five times more it flew out of the window and came back with a leaf in its beak. This time, though, it didn't lay them on the dress but on the floor at my feet. Where the first leaf landed, a pair of beautiful cream-coloured dancing shoes appeared; where the second leaf landed, a pair of ivory silk stockings as fine as lace materialised; in place of the third came a swirling satin cloak of mint-green, lined with a deeper shade; fourth, an exquisite little embroidered evening bag; and last of all was a crown of pale gold roses interspersed with white pearls, threaded on a fine, filigreed gold band.

The finch flew out one more time and when it returned it did not have a leaf in its beak – but a key. The key to my room!

Ten

I waited for about an hour till I could no longer hear a sound from the kitchen. The staff had been given the rest of the evening off and I knew most of them were planning to go to the night-fair that was being held to celebrate the Prince's visit. No-one remembered me, in their eagerness to go off and enjoy themselves. And no-one would be around to see me creep out of my room.

After I was sure I was alone, I unlocked my room and went into the kitchen. I warmed some water on the big wood stove, added a few drops of the rose water used for flavouring sweets and, taking it to my room in a jug with some soap, stood in a tin basin and poured the water all over me. After a thorough wash, I dried myself and put on the underthings and stockings, then slipped into the dress, which fell in perfect folds around me, and shoes. I brushed my hair till it shone, and pinned it up so it fell in a soft roll at the back of my neck. I then placed the crown of roses carefully on my head and put on the cloak. I looked at myself in the bowl of water.

I'm truly touched with magic, I thought, as I looked back at myself in the soft light of the moon that came through the window. My hair shone, my eyes sparkled, my lips were alive with a coral shine. My skin – now with a honey glow – gave off a perfume of roses much stronger than the few drops of rose water could have provided. Even my hands, that usually bear the marks of my drudgery, felt soft once again. It was strange, like seeing oneself in a beautiful dream. I wondered if my stepmother and stepsisters would recognise me, as I hardly recognised myself. My mother had promised me everything would change. It was now up to me to make sure it would, and not to let fear or doubt stand in my way.

Before I left my room and ventured into the moonlit streets, I took one last thing – Maria's locket – and fastened it around my neck. She had thought it too poor to wear but I felt differently. And when I looked into the watery mirror and saw that it too glowed with the same glamour, I knew I had been right.

I closed the door of my room and locked it behind me, replaced the key on the nail and set off into the patch of woodland. As soon as I saw the hazel tree, I realised it had stopped growing. No, it had actually shrunk, as if the effort of the magic had taken some of the vitality from it. I gazed at it, a little anxious; then, suddenly, from the tower in St Hilda's Square, came the sound of the clock striking nine and as it did so my mother's voice came into my mind and said, 'When the clock strikes twelve, you must leave or be discovered, my darling daughter.'

'I will, Mama, I promise I will,' I said aloud. I slipped out through the door in the garden wall and into the street. I had half-thought that perhaps there might have been a carriage waiting for me, a vehicle born of the same night-magic, but there was not. I'd have to walk through the backstreets to avoid attracting attention, for St Hilda's Square and the main bridge across the river were full of people going to the night-fair. In this part of the town, though, it was quiet. As I sped up the hill towards the castle, my feet, in those lovely shoes, seemed to skim over the cobblestones as though they had wings, and in hardly more time than it takes to write it, I was at the gate.

Quite suddenly, I was frightened that my stepmother had somehow contrived for me to be refused entry, so when the guards asked me my name I gave them the name of a character in one of my mother's favourite novels – a young Champainian woman who was a mistress of disguise and who worked as a spy for her government. And as citizens of the Republic of Champaine, a country far to our west, have a romantic reputation for glamour, I thought it appropriate.

'My name is Mademoiselle Camille St Clair,' I announced loftily, 'and I am expected.'

I don't know if it was my confident tone or my borrowed glamour but the guards offered no resistance or protest. They only nodded a little bemusedly and let me through without even asking me where my carriage was.

I went through the courtyard towards the lights and music of the ballroom. At the door a footman took my cloak while another asked who he should announce, then

I was sweeping in, straight into the bright hubbub of the ball.

Couples whirled about the floor and for a moment I could not see my family amongst them. I spied Odette first, whirling in the arms of burly Count Otto (I recognised the 'face like a bulldog' at once!). Then Babette, dancing with a man I recognised at once to be the Prince. Dressed in the sky-blue uniform, he was just as I'd seen in the miniature, with golden epaulets on his shoulder. He was blond and good-looking, though not quite as handsome as in the pictures. His eyes were a paler shade of blue, his hair less golden, his lips a little thinner and the expression on his face not as appealing. Still, he was a handsome man. Of my father there was no sign but I caught sight of Grizelda, sitting at a little table on the opposite side of the room with the ladies she called her dearest friends. She was looking like the cat that got the cream and they were looking like that same cream was choking them!

It would have been quite amusing if I hadn't been so nervous. All my old doubts and fears came rushing back and suddenly all I wanted to do was to turn around and walk away. But at that moment the dance stopped. As the Prince bowed to Babette, the footman stepped forward to announce me and the Prince looked straight at me. He smiled and, leaving Babette standing there, he came towards me.

'May I have the pleasure of this dance, Mademoiselle St Clair?'

'It would be an honour,' I stammered, aware of all the eyes on me, especially those of my stepmother and stepsisters. But I need not have worried; though an expression of slight puzzlement flashed across Grizelda's face, neither Babette's nor Odette's expressions showed a flicker of recognition – only spiteful curiosity. The protective glamour of the hazel tree must have dazzled them so that they did not see any familiarity in my face or what I was wearing. I offered up a silent thanks to my mother as the Prince took my hand and led me to the centre of the room.

Fortunately my mother taught me to dance – although I think the shoes would have helped me if I had needed it, for I felt as though they hardly touched the floor as the Prince and I glided around the room.

Close up, those first impressions were reinforced. Yes, he was handsome – even *very* handsome – but there was a hint of temper to the tight lips and a touch of arrogance in his blue eyes that made me feel a little wary. He was an excellent dancer and he soon set out to be charming as he whirled me around the floor, asking me about myself (I said I was a visitor from Champaine) but mostly showering me with compliments and claiming that his evening had been dull till I had walked into the room. I can't say I disliked what he said – I especially liked imagining how furious Babette would have been had she heard – for it was sweet balm after so many years of spite and disregard. But it did not go as deep as my heart, for despite the fine words and the admiring looks, there was still something about him that I did not warm to.

But when the dance ended, he asked me for another. And by the end of the second dance just about every mother in the room, and most of their daughters, were looking daggers at me – especially Grizelda and her daughters. I could see them whisper to each other, probably wondering who this interloper was who had captured the attention of the Prince. Feeling more and more uncomfortable, the pleasure I had first derived from being singled out changed to an anxiety that I would be found out if I kept attracting so much attention.

To my relief, before he could ask me to dance again, a footman came over bearing a folded slip of paper on a silver platter. The Prince took the paper and read it, then bowed to me and said, 'Mademoiselle, I must regretfully leave you for a moment as there is an urgent matter awaiting my attention.'

I gave him a deep curtsey. 'Of course, Your Royal Highness.'

'Don't go away, though, Mademoiselle,' he said with a dazzling smile before he strode off through the crowd that parted before him, the men bowing and the women curtseying as he passed.

After he had gone, a great many curious eyes turned back in my direction. I made as though I did not notice and, with my head held high, moved in the direction of the supper room just beyond the ballroom. I was famished and dearly hoped no-one would waylay me with questions or an offer of another dance before I got to those tables groaning with delicious food. Reaching the supper room without incident, I was able to fill a plate without too many people looking at me (though I could feel their eyes burning on my back). I slipped away, not wanting to eat under their stares, and went from room to room till I found a quiet little antechamber which contained a small table, a chair and not much else. The lamp on the table was unlit but that did not matter for the room was bathed in moonlight coming through its one window so that everything was nearly as bright as day.

I sat down and with a sigh of relief started on the food. Just as it had looked, it tasted wonderful: caviar on croutons, lobster in tarragon cream, steamed young asparagus with a lemony sauce, tiny pheasant pies, some anchovy eclairs and a preserved artichoke salad which tasted of the sun. It was the kind of thing I could normally only dream of and I took my time to savour each mouthful.

'Well, here I was thinking I'd get some quiet in here,' came a soft, amused voice behind me, making me jump. I turned to see that someone had noiselessly come in through that door at the other end of the room. He was a young man about the Prince's age, as tall and broad-shouldered as Leopold, his eyes also blue but veering more towards grey, while his hair was coal-black. He had a pleasant face but wasn't particularly handsome. He was dressed for the ball in a smart dark brown uniform with silver epaulets, but carried a book under his arm. He saw me look at the book and smiled ruefully.

'I'm not much of a one for parties and crowds. I thought I'd just hide in here and read awhile.'

'I'm sorry,' I said, flushing, 'but I thought nobody would come here so I –'

'Don't apologise, it is I who should do that,' he said. 'Coming in like that and frightening you away from your food.'

'Oh no, you didn't, I had already finished,' I lied, embarrassed to have been caught gluttonising like that all on my own.

He raised an eyebrow. 'Are you sure?'

'Quite sure.'

'Well, then you won't mind if I eat one of those eclairs, will you? They're one of my favourites.' I nodded and he took one and popped it in his mouth. 'I wasn't as clever or as far-sighted as you to get myself a plateful of food before I fled that ballroom,' he went on, and picking up a pie, ate it as well. 'Did you ever see such a crush! Glad I'm not in Leo's place and can escape without anyone noticing.'

Leo. He had called the Prince 'Leo'. He must know him very well. Not just a courtier, then, but a friend who had come with him from Faustina.

He must have read my expression, because he said, 'Forgive me. I'm being rude again. My name's Maximilian von Gildenstein. Everyone calls me Max.'

So this was Count Otto's son, the Prince's childhood friend! Surprised, I blurted out, 'You don't look much like your father.' I could have kicked myself for being so impolite.

But he laughed. 'No. I take after my mother, I'm told.'

'Oh.'

'And you, mystery lady, what is your name?'

'St Clair,' I said, promptly, 'er . . . Camille St Clair.'

'Goodness,' he said lightly, 'just like my mother's favourite heroine.'

My cheeks burned. Trust me, I thought to myself, to meet someone whose mother had the same taste as Mama! Hastily, I said, 'My mother was also a fan and as our family name is St Clair, she thought it would be nice if I was called Camille.'

'Mothers, eh?' said Max, his eyes twinkling at me from behind his glasses as he cheerfully grazed on the rest of my supper. 'Still, it is a nice name and it suits you.'

He smiled, and popped the last of my lobster thoughtfully into his mouth. 'So what do you think of the ball?'

'It's lovely,' I said weakly. 'I am having a very good time, thank you.'

'You should be out there, not skulking in here, you know,' he said seriously. 'Or you might miss your chance.'

'My chance?'

'There are more pretty girls out there than fancy buttons in a draper's shop,' he said, 'and every one of them hoping to catch Leo's eye.'

I drew myself up and looked at him. 'If you are quite finished, I would like to be alone again, thank you.'

'Oh dear, I've done it again, haven't I?' he said disarmingly. 'I didn't mean to offend you, Mademoiselle St Clair. It's just that it can be a bit much . . . knowing that all those people – they don't see Leo, they don't see my friend. They see the Crown Prince, the most glittering prize in the whole empire if only they could land him.'

'And so what if they do?' I snapped. 'It doesn't mean *I* do. And it doesn't mean that your friend is always just your friend. I mean,' I added, as he looked confused, 'out there he is the Crown Prince and everyone bows and curtseys to him and has eyes as you say only for him. And it looks like he likes it.'

'What would you know of that?' he said, sounding annoyed. 'You do not understand what it's like, nor know him as I do.'

'And nor do I wish to,' I said sharply, 'for I have no desire to land that "glittering prize", as you put it, sir. You say I do not understand his situation, well, you do not understand mine. And you know me and my reason for

74

being here no more than I know the Prince as a person. Now, goodnight to you.'

'No, wait, Camille, I only meant . . .'

But I did not turn around and he did not follow me, yet the sting of his words lingered. I wasn't royal, but I knew well enough what it was to be fawned over because of your social standing. And I knew well enough how shallow it was, too. But the Prince clearly did not. He might complain to his friend in private, but you could tell he enjoyed the attention and adulation.

'Oh!' Rounding a bend in the corridor, I had almost run straight into Prince Leopold himself and Count Otto, the two of them deep in conversation. The Count looked cross at the interruption but Leopold gave me a dazzling smile. 'Mademoiselle St Clair! Are you going back to the ballroom?'

I wanted to say no, but instead mumbled, 'Er, I . . . yes. But, that is, I was just planning on exploring a little first . . . I have heard Ashberg Castle is one of the great wonders of this land and as this is the first time I have been here, I just thought . . . I hope you don't mind.'

'Of course I don't mind,' said the Prince laughingly, 'and if I don't, nobody will. Will they, Count Otto? Baron Tomas must do as he is told by us, isn't that right?'

'Yes, indeed, Your Royal Highness,' said Count Otto stolidly. His glance at me was not altogether friendly.

'That being so,' said the Prince, 'I've decided to show you around myself. What do you say?'

'But Your Royal Highness,' began Count Otto, 'the guests will be waiting for you to return and –'

'Hang the guests!' said the Prince. '*I'm* the guest of honour and can do just as I like. And what I would like right now is to show Mademoiselle St Clair around Ashberg Castle, is that understood?'

Count Otto's face was impassive, though I noticed a tiny pinch of white at the corners of his nostrils. He flashed me a hard look, then turned to the Prince. 'Very well, Your Highness, as you wish.'

I've made an enemy, I thought, uneasy. If only I could have kept my mouth shut! It would just have been better to go back to the ballroom. Now, not only had I helped to annoy Count Otto, but I was forced to follow Prince Leopold on an unwanted guided tour of Ashberg Castle.

Eleven

As we walked along, with the Prince rather pompously – and inaccurately – recounting the history of the castle, I couldn't help but think that Max would have done a better job of telling it. He might have been cheeky about it, I thought, but I didn't think he'd have been boring, and sadly, that could not be said about the Prince. He rambled on, seeming to enjoy the sound of his own voice more than the subject he was supposedly enlightening me on.

I was certainly paying the price for lying, I thought as we entered the council room where, centuries ago in the days before the Faustine Empire had annexed our country, the Lords of Ashberg had held court. One of the oldest parts of the castle, it was small, dark and rather grim.

'Mademoiselle St Clair, you are looking a little tired,' said the Prince, unexpectedly interrupting himself in the middle of a dull monologue on the history of the Lords of Ashberg, only half of which was true.

I started. 'Er, no . . . yes, that is . . .'

'Please sit down for a moment.' He motioned me to a chair. What else could I do? I sat down, and he sat next to me and smiled.

'Better?'

'Thank you, yes.' It wasn't. The seat was long and my skirts were quite full but the Prince had still managed to sit uncomfortably close to me.

'It makes you think, doesn't it?' he said.

'Er . . . yes?' I didn't know what he meant and I heartily wished he would get up and that we could move on.

'One must seize the day,' he said. 'The past belongs to the past, the future belongs to the future, but the present is ours. Don't you think so?'

'Um, I suppose so.'

'I'm glad you do,' he said, and he closed in, one of his arms around my waist, his other hand tilting my face up to his. His eyes looked into mine and he murmured, 'Sweet creature, you would tempt a saint,' and then his lips came down to mine.

'No!' I cried, jerking my head away violently. 'No,' I repeated, less harshly, as I saw the stricken look on his face. 'I mean, Your Royal Highness,' I quickly added, 'I was not expecting this.'

'Are you playing with me, girl?' His voice was cold now, the stricken look gone.

'No, of course not. It's just that . . . if someone saw . . .'

'So what if they do? I am Prince Leopold. It is my right to kiss whoever I please.'

And what of my right, I thought angrily. Instead, quietly trying to sidle away, I said, 'Your Royal Highness, I am flattered, but I can't –'

'Why not? You seemed eager enough to be alone with me.' The blue eyes now like ice, his thin lips set like the blade of a dagger.

'No, that is, I –'

'Stop this game,' he said roughly and grabbed me by the shoulder. I struggled to free myself but he was stronger.

'No, please, don't –' I cried.

'What is going on here?' came a familiar voice at the door. Leopold dropped my arm and I seized my chance. Dishevelled, panting, I raced for the door but Max blocked it. 'What just happened?' he said coldly.

I swallowed, unable to speak.

'She's been flirting with me all evening, the little witch,' said Leopold calmly. 'What else was I supposed to think?'

Max looked at him. There was a strange expression in his eyes and he finally said, biting off the words, 'This isn't the way for a prince to speak – or behave.'

Leopold's face stilled, an unpleasant gleam in his eyes. 'You forget yourself,' he said softly.

'I most certainly do not,' said Max in the same tone. They looked at each other like two wild animals sizing each other up before a fight.

I said, 'Please stop, both of you. I'm ... It doesn't matter. I just want to go, please let me go!'

'No,' said the Prince, but Max stepped aside. I dashed past him down the corridor, holding up my skirts and running away as fast as I could, the enchanted shoes racing me towards an exit. I suddenly realised that in my hurry I'd left my evening bag and cloak behind, but that didn't matter – they'd turn back into leaves at the stroke of midnight so even if someone thought to check the cloakroom for clues as to my identity, they would be none the wiser. It wasn't until I was well out of the castle and down the hill that I realised my locket was also missing. When the Prince had grabbed me he must have snapped the chain, I thought. It might have been enhanced and enriched by the magic but it was real enough, and if the Prince found it and made enquiries there was a faint possibility it might lead him to me. But there was nothing I could do about it now. I was certainly not going to go back for it.

Once again, I avoided the areas where I might be seen. The night-fair was still in full swing. The clock in St Hilda's Square began to count down the twelve strokes to midnight and by the time I'd got to the streets near my house, the last stroke sounded. All at once I was barefoot and stockingless on the cold cobblestones. To my immense relief, the dress did not fall away in shredded rags but just lost its magical glamour, returning to the simple muslin dress it had once been. At least that was something, I thought miserably as I trudged homewards. My evening was ruined and the magic of the hazel tree drained for no good purpose, but at least I wouldn't break Maria's heart as well.

I'd tell her I hadn't had the courage to go to the ball.

I shivered, suddenly. I'd thought myself so clever, under my borrowed identity. But it might well have been my undoing, for if Leopold had thought I was a member of a great and important Ashberg family, he might well not have acted like he had. But I had come on my own, a supposed foreigner with no family and no reputation. If Max hadn't come in at that moment, what might have happened? It might not have just ended with a stolen kiss . . .

I thought about what Max had said. Had he been warning me rather than scolding me? But if that was the case, why hadn't he said so? Because 'Leo' was his best friend, and also the Crown Prince; when all was said and done, that trumped everything.

Passing through the woodland to the hazel tree, I saw that it had shrunk a great deal. It now only just reached my knees and its branches were almost bare. A few hours ago, the sight would have deeply dismayed me. Now, it hardly affected me as I walked listlessly back through the garden to the house, fortunately without attracting attention.

I got myself some cold water from the kitchen and washed my dirty feet and undressed, folding Maria's dress carefully and hiding it under my bed. Shivering in my thin nightdress, I washed the underthings and hung them inside my cupboard to dry. I locked my door from the outside, replaced the key on its nail and, climbing in painfully through my window, crept into my cold and lumpy bed.

I tried to sleep. But everything kept going round and round in my head and in the end I gave up, lit a candle and sat up to read one of Mama's books till, bit by bit, I began to calm and finally see that things might not be as bad as they seemed. I had escaped the Prince's clutches, he had no idea who I really was, and neither he nor Max would guess the truth in a million years. At least I'd had a few moments of fun and glamour, and eaten some nice food, and Maria's daughter could still dance at her wedding in her pretty muslin frock.

By the time I heard the first stirrings in the house as the servants then the family returned from their various outings, I was feeling a good deal better and even managed to fall asleep for an hour or so before my door was unlocked and a rough voice told me to get my 'useless bones' up for the first of my morning chores.

Twelve

Mrs Jager was in a foul temper (the whisper in the kitchen was she'd overindulged in wine at the night-fair) and made me and everyone else run ragged. I had to get Maria's dress back to her as soon as possible, in case Grizelda should get it in her head to search my room. Neither she nor her daughters surfaced till well past the hour when lunch should normally have been served. But I didn't have a chance to slip out and return the dress till quite a while later.

In the meantime, I kept an ear out for gossip about the ball. There was a good deal, for it appeared the whole town was buzzing with news about the 'foreign hussy', who had turned up alone at the ball and who had danced more than once with the Prince only to then vanish. A footman had heard about it from a friend of his who'd got it from someone else who knew someone who'd been working at the castle that night. I could hardly recognise the picture he painted of the whole thing, for the story had been vastly embellished so that now the rumour that ran amongst the staff was that the Prince had fallen deeply in love and that he would not rest till he found the mysterious girl who had stolen his heart. The open-air address in the Square had even been cancelled as the Prince apparently no longer felt up to it. The whole thing divided the staff: some relished the romantic story while others thought the foreigner was up to no good and suspected her to be part of a dastardly plot to humiliate Ashberg and its finest families – some hostile foreign power or Faustinian snobs who wanted to ruin Ashberg's reputation, depending on who you listened to. Because, as everyone knew, there was no way the Emperor would allow his only son to marry some foreign nobody, no matter how pretty she was or how much the Prince had fallen for her. Leopold had to make a good marriage, and while a girl from one of the top Ashberg families might at a pinch be suitable, somebody bowling out of nowhere with a foreign name and no reputation certainly wasn't.

I listened to all this talk with some amusement, hugging my secret to myself. For the first time in a long time, I felt as though I had some power – the power of knowledge and of the truth. All these people gossiping and speculating, people who had helped to make my life a misery, or who had at least looked the other way. I was the only one there who knew what had happened. I was the only one there who knew the truth about the Prince. It was a bitter knowledge, but it made me feel strong. Stupidly so, as it turned out.

It was very late in the afternoon when I finally hit on the perfect excuse to slip away. Every month or so it was my job to gather up all the household rags and dusters that had become too tattered to use and take them to the rag-and-bone man. It wasn't really time to do it yet but because of all the extra cleaning and polishing that had had to be done for Count Otto's visit, I soon gathered up enough rubbish to convince the head kitchen maid that it should be done. It was easy to hide Maria's parcel under the pile of rags and, with the heavy bundle on my back, I went out without anyone the wiser. Passing the hazel tree, I saw with a pinch of the heart that it was still quite bare and had shrunk and withered so much that it looked like nothing more than a dry, dead stick. There would be no more magic to come from it, I thought sadly. Everything was back to what it had been before.

As the rag-and-bone man's shop was in a dirty backstreet a good way from the house I decided to deliver the dress and underthings safely back to Maria first. I dumped the rags in some bushes on the way and hurried in the other direction. I knew that at this time Maria was likely to be finishing up her afternoon duties in the Angel's kitchen but, as I couldn't risk being seen by the other workers, I intended leaving the parcel in her room with a note, then rush back to my rag duties before anyone wondered why I was taking so long.

I'd almost reached the narrow street that runs along the back of the Angel when disaster struck. I was racing along without taking much notice of what was going on when I suddenly spied another Mancer carriage – or was it the same one? – drawn up outside a house. Instinctively, I turned and went in the opposite direction, emerging on a street lined with elegant boutiques, outside which smart carriages were waiting for even smarter passengers. I had no other way to go. Clutching my parcel tightly, I scurried past the coachmen with head bent and heart beating like a drum. I tried to tell myself I had nothing to fear, that nobody knew, when suddenly –

'What on earth are *you* doing here?'

Horror-struck, I stared at Odette, who had suddenly emerged from a hat shop. Only for a second did I stare; the next, I took to my heels and fled, with her lying shouts to 'Stop! Thief!' echoing behind me. I didn't make the end of the street before I was tackled by two burly coachmen – my parcel sent flying, the brown paper bursting open to reveal its contents.

The coachmen stared. 'And what's this?' said one of them sternly.

'Please, please let me go. It's not how it looks, I promise. Please –' I was almost sobbing, but it made no difference. I was obviously poor. I'd been caught fleeing while carrying a parcel of clothes in a street full of dress shops. I'd been called a thief. Guilty as charged, as far as they were concerned.

I had to get away. Struggling desperately against their iron grip, I managed to reach down and bite one of them on the arm. He howled but instead of letting me go, gave me such a cuff on the side of the head with his other hand that my ears rang. 'You little hellcat,' he said between gritted teeth. 'You vicious little hellcat.'

'What's going on?' said Odette, coming up towards us, her sister close on her heels. Her eyes widened as she took in the contents of the parcel. But it was Babette who, baffled, said, 'I don't understand – it can't be – it looks just like that other dress. But Mother saw to it, didn't she? So how could Ashes . . .?'

Odette said nothing as she looked at me, her eyes gleaming with a nasty light. And suddenly I was filled with terror, and it gave me a mad idea. I couldn't pretend *nothing* had happened. But Odette and Babette were not – at all costs – to suspect the truth. Better to be thought of as a thief. I said, desperately, 'I – I wanted to replace the other one. And, you see, it was . . . it was so tempting to . . . when I saw it, I just could not help myself and –'

'She admits it, the shameless thing,' said Babette.

Odette, a younger version of her mother, still said nothing but continued to stare at me as if she were trying to see inside my heart to my deepest feelings. Yet she was still young, not experienced like Grizelda at unpeeling a person. After a moment she said, 'She's certainly shameless, and she's got to be stopped,' and, turning to one of the coachmen, ordered, 'Go and get a policeman and come back quick smart.'

Off he went while the other coachman held me tight.

'Mother won't like this, Odette,' Babette said. 'It's embarrassing for our reputation to have a scandal played out in the street.'

'No, no, Mother will understand,' said Odette, impatiently. 'See, Ashes will be thrown in prison like she's deserved for a long time.' She went over to the parcel. 'Look – it's not just the dress she's pinched, but underclothes, too.'

'It's strange – it looks almost the same as that dress Mama destroyed yesterday,' said Babette with a frown.

'It's the same pattern,' I said, quickly. 'A popular pattern, you see, and –'

They looked at me in disgust. Babette said, loftily, '*No high-class fashion house makes two dresses exactly the same – it's just not done.*'

'It won't be a high-class fashion house,' snorted Odette. 'She couldn't have even gotten a foot in the door! And look at that material – it's not top quality. No, it must be from one of those places that make cheap copies of fashionable frocks for shop-girls and waitresses. Am I right?' she said, staring at me.

I hung my head and nodded reluctantly, glad for her mistake.

'Where is this place?' snapped Odette.

'I . . .' I swallowed. 'I don't want to say.'

'You'll have to, you little thief, when the police ask you,' said Babette.

'You're not the police,' I said tightly. 'I don't have to tell you anything.'

'How dare you!'

'Easily,' I said, beginning to enjoy myself in a miserable sort of way. 'I don't care what you think, you jumped-up clothes horse with sawdust for brains.'

Babette's jaw dropped. Her eyes bulged. She squeaked, 'Odette! Did you hear what she said?'

Odette smiled thinly. 'Don't worry, Babette. She'll soon have time to ponder her bad manners when she's locked up in the dark with only rats for company.' She turned to me. 'You're such a fool, Ashes. Don't you even see what you've done? You've shown exactly what you are – a common criminal. No-one can protect you now. Our father will completely disown you. Even if they don't hang you, which they should, you might as well be dead.'

I looked into her pretty face, into those nice dark eyes that were bright with malice and cruelty, and said quietly, 'Being dead would be better than ever seeing you again. But listen well, both of you – the day will come when you will pay for what you have done. You will beg for mercy. But it will be too late.'

Though the words were quiet, they came from the darkest part of me, from the boiling heart of the rage and hatred I'd held down for so long, and they had an unexpected effect on the girls. Babette gasped, stepping back, and Odette's eyes widened in shock, even fear. But before either of them could say anything, the coachman came back with three policemen. It seemed like overkill for one scrawny little street thief. Two of them grabbed me, while the third policeman picked up the parcel and took a statement from my stepsisters.

As I was dragged away, I could feel the girls' eyes on me. Now they and their mother had exactly what they'd always wanted – to be rid of me – and I was the fool who'd made the noose for her own neck. Odette was right, my father would certainly disown me when he heard what I was alleged to have done. The last shred of his protection would be gone.

I tried to tell myself that things could have been worse; that they could know the actual truth, that I could have been dragged off not by the police but by the Mancers – that it was better to be thought of as a thief than a witch. But it was cold comfort because I knew that my desperate story had only bought me a little time. I'd have to answer the policeman's questions, and even if I made things up – which I had to – sooner or later they would come to realise I was lying. And then what was to happen to me?

Thirteen

The police station was crowded and noisy, and stank of old cabbage soup and old socks. My captors handed me over to a sergeant who wrote down my name – or at least the name my stepsisters had given, Ashes – which I did not challenge, not wanting to attract any more attention to myself, and the charge: stealing. Then I was marched down to the women's holding cell, which was full of women of every age. Most seemed unfussed at being there: a big group played cards, one or two paced around, a couple of inmates huddled in corners, their heads in their hands, while the rest chatted or dozed.

I was nervous at first. Many of these women looked pretty tough – the sort whose eye you really wouldn't want to catch – but I soon realised that no-one was interested in me. They all had their own problems and many seemed to know each other. As I sat quietly listening to their conversations, I learned that most of them were pickpockets, card sharps or brawlers who had been picked up during the night-fair. Even though this was clearly only the minor league of the underworld, it felt strange to have suddenly been thrust into the company of those who thought nothing of the law. Servant I might have been, disregarded and oppressed, but though the work was backbreaking, it was still respectable. Now I had fallen far beyond even the humblest servant. I was a common thief, like so many of the others here, and I could never claw my way back up, no matter what happened. My throat thickened with the bitterness of it and I could feel foolish tears starting. But I blinked them fiercely away and tried to concentrate on working out what I must say when it came time for my interview before the magistrate.

But it was hard for I was quite out of ideas and after a time I gave up, listening instead to the others' conversation, pricking up my ears when I heard mention of the Prince. But it was just gossip about the 'mysterious girl', nothing more illuminating than what the servants had been saying.

By and by dinner came – tin bowls filled with thin, greasy cabbage soup and hunks of dry, dusty black bread. It looked disgusting but I was hungry. I was just starting on the bread, having gobbled down the soup, when suddenly there was a yell and one of the card players, a big woman with a face like a cracked old boot, launched herself at a figure in the corner, punching and kicking her. Someone told me that she had tried to sneak the big woman's bread when she wasn't looking. The whole cell was in uproar, enjoying the fight.

I don't know why I did it – everything should have warned me not to. And the big woman was in the right, after all. But the sound of that baying crowd – and the sight of that woman's huge fists and feet smashing into the helpless thief, who was about half her size, and who had rolled into a ball to try to escape the blows – aroused a volcanic reaction in me, so that I screamed, 'Stop that! Stop it at once!'

The big woman paused, looked over her shoulder at me and smiled unpleasantly. 'What did you say?'

'Let her be,' I said, swallowing.

The big woman dropped the thief, who stared at me with wild green eyes from under a tangled mass of dark hair. The big woman lumbered towards me and the crowd in front of her parted, everyone staring at me.

Trembling, I held out my hunk of bread. 'Take this. She shouldn't have done it but, please, let her be.'

The big woman stopped and stared for a long moment, then snatched the bread from me and said, 'You're a fool,' just as a couple of policemen, alerted by the noise, came running to see what was going on.

Nobody told them what had happened, only the big woman, who said that there had been a bit of 'high spirits and larking about – nothing to worry about, officers'. The policemen were easily satisfied – it was clear they had no stomach for trying to find out what had really happened. Once they were gone, the big woman turned to the thief and said, 'If you try anything like that again, I'll rip your guts out.' Then she looked at me, raised her eyebrows, shrugged, and went back to her friends and her card game – devouring my hunk of bread. The others whispered about it for a little while but soon lost interest and returned to their own concerns, though from time to time I would catch someone glancing at me and at the thief.

The thief didn't try to come near me, and I let her be. She'd given me one wild glance of uncomprehending gratitude, then had huddled down again, putting her head in her arms. She was thin, her filthy feet bare, her nails ragged and bitten to the quick. Her clothes were dirty rags much worse than my own patched dress – she looked altogether a most miserable creature. She was young, too – probably only a year or two older than me. And I hadn't heard her speak once. Even when the big woman was bashing her, she hadn't made a sound.

Time passed and as darkness began to fall the card players put away their games. It grew quiet in the cell, warm because of the many bodies. People fell asleep on the straw strewn over the stone floor. Some snored – the big woman the loudest of them all. But I couldn't sleep. I had no space to lie down so I sat with my arms around my knees, thinking and thinking and not getting anywhere.

Still, I must have dozed off, for when the barred door was flung open and the lantern light fell upon us, I came to with a start and saw that four large policemen had come into the cell. But they weren't alone. With them was a tall dark-haired man wearing elegant evening dress, a cloak and a black eye mask, carrying a smart silver-topped walking stick. In the wavering light of the lantern, the part of his face that could be seen was pale as death, and the silver top of his stick, with its sinuous serpentine curves, glowed with an odd light.

Though everyone had been woken by the entrance of the five men, no-one said a word. It wasn't the sight of the police that stilled the tongues of even the toughest of the prisoners. It was the sight of the other man. Nobody needed to be told who he was or, rather, *what* he was. A Mancer!

I was sure my last hour had come. They had found out and were after me. I was so scared that I was beyond fear. I sat as still as a frog hypnotised by a snake, but I knew it would do me no good.

The Mancer did not speak. He walked amongst us, swinging his lantern, examining every frozen, frightened face. Each time, he passed on. Now, the moment had come – the lantern swung towards me – and my heart nearly stopped. He looked at me and I felt the cold fire of his pale eyes burn into me, even though I kept my own eyes down. And then . . . he passed on to the next person, the next face, until he reached the thief.

I could see what he was doing out of the corner of my eye. He swung the lantern over her, made a clicking sound in the back of his throat – audible to everyone in the deathly silence – and bent down to her. He forced her face up and looked into her eyes. He sniffed. He straightened and called to the policemen. 'This one,' he said sharply.

The thief shrieked and tried to twist away but he was too quick for her, grabbing her by her long tangled hair. In an instant two of the policemen were on her. One held her down while the other tied her wrists and ankles with rope. She had gone quiet and limp, her head on her chest. Nobody said anything. I felt nauseous, my palms were prickling and my heart was thumping so much I was sure it could be heard.

The Mancer held the lantern up and looked at us. 'Do any of you know anything about this girl?' His voice was soft, pleasant and educated, yet there was a tone in it that sent shivers down my spine. Nobody said anything so he repeated the question, adding, 'If I find out that any of you have withheld information, it will be so much worse for *all* of you.'

The big woman said, in a voice that was a mere shadow of her former booming tones, 'She . . . she's a thief, sir.'

The Mancer smiled thinly. 'So are you all.'

'No – you see, sir,' stammered the big woman, 'she's the worst – she steals from her own fellow prisoners – took my bread.'

'I see.'

'And . . .' Her panicked gaze swung over to me. 'That one over there came to her aid, heaven knows why.'

'Really?' said the Mancer, his pale gaze was on me again. I was overcome with horror and terror. I called out cowardly words that, though true enough, resounded shamefully in my head afterwards. 'No! She's nothing to me! I've never met her before in my life! You must believe me!'

'We'll see about that,' said the Mancer and he signalled to the other two policemen, who pinioned my arms behind my back, tied them with rope and stuffed a gag in my mouth as I was trying to protest my innocence. The Mancer turned to the other prisoners. 'Not a word about any of this, or I'll be back for more of you,' he said quietly. 'Is that understood?' Every head nodded, fearfully; every mouth was shut, every head was bent as I and the other girl were picked up and carried out of the cell in utter silence.

Fourteen

He had a carriage waiting and we were flung inside it, into a hinged compartment at the back of the seat. It was dark and suffocating, like being in a coffin, though at least they'd ripped off my gag. Each bump of the carriage over the cobblestones made our teeth rattle in our heads, but neither of us spoke a word. I could hear the other girl's breathing, regular and soft, not sharp and ragged like mine. She wasn't afraid, I thought, suddenly. Or maybe she was beyond fear – scared into a numbed acceptance. But I wasn't ready for that. I wasn't ready to disappear. And yet that was what would happen if the Mancers found out my secret. There were never any reports of the arrests of illegal witches and magicians, and no public trials; one simply knew that if they were ever caught, they would vanish never to be seen again. Whether they rotted in prison for ever or were executed or experimented on (as rumour had it), no-one was quite sure. And no-one wanted to find out. Unless I was very, very careful, I was going to find out in the worst possible way. But I had one thing going for me: I had been picked up by chance – the Mancer had not come looking for me.

But he had for the other girl. Why? If she was an illegal witch, she surely wouldn't have been in the ordinary holding cell. She'd clearly been arrested along with the others at the night-fair and, remembering how she'd stolen the big woman's bread and the starving look of her, I thought it most likely that her arrest had been for stealing food. But ordinary thieves are of no interest whatsoever to Mancers, so somehow they must have learned she was more than what she seemed to be. I remembered how the Mancer had gone amongst the prisoners, checking each one of us, and then when he reached the girl, how he had looked at her for quite a while before saying, 'This is the one.' So he must have had some description of her but hadn't been sure which one he was looking for. What did that mean? Was she a witch, or something else? The Mancers looked after the royal family's security, after all, which included all threats, magical or not. And the last time a member of the royal family had come to Ashberg, the Emperor had been shot at. Maybe the Mancers had information of some plot against the Prince. Maybe that explained their unusual activity in the days leading up to the visit. Maybe this girl was some kind of assassin.

But whatever the truth, whether she was a witch or a would-be assassin or simply a person of suspicion, it didn't bode well for her. Or for me, as I was now associated with her by mere chance. The only way for me to get out of this would be to convince the Mancers that it really *was* chance, that I really had nothing to do with her and that my only crime had been to take pity on her in the cell. There would be no escape for her, but there might be for me, perhaps, if I was very lucky.

The carriage came to an abrupt halt. Rough hands pulled us blinking out of the dark and untied our legs so we could walk. We found ourselves in a large courtyard, enclosed on three sides by blank, windowless walls. On the fourth was a big barred door guarded by large men who wore the black and white livery of Mancer servants and who carried guns. I was disoriented by the trip, but knew we must be somewhere in the Mancers' quarter of the city, though I had never been inside it.

The policemen marched us to the barred door and left us with two burly Mancer guards, who held us in an iron grip while the Mancer who'd brought us from the prison rapped three times on the door with his walking stick. It opened, and we stepped through . . .

Into Hell, I thought at once. Behind the door was a long, dark corridor, fitfully lit by a red glow from down the end, from which I could hear clanking noises as well. We were marched down this corridor, the main Mancer leading the way, the guards behind us. Nobody spoke. The girl stumbled along beside me but she made no move towards me, she didn't even look at me. I was desperately racking my brains trying to remember every last thing I'd heard about the Mancers. Theirs was a closed world. You couldn't become a Mancer just like that, you had to be either born into an old Mancer family, or on rare occasions, be chosen by the General Secretary of the Mancer Council or one of his talent scouts. It was said the Mancers held every spellbook and volume on magic that had ever been written (all such literature was banned for everyone else). Yet they did not rely solely on old magic, it was said, but also experimented to find new forms. Their methods were shrouded in absolute secrecy, however, for their magic was built around one objective: the protection of the Empire and the elimination of its enemies. Mancers were forbidden from using their magical knowledge for any other purpose. They could not sell spells or go into business as public wizards, and they were banned from practising magic for personal gain such as for fun or relaxation, or for love or hate. They were kept away from normal society and lived in special quarters, they went to special schools and could not travel or marry without the approval of the Mancer Council. At the age of nine, a Mancer swears an unbreakable oath of secrecy – the betrayal of which was punishable by death. They were anonymous – only the General Secretary of the Mancer Council ever appeared at public occasions. But even he made no public statements on Mancer matters; only the Emperor could do that and he hadn't done so for many years.

What use were any of those scraps of information, when I knew nothing whatsoever about how Mancer magic worked – not even a hint of something that might help me to armour myself against it? They must be able to read minds, I thought, at least at some level. They couldn't be infallible, or there would not have been such incidents as the attempted assassination of the Emperor years ago, or any possibility of illegal witchcraft. But that didn't comfort me much. I was just a sixteen-year-old girl with a guilty secret. I'd played with fire like the idiot I was and,

100

under interrogation, they'd know that in seconds. I was no enemy of the State but I was certain they'd see me as such. Unless . . .

The finch. The hazel tree. My mother. If only . . . I did not even dare to put my desperate wish into thought. Not in this place, not in the dark heart of the most powerful magic, beside which the magic of the hazel tree seemed like a frivolous fancy. A frivolous fancy that could soon see me swinging on the end of a rope – or worse.

We reached the end of the corridor and found ourselves in a round, echoing stone room, with a metal door down one end. It was garishly lit by red lanterns hung around its walls and in the very middle of it, perched on a stool, sat a Mancer scribbling at a tall desk, his fingers stained with ink, with a pile of ledgers beside him. Behind him, near the door, was another table with what looked like a goldfish bowl. However, instead of fish, it contained a confused mass of objects that made no sense to me. It must be some sort of magical item, I thought.

The Mancer at the desk was small, wizened and grey. He didn't wear a mask but steel-framed pince-nez on his nose. He didn't have a cloak but was dressed in an ordinary dark suit like that of a clerk. But from the respectful way the elegant Mancer addressed him as 'Sir', the wizened one must have been of higher rank. They conferred briefly in low voices and I strained to hear what they said. But I could not.

Shortly afterwards, the little man pressed a lever under his desk and the door at the end of the room opened with a grinding of cogs. We were hustled towards it by the guards and the elegant Mancer followed. Just before we got to the door, he pointed to the bowl and said, 'Empty out your pockets and put the contents in there.' Now I knew why it contained such a confused mass of objects, everything from coins and buttons to handkerchiefs and pocketknives and sweets and . . . my heart nearly stopped as I caught sight of something familiar.

'Didn't you hear me, girl? Empty your pockets,' said the Mancer roughly, and I realised with a start that they were all waiting for me, for the other girl must have already done as she was told. I rummaged feverishly in my pockets, pulling out their meagre contents: my old mittens, a twist of coloured paper, an apple core and the stub of a pencil. In my agitation I dropped the pencil and had to scrabble for it under the impatient glare of the Mancers and the guards. I put the pencil in the bowl with the other things, trying hard not to stare at what lay there amongst the nest of other people's belongings. A locket – a small, green, enamelled heart-shaped locket. It looked exactly like mine, the one Maria had given me, the one I'd lost at the ball . . .

My head whirled. How had my locket got there? But wait. Wait. How did I even know it was mine? How many of those cheap little lockets had been sold, I told myself, wildly. You could buy them at any fair. And the night-fair had just been held. There was sure to have been a stall selling that kind of thing. Someone could have bought one and then been arrested by the Mancers. No, it couldn't be mine.

Through the doorway was yet another door, wooden this time, then a grille gate, which was unlocked by a large warder who loomed out of the gloom with a bunch of keys. He'd clearly emerged from having his dinner, for the napkin with which he'd just wiped his mouth hung out of his pocket. As we passed the open door to his quarters, a little boy stuck his head out and looked at us briefly before being called back in by a woman's voice. He was a small, fair child of about seven, with bright, pitiless eyes. His glance was the same kind an ordinary small boy might give a fascinating insect.

We walked on, through another grille, and finally down a corridor lined, at regular intervals, by cell doors. Everything was neat and clean, with none of the noise and stink of the police station cells, but there was a feeling here that almost made me look back on that cell with nostalgia. For you knew there were people here, behind those thick metal doors; but there wasn't a sound. Not even a whisper. It was quiet as a graveyard, but not as peaceful for it was a place where the very air seemed to breathe living despair.

We descended a winding stone staircase which twisted into darkness, and down another corridor, where the old Mancer stopped. He gestured for the warder to unlock the door and waved us in.

The cell was small and damp but it was empty at least. There was straw strewn on the stone floor and a couple of grey blankets and a bucket in one corner. Air came in through a small, barred window high above our heads, and though that air was a little stale, it was better than that suffocating compartment in the carriage, which was what I'd feared these cells might be more like. For some reason I had the impression that this wasn't the kind of cell you'd put a really dangerous person in, which made my heart lift a little, and that impression was confirmed by the elderly

Mancer's words to us as he left the cell. 'You'll be fetched first thing tomorrow morning,' he had said, and then he went out without looking back. The door was slammed shut and locked behind him, and we were alone at last.

Fifteen

I looked over at the other girl. She was sitting in the same dejected position she had been in at the holding cell – her knees drawn up to her chin with her head resting on them. She looked as though she'd given up already.

I hadn't, though. No way was I just going to meekly give up and go like a lamb to the slaughter. I paced around the cell looking for any way to escape. I tried the door and, of course, found it to be thoroughly locked and immovable. I looked up at the narrow window high above us and thought if I could somehow take a flying leap up to it, I might be able to – what, exactly? Turn myself into a snake and slither out through the narrow bars? Or a bird and fly out of the window? I rapped on the thick walls, only succeeding in scraping my knuckles. I lifted up the straw to look for a grate in the floor underneath, finding nothing but the tightly packed flagstones with not a chink between them.

It was as I was replacing the straw that the other girl spoke for the first time.

'I take for you.' Her voice was low, a little raspy, with a strong foreign intonation.

I started and turned around to find her looking at me, her green eyes quite unreadable. Weakly, I said, 'What did you say?'

She shrugged and held out a hand, in which something small and green and heart-shaped glittered. I stared, unable to believe my eyes. I stammered, 'Wh– what? How?'

'I see in your eyes you like this. So I take when they not watching,' she said, flashing a little smile.

It must have happened when I dropped the pencil, I thought. She must have been very fast because I'd noticed nothing. Some thief, indeed! 'Thank you.'

'You kind to me. I want to repay.'

I took the locket and slipped it in my pocket. I said, 'You're different. From before, I mean.'

She smiled. 'I think if they think I am meek and scared, they not watch me too much.'

I smiled back. 'Good plan. Pity you forgot about it in the police cell.'

She shrugged. 'Make no difference. They come get me anyway. And I too hungry,' she said.

'Yes,' I said, 'but if you hadn't done that –'

'I know. You not here,' she said, her green eyes shooting me a sharp glance. 'I am sorry. This also why I want repay.'

I made up my mind and put out a hand. 'I'm Selena. And you are?'

'I am called Olga,' she answered promptly, shaking my hand. 'Olga of the family Ironheart.'

An unusual name – obviously foreign. I wanted to ask why the Mancers had taken her, but she forestalled me by saying, with a sideways glance, 'You hear of *garwaf*?'

'I don't under—' I began, then gasped as I realised what she'd said. Her pronunciation was unfamiliar but I'd seen that word before in one of my mother's old books. I could see the actual line swimming in front of my eyes: *Garwaf: an old term for a werewolf.*

'You – you can't be . . .' I whispered.

It wasn't possible, it just wasn't. Werewolves and other shapeshifters had been extinct in the Faustine Empire for more than a hundred years since the defeat of the Grey Widow. They still existed in other countries, of course, especially Ruvenya, but even there I'd heard they weren't exactly thick on the ground. They lived isolated from ordinary people and kept to themselves except in rare circumstances. They had very few children. And they most certainly couldn't get visas to enter the empire. I could not even remember hearing any rumours of werewolves entering our lands within my lifetime.

All these thoughts flashed in my head as I stared at Olga Ironheart – at the sharp green eyes, the tangled black hair, the long nails and scrawny body, and remembered the flash of sharp white teeth when she'd smiled. I knew in an instant that the impossible had happened and that I was shut up in a Mancer cell with a werewolf – with a *hungry* werewolf.

She read my expression at once and said, sounding hurt, 'You mistake, Selena. Family Ironheart never eat people and never, ever hurt friend.'

'I'm sorry. I didn't mean, that is, I . . . it's just a shock,' I said lamely. 'I never expected ever to meet – I mean, I know nothing really about your people. Only the little I've read in books. I thought your people weren't allowed to come here?'

She shrugged. 'Not allowed does not mean not possible. They cannot guard whole border always.' She paused. 'Family Ironheart from Ruvenya, you see. But long, long, long ago my great, great, great grandmother, when she young, she come from here. She flee your country when great killing going on. My great, great, great grandfather – he find her in forest near border. She nearly dead, he nurse her until she well and then they marry. You see?'

'I do.' It must have been after the Grey Widow's rebellion, I thought, with a strange flutter of the heart. Oh, Olga Ironheart, you and I share more than you know! But I could not tell her – dared not tell her – that in my veins flowed the blood of the moon-sisters, who were outlaws like the *garwafs*, but in a worse situation, for werewolves had always existed in all kinds of places, while moon-sisters were indigenous to Ashbergia and had never settled elsewhere. And even though Olga had entered the country illegally, her government might help her if they found out where she was. But if the Mancers discovered the truth about me, nobody would help me. I'd be branded a traitor merely by virtue of my blood, and be made to disappear.

I said quietly, 'Ashberg's a dangerous place for someone like you. You were bound to get caught.'

She shrugged. 'I did not think this would happen. I slip in unnoticed. And I have money. Plan to be careful. But my money, it all stolen in hotel and I am starving and take food from shop – and then am arrested. I think at first police not know truth about me. But somehow Mancers find out.'

'But why did you come in the first place?'

'I am curious to see this country, home of my long-ago grandmother.'

Simple as that, yet utterly reckless, I thought. How could she think she'd pass unnoticed? But then she was Ruvenyan and werewolves were not outlawed there; she mustn't have fully realised what danger she was really in. 'The Mancers,' I said, 'I'm sure they have ways of finding out if a shapeshifter is in the country illegally.'

She nodded. 'I know this now. And I very careful but, well, once it is full moon and I go to hills and . . .' She broke off, looking a bit embarrassed, and I suddenly remembered hearing a wolf howling that moonlit night I'd planted the hazel tree. How strange if that had been Olga in her wolf-shape roaming the hills behind the city!

'Oh my God!' I exclaimed, as another image burst in on me – something also from that night.

'What is it?' Olga said anxiously, as I feverishly fumbled for the locket in my pocket. Please, please let it be mine. If it was indeed mine, then there would be . . . With trembling fingers, I sprang open the catch of the locket and only just stopped myself from giving a cry of delight – for in it lay the hazel leaf. It looked just as fresh and green as the minute I had placed it in the locket, when I'd found it in my hair, after that vivid 'dream' I'd had of dancing in the moonlight!

'Olga, we're saved! We're saved!' I said wildly. 'Oh, we're saved!'

She looked at me as though I were mad.

'It's not what it seems,' I gabbled. 'It's from a magic tree which grants wishes . . .'

Olga's eyes widened. 'Wishes? Magic? You are witch?'

'It's not like that. It's . . . Look, I'll explain later, it'll take too much time otherwise. Anyway, what matters is that the leaf can turn into something else – something we want.'

'We want get out,' she said promptly. 'So you can wish for prison key, yes?'

'I suppose so,' I said hesitantly. 'But I'm not sure if –'

'You try,' she said bossily. 'You ask for escape from here. Not to forget me, please.'

'Of course I won't.' I held the leaf and closed my eyes. Come on, dear hazel tree, I thought desperately. Please help me, just this last time, please. Make the leaf turn into a master key or a flying carpet or sticks of dynamite or anything that will get us out of here!

Nothing happened at first and then quite suddenly I felt the leaf give a little skip and become heavier. I opened my eyes and there in my hand was not a key *but a top* – one of those little toys you set spinning. It was shiny and green and new but there was no getting around it; it was a top and about as much use at opening locked doors and helping us out through barred windows as, well, a leaf.

The disappointment was crushing. I really had expected a miraculous escape. Instead I'd been given one of the hazel tree's little jokes, like the handkerchief it had given me that first time. Only this was much more serious, for metaphorically speaking I was in very hot water and I would be boiled alive come morning when the Mancers came to fetch us for the interrogation. I looked at Olga and, throwing the top on the straw, said, bleakly, 'I am so sorry.'

Olga shot me a look. Then she picked up the top and stood looking at it, examining it closely. She said, 'Maybe if you spin, wish comes true?'

I shrugged. 'I doubt it, useless thing.'

But she set it spinning anyway. It spun better than any top I'd ever seen, flashing brightly so that your eye was drawn to it. At its fastest, it began to whistle so musically that it sounded like a tune. Then suddenly a flap on its side opened and out popped a little yellow toy bird on a spring. I held my breath, my palms prickling with excitement – but then the little bird popped back in, the flap closed, the whistling stopped, the top slowed down, down, down and then stopped completely.

Olga and I looked at each other. 'So that's no good either,' I said.

She shook her head. 'Me, I do not know magic. It is you who is witch –'

'I am *not* a witch!' I said crossly. 'I have no idea how to make magic work. It does just as it wants and I . . . Wait a moment.' I had been angrily scuffing my shoes at the place where the top had been spinning when my eye had been caught by something – a crack through which I could see a chink of light . . .

I scraped the bits of straw off the place to reveal the flagstones underneath. So far, so normal – but there, on top of one of the flagstones exactly where the sharp point of the top had spun, was a hole bored into the stone. It was about the size of a keyhole and there was light coming through it from beneath. I put my eye to it. I was looking down into a cell identical to this one. There was a man sitting on the straw, his head in his hands.

Behind me, Olga said, 'What you see?'

I told her and she waved me away to have a look for herself. 'Who is he?'

I shrugged. 'A fellow prisoner. Can't see him properly.'

'He wear nice clothes,' she said, looking through the peephole again. 'He not poor like me and you.'

'So what? He's still in a Mancer prison. So he's in trouble just like us.'

'Ah, wait – he turns now, I see his face. He is young man. Black hair. Grey eyes. He look very sad and very angry.'

'Let me see,' I said. I put my eye to the peephole and looked straight down into the startled grey gaze of Maximilian von Gildenstein.

Sixteen

If he was startled to see a disembodied eye suddenly staring at him through a hole in the ceiling, then I was utterly shocked by the sight of him. I felt as though I were dreaming. Why on earth was the son of one of the most important men in the empire – a member of the Mancer Council, at that – locked up in a Mancer prison? Surely they couldn't suspect him of anti-empire activities or being an illegal wizard! The whole thing was quite unbelievable. Surely Count Otto could not know what had happened, because what kind of father would deliver his only child into the clutches of the Mancers? And if the Mancers had done it behind his back, what could it mean? Then a shocking thought struck me – what if Count Otto himself had also been arrested?

My thoughts fled as Max called up anxiously, 'Who's there? Please, who's there?'

'Friends. Oh, Max, are you all right?'

'No,' he said, 'I'm –' And then he broke off and said in quite a different tone, 'How the hell do you know my name?'

I swallowed, aware of Olga listening. I wanted to lie but somehow I couldn't. 'I'm – I've met you. Once. You probably won't remem–'

'Oh no,' he said, interrupting me. 'I know that voice. Of course I remember. It's you, Camille. Oh my God, I'd so hoped –'

'Hoped what?' I said, and I could feel my heart thudding painfully for reasons I didn't quite understand. I clutched the locket in my pocket, thinking wildly that he must have picked it up the night of the ball and kept it with him. That's why it had been in the bowl.

He said, quietly, 'I hoped they hadn't found you.'

I looked up at Olga. Her eyebrows were raised and I made a sign to her meaning, I'll explain later, and turned back to Max. I said, gently, 'Max, why did they arrest you?'

He was silent for a moment, then said, 'Better you don't know. It's . . . too dangerous.'

'Was it anything to do with what happened that night with me and the Prince? Please tell me, yes or no?'

'No,' he said, a little too quickly. But I let it pass for the moment. I said, 'Was it . . . was it your *father* who had you arrested and brought here?'

'My father? Oh no, no, he doesn't even know it's happened,' he said firmly, and this time it had the ring of truth.

'Then who –'

'I can't tell you,' he said. But I knew – he must have been arrested on the Prince's orders, no-one else would have had the authority.

'If your father doesn't know,' I said, 'then you must get word to him.'

'How?'

'The warders – bribe them, threaten them, whatever you have to do.'

'It won't work,' he said. A shadow crossed his face. 'You don't understand.'

'What I do understand,' I said crossly, 'is that you're just sitting there waiting for the Mancers to . . . to do whatever they're going to do to you. You're giving in without a fight. I thought more of you than that.'

Colour rushed into his face. 'And what about you, Mademoiselle St Clair, if that is in fact your real name? If I am not mistaken you too are stuck in a Mancer cell with no hope of escape.' His voice hardened. 'Or are you so chirpy because you know that the people you work for will get you out?'

I was struck dumb. 'What the devil is that supposed to mean?'

'For God's sake! You appear out of nowhere, giving a name identical to that of a fictional spy. No-one knows anything about you, and when the border records are examined, no-one answering your description has entered the country from Champaine or anywhere else.'

'They did that?'

'They did indeed. Do you wonder that it's easy to make a case against you?'

'You think I'm a spy,' I said blankly.

'I didn't say that.'

'Didn't you?'

'For God's sake,' he said wearily. 'Do you think I'd be talking to you right now if I really thought it? I'd never do anything that might endanger the empire.'

'And yet you're in a prison reserved for enemies of the empire,' I said.

He sighed. 'Yes. But then so are you.'

'Not for that reason. Whatever you might think, I've not been arrested as a spy, but for quite another reason.'

'What, then?'

'If you can have secrets, then so can I,' I said tartly.

He smiled for the first time. It lit up his whole face with great warmth. '*Touché*.'

I took a deep breath and said, 'I have to ask you – I lost ... something the night of the ball –'

'Yes. The locket,' he said steadily. 'I found it after you'd gone. It intrigued me that such a fashionable young woman should wear a simple enamel heart. It made me think I had misjudged you.'

'You didn't open it?' I said.

'Yes.'

'It's a memento,' I said hurriedly, replying to the questioning note in his voice. 'A leaf from a tree on my mother's grave. She ... died a few years ago. I miss her very much.'

My voice must have cracked a little as I spoke because he said, gently, 'I am sorry, Camille. I did not mean to –'

'It's all right,' I said awkwardly. 'I ... did you tell the Prince – about finding it, I mean?'

'Not him and not another living soul,' he said. 'He hadn't noticed you lost it. I thought ... I thought the locket could be a clue. That it might help me find you – before *they* did.'

My palms were prickling, my heart racing, my veins singing with a strange sweetness I had never experienced before. I said weakly, 'Oh. I see.'

He sighed. 'And now I've found you, but too late . . . Oh, Camille. We're in a pretty fair pickle the pair of us, aren't we?'

'Yes,' I said quietly. 'But we're not alone.' I motioned Olga over. 'Max, this is my friend Olga. She's from Ruvenya.' Let Olga tell him herself about the werewolf thing if she wanted, I thought.

She didn't. 'Hello, Max,' she said shyly, peering down.

'Ruvenya, eh? I have visited your country. It is beautiful.' He paused. 'I am pleased to meet you, Olga, even if it is in this place.'

'And I you,' said Olga. She added, hurriedly, 'Max, my friend Selena she is a very brave person and she –'

'Ah,' he said, interrupting. 'So that is her real name! *Come dance with me, Selena seen by moonlight,*' he quoted. It was a line from a well-known song. 'So not Camille, but Selena. And not Champaine but Ashberg, right?'

'Right, but never mind about all that for the moment,' I said impatiently. 'What we should be thinking about is getting out of here.'

'Indeed,' he said wryly. 'What are you proposing? That we walk through walls? Fly through the bars? Squeeze through the keyholes and swim out through the river?'

'The river?' I echoed.

'Yes. Part of this dungeon is built on the river. Below me somewhere there's an entrance to some steps that go down to the water. They sometimes bring in prisoners that way if they don't want anyone to see them.'

'How do you know that?'

'Because they brought me that way,' he said simply.

'Well then that's the way we'll go.'

He laughed. 'Really! And how do you propose we get through the solid walls and the locked doors and all the rest? And it's not just a question of locks and keys, either.'

'What do you mean?' I said sharply.

'I heard my father speak of it once. All doors in Mancer prisons have a spell on them. That is why they do not need to employ as many guards as in an ordinary prison. You see, not only do you have to have the key, but you must have the words to unlock the doors. And even if you have both, it will do you no good – they only respond to a Mancer.'

'Well then, we'll have to get a Mancer to do it for us,' I said firmly.

'Oh, Selena, why not ask for the moon too while you're about it?'

'Good idea, I might try that,' I said.

He laughed. 'You are quite the most unusual girl I have ever met.'

'You can't have met many girls then, Maximilian von Gildenstein,' I retorted.

'I can assure you that –' he began, then in a different tone said, 'I can hear someone coming, talk to you later.' He walked rapidly away to the other side of the cell, and I hurriedly covered up the hole in the flagstone with straw so the chink of light couldn't possibly be seen from below.

Olga said, with a sidelong glance at me, 'He is nice man.'

'Yes,' I said quietly.

She looked a little severe. 'But you have not told me who this Max is and how you meet, and how it is that you say you are not witch but still you have magic leaf.'

'Look, it's rather a long story and we should be thinking of –'

'All the family Ironheart like long story,' said Olga firmly, patting the straw next to her. 'You sit here, Selena, and you begin from beginning.'

So I sat next to her and I began from the beginning or, rather, from my mother's death. I told her just about everything except the secret my mother had told me about her moon-sister ancestry, for I was still afraid of voicing that to anyone. Olga listened without interrupting me, her great green eyes fixed on my face. When I finished with how I'd been arrested for stealing, she looked at me and said, 'You are not witch, you say, yet you can work magic.'

'Correction,' I said. 'I can't work magic, it works *me*. Big difference, Olga.'

She shook her head. 'In this country where only Mancers may know magic, people forget it come in many ways. It is not only in books and spells. No, the best magic – the very best – you do not choose it, *it choose you*. And it choose to grow in deep soil only – in fine, strong heart. And this is you, Selena.'

'What do you mean?' I said, startled.

'I am of the family Ironheart,' she said seriously, 'and we are brought up to be strong. But I cannot endure such a thing as you suffer with those wicked ones.' Her eyes glowed. 'Long since, I would have killed this Grizelda and her daughters, I would rip their throats out and leave them to the crows, I would cast out my father. But not you – you give your word to your Mama, and this word you keep. Not because you are weak, but because you are strong. And this is why magic grow in you.'

'No,' I said. 'I had nothing to do with it. It was my mother, in a dream.'

'This you tell me,' she said, 'but this also I believe: that in other hands this hazel twig, it stay a hazel twig; in yours, it work magic. You may not understand now why or how but magic choose you, that is certain. And that is how I know you get us out of here, like you tell Max.'

I squirmed. 'Oh, Olga, I was just speaking off the top of my . . .' I trailed off because she wasn't listening. She'd picked up the top again and was turning it over in her hands.

She said, 'This come to you for reason. It show Max was here.' She looked at me. 'Maybe there is more, Selena?'

'Maybe,' I said slowly, her bright hope contagious. 'Let's try another spin,' I said, and did so. The top bounced along merrily, spinning faster and faster till it started whistling and the mechanical bird came out. We watched it intently, hoping something would happen. But all it did was slow down and come to a stop. We pulled up the straw around where it had been spinning, in case it had deposited some useful item for escape, or even that it might have transformed some of the straw into gold with which to bribe the warders. But there was nothing. The straw stubbornly remained unchanged and all we found in it were some definitely non-magical fleas, which we promptly squashed.

'So what we do now, Selena?' said Olga.

I shrugged despondently.

'Maybe when warder come, I kill him,' she said.

I sighed. 'Don't be silly. You might be a werewolf, but he's at least twice your size and much stronger. And he's a Mancer, even if not of a very high rank. You'd probably be dead the instant you sprang at him. No, we've got to use our wits, not brute force.' I sighed. 'And the top won't last, anyway.'

'What do you mean?'

'The hazel-tree magic only lasts for a few hours. By morning it will be a leaf again – a dead leaf.'

'Then what good is this stupid toy?' said Olga fiercely, and she was about to snatch it out of my hands to throw it against the wall when all at once we heard voices just outside the cell, and then the heavy keys rattling in the keyhole. I only just had time to shove the top well out of sight, deep in my pocket, when the door crashed open.

Seventeen

The warder stood framed in the doorway, carrying a tray on which reposed two steaming mugs of fragrant tea and a plate of seed cake. 'Supper,' he grunted, and came into the room. And that's when I saw that his little son was behind him, staring at us with great curiosity.

An idea flashed into my mind – an idea so desperate and chancy that I knew it had very little likelihood of working. But I had to try. I shot Olga a glance, patted my pocket and gave a minute jerk of the head towards the child. To my relief her face lightened. She had understood. And as the warder put the tray down on the floor before us, she flung herself at the man's feet, clutching at his boots. 'Oh sir, you so kind,' she sobbed, her words even more broken than usual. 'You such kind man to miserable prisoners. We thank very much, kind sir, kind sir –'

'Stop that, stop,' said the warder, waving a hand at her as though she were a pesky fly. 'Stop it, show some dignity at least, Ruvenyan vermin.'

'Oh sir, but I so grateful, so grateful ...' And on she went, clutching at him all the while.

I had my chance. I took the top out of my pocket and, concealing it in my hand, sidled over to the boy and whispered, 'Look.' I opened my hand. The top gleamed softly, appealingly. 'You like?'

He looked at me and nodded.

'It's magic,' I breathed. 'It grants wishes.'

The little boy's eyes widened.

I whispered, 'Do you want it?'

He looked quickly at his father, who was still busy trying to extricate himself from Olga's noisy clutches. He looked at the top. There was deep longing in his eyes as he murmured, 'I'm not allowed.'

'Then come later when everyone's asleep and I'll give it to you. No-one will know. Agreed?'

A sly look came into his eyes. He nodded. I slipped the top back into my pocket. His eyes followed the movement. I gave him a wink. He swallowed. I could see he was hooked, and wouldn't rest till he had that shiny magic toy in his hot little hands.

His father had finally managed, by dint of pushes and kicks, to free himself from Olga, who lay rolled up in a ball on the floor hiccupping and sobbing. He looked at me and snapped, 'Get it into your thick heads such shameful displays won't do you any good. Have your supper and get some rest. They come for you at dawn,' and without waiting for an answer, he marched out, the child following meekly at his heels.

When the door was firmly locked again and their footsteps had receded away down the corridor, Olga immediately unrolled herself. Her face was streaked with tears she'd forced out, but her eyes were gleaming with mischief. 'Well?'

I told her what had happened and a smile slowly spread over her face. 'Selena, you are genius!'

'No, just desperate. And it probably won't work.'

'Why you say this? Max say only a Mancer can unlock doors and that is a Mancer brat.'

'Yes, but I don't know if you need to be a certain age before you can work magic. He said he wasn't allowed to have the top, which probably means he's not allowed to own magical objects. So that probably also means he's not yet of the age to open those doors by himself.'

'Piffle,' said Olga, 'that brat live here, he sees his father open these doors every day, and I bet he knows what is what. Besides, he want that top badly, I am thinking, and will do anything to get it for himself.' She rubbed her hands and, going over to the tray, picked up a mug and a piece of cake. 'Let us have our supper and then tell Max what is to come.'

'We might as well do . . .' I began, and then broke off. Something had come back to me – the sly look in the Mancer boy's eyes. 'Don't eat that!' I cried, as Olga put the cake in her mouth. 'Don't!'

'Why not? It smell wonderful!'

'Exactly. Why would they lock us up in a stinking prison and then give us delicious tea and cake for supper? Think of the rubbish they gave us in the police cell. This doesn't make sense, Olga, can't you see? Leave it.'

She looked at the cake and at the tea. She said, uncertainly, 'It is poison, you mean?'

'Maybe. Or maybe just something to make us sleep.'

'How can you know this?'

'I don't. The boy – he had a look in his eyes when I suggested that he come later – he looked as if he knew something I did not. I mean, he is young but he is still a warder's son. He must know a prisoner wants to escape and that that was my plan. But he knew I couldn't because I wouldn't be awake, and that he could just take the top and no-one would be any the wiser.'

Olga stared at me. Then she threw the cake down and ground it underfoot, followed with the tea. It hissed like a snake as it touched the straw and an ugly pale scum appeared in place of the cake crumbs, the straw where it had fallen instantly shrivelling as though in a hard frost.

We looked at each other. Fists clenched, Olga growled, 'Evil mangy Mancer mongrels – give me one chance and I tear them to pieces, send them to Hell where they belong . . . and that spawn of the Devil with them. That vile brat . . .'

'If it hadn't been for him, we'd have drunk that tea and eaten that cake,' I said. 'So he has done us a favour. Oh no, Olga! I've just thought – Max – they came to Max, first!' Without waiting for her answer, I frantically shovelled the straw away from the hole in the flagstone. I peered down and saw Max sitting by a tray identical to ours. He had the mug of tea in his hands. But of the cake, there was no sign . . .

I called down, wildly, 'Max! Max! Don't drink that!'

He looked up and my heart sank. His eyes were unfo-cussed and there was a foolish smile on his face. 'Hello, my dear, and how are you this fine evening?'

'Max, please – don't drink any more! Please, I beg you, don't.'

'Why? It is good and hot,' he said, 'and it smudges my mind and makes me forget how I was betrayed and how it can never, never be put right because you see, my dear – my very dear, it is too late, far too late –'

'No! No, it isn't, Max! We're getting out tonight, I promise. Tonight I will come for you and we will get out of this place and we will go to your father.'

His mouth twisted bitterly. 'They will not let us reach him and even if by some miracle we do, it will be no good. He will never believe . . .' He stopped abruptly.

'Never believe what?'

'Never believe this could happen,' he said sadly.

'Don't be so weak, Max!' I shouted. 'You're getting out whether you like it or not so stop drinking that horrible tea right now and throw it away!'

His head jerked up. There was the beginning of a smile in his eyes. 'What a spitfire you are,' he said.

'Call me what you like, but just get rid of that stuff. Please, Max.'

'If I do, will you promise me something?' he said.

'Depends what,' I said sharply, feeling hot and cold, annoyed with myself and with him. This was no time for silly romantic notions. If he asked for a kiss or a vow of true love or something absurd like that I would tell him smartly to pull his head in and stop being such a –

Then he took the wind out of my sails completely by saying, 'Promise you won't hate me.'

'What are you talking about? Why on earth should I –'

'The truth,' he said. 'You might hate me when you know the truth.'

'You're raving,' I said, shaken.

'That may well be. I feel more than a little mad already,' he said quietly. 'But do you promise?'

'Of course I do,' I said. 'There, now, do you feel better?'

'Yes,' he said and deliberately tipped his tea into the straw.

'See?' I said, when he gave a little start as the pale scum appeared. 'How much of that rubbish did you drink?'

'Only a few sips,' he said.

'And the cake?'

'Oh, I've never liked seed cake, ever since I was a child. Left it in the corner for the rats.'

Relief washed over me. 'Good. It *is* only fit for rats. Look, Max, don't go to sleep, whatever you do, all right?'

'All right,' he said and gave me a big smile. His gaze was still a little unfocused but not as much as before, I thought. He was returning to his senses and his wits. 'I'll do long division in my head or mentally compose an essay analysing our predicament or recite to myself the most pompous and ridiculous poems I learned at school.'

I laughed. He was definitely on the mend, I thought. 'Careful you don't bore yourself to sleep,' I said.

'I won't. And you stay awake too,' he said.

'I will. See you soon,' I said, my heart lighter than it should have been. I turned back to Olga.

'He's all right,' I said, and explained what had happened.

She said, 'That promise he asked you – why do that? It is strange.'

'I just think it was the spell in the tea working on him,' I said. 'He said it smudged his mind and helped him forget the way he'd been betrayed. Perhaps he doesn't realise

I already know the truth – that, of course, it can only be the Prince, his lifelong friend, who has betrayed him and had him arrested and locked up.'

'But why he think you hate him for this? You did not like the Prince.'

'No, I certainly did not,' I said, 'but you know Max is from the Court and he is used to thinking of the royal family as the centre of the universe and, besides, I think he is still loyal to that creep of a Leopold and does not want to believe what has happened himself. He even thinks it might be his fault and – oh, it is all muddled in his head.' It sounded muddled to me, too, but it was the only way I could explain what I was sure was going on in poor Maximilian von Gildenstein's mind. I was sure because I had felt the same things myself. I knew what betrayal was. I knew how it felt when someone you trusted turned out not to be worthy of that trust. I knew how you could take nothing for granted and that overnight your life could change from sunshine to shadow. And I knew that at first you did not want to believe the worst and that it took time, bitter time, for the iron to really enter your soul.

Eighteen

We got rid of the rest of the tea and cake and settled down for a wait whose length we could not guess. At first we talked round and round the possibilities. If the Mancer boy decided to come back – and it was a big if – he'd have to wait till his parents were asleep, and that would likely be pretty late. Would a child of his age be able to keep his eyes open that long?

I wasn't exactly feeling fresh as a field flower after a spring shower either and Olga did not look too much better. The exhaustion of the last few days was setting in with every slow, dragging minute as the cell grew darker and darker and the space between our words grew longer until finally silence fell. I had tried to stop myself from sleeping by sitting bolt upright against the hard stone wall but as time passed I could feel my limbs turning to melted rubber and my head bending further and further towards my chest. Though I pinched myself several times to stop the treacherous sleepiness from invading me completely,

I could feel it was getting to be a losing battle. Never mind the spell-laced tea, nature was doing her stealthy work, and all I could think of was sleep, sleep, sleep . . .

It was Olga who saved us. The boy had opened the door so quietly that I would certainly not have heard it in my state if I'd been alone. Although she was so tired in her human shape, Olga's buried wolf-instinct must have pricked up her ears at the tiny sound the boy made, waking her instantly from the light doze into which she'd fallen.

She told me later how she'd done it. He had come in, his footsteps as light as a feather, and stopped to see if we were asleep, then had headed straight to me. He had his back to where Olga lay and, as he reached stealthily for my pocket, she sprang, knocking him down and making the small bunch of keys he was carrying fly out of his hand. I woke with a start to see Olga with her knee on the child's chest and her hand over his mouth as she said, 'Your Mama tell you stories of werewolves, boy?'

A frightened nod.

'She say they kill and eat little children?'

Another scared nod.

'Well, boy, you better believe it. If you scream or you try to warn anyone or you don't do what we say, I'll . . .' And she bared her sharp white teeth in a menacing snarl. I felt a little sorry for him then because I knew Olga would never carry out her threat. But it would keep him quiet – of that there was no doubt, seeing the terror on his face.

No time to lose now. We picked up the keys and slipped out with the boy still held in Olga's grip. We made him lock the door of the cell again, with the key and the magic words which he murmured under his breath. If there was a delay in them finding out we'd gone, so much the better.

Our corridor was empty and unguarded; the prisoners on this floor were obviously considered low-risk and of low value. I would've liked to open every cell door but it was too risky. We had to get away quickly.

We reached a flight of stairs and went down, pausing in the shadows of the landing to spy out the territory. Two corridors: one leading right, one left. As Max's cell was directly under ours, it would be in the corridor on the left. Alas, the way was barred by an enormous guard who sat at a table with his back to us facing the line of cells, reading a newspaper in the light of a lamp. Somehow, we had to get past him. Someone had to cause a distraction and allow the others to get past. But then that someone would be caught, and . . .

'The top,' Olga whispered in my ear. 'The top, Selena.'

Of course! I pulled the top out of my pocket and hurled it down the corridor on the right as hard as I could, then pressed back in the shadows under the stairs with the others.

For such a small object, the top made an unholy noise, clattering on the flagstone floor with a metallic screech. The effect was spectacular. The guard jumped to his feet, knocking over his chair. It then fell into the table, which crashed and knocked the lamp over, shattering the glass and leaving the corridor in darkness. The guard swore loudly, and ran unseeingly past us down the right-hand corridor where the top had started spinning madly, whirling rapidly away.

It was our chance and we took it, hurrying to Max's cell. The boy unlocked the door, it gently swung open and Max jumped out, having heard the noise.

Quickly, we had the boy relock the door and raced down the corridor, with Olga still hanging on to the child. We went through another door, down to the end of a short corridor where a grate led to a flight of steep stone steps. At the bottom was a swish and lick of water. The river!

I'd hoped there might be a boat tied up there. Indeed, there was a mooring spot but it was empty.

'They're probably out on patrol,' Max said. 'Hopefully they won't come back too soon. We'll have to swim. The Golden Bridge isn't far, by my reckoning. I think we should head there and take the first coach or train out of the city.' He pulled off his boots and stripped off his heavy coat. 'That is, if you can both swim?'

Olga and I nodded. I could swim but not well and the trouble was that the thought of deep water frightened me. And the river could be treacherous in the dark. You don't know how deep it is till you're in it. But what choice did we have?

'I don't think we should go to the Golden Bridge,' I said. 'It's the closest, yes, but for a start it's likely the patrol's gone that way – where the crowds are. We've gained a bit of time locking those doors and we should throw those keys into the river to delay them further.' I threw them in without thinking twice. 'But once the guards discover we're gone, they'll instantly get word to the patrol, who'll start hunting for us around the Golden Bridge because it's close and because they'll think we'll be heading to the main road or the railway station.'

'What do you think we should do then?' said Max.

'Head in the opposite direction to the Cargo Bridge where the barges come in. It's a fair bit further but we could hide amongst the barges and rest while we decide what to do.'

'You're the local,' said Max. 'We'll do as you say, Selena.'

I looked at the dark, heaving water, my heart pounding. 'All right then. Leave the boy behind, Olga, and let's go.' Without waiting for an answer, I threw off my shoes and stockings, rucked my skirts up to the waistband of my cotton drawers and, taking a deep breath, dived straight into the black water.

I supposed it was lucky that my clothes were so thin and worn because at least they didn't weigh me down and I was able to kick my legs freely enough. The water was cold and unpleasantly oily. I tried not to think of beasts that might be lurking in the depths or currents that would pluck one down to a watery grave ... Oh, for pity's sake, what a fool I am, I thought, worrying about imaginary dangers when the very real threat of the Mancer prison was still not far behind us!

Max swam up beside me with an assured stroke that spoke of long practice. 'Are you all right?'

'I am perfectly fine,' I said, crossly treading water, 'and you should ...' And then I stopped speaking, for Olga had come into view – and she wasn't on her own. On her back, clinging desperately to her as if she were a lifebuoy, was the Mancer boy!

'Olga, for God's sake, you were supposed to leave him behind!'

'No, no,' said Olga scornfully. 'He know too much. He tell them where we go. He tell them what we do. I think maybe I drown him like keys. Then I think, no, we take boy. Maybe they pay to get him back. Give us safe conduct, even.'

I looked at her and at the frightened boy. 'He can't swim,' I said.

'No, the little fool, he cannot. So Olga of the family Ironheart have to carry Mancer brat. And he have sharp claws – ow!' she said fiercely, as the child clung to her ever harder.

'I'll take him, if you like,' said Max.

She did, and in a trice the child was on the young man's back and we swam on. The boy looked slightly less scared and I felt a surge of pity for him. Mancer or no Mancer, he was still just a child. How would I have felt at his age?

Stop it, Selena, I thought. Little Mancers grow into big Mancers, and big Mancers think people like you and Olga ought to be imprisoned if not outright exterminated. All his life the brat must have heard that sort of thing. And he had known what we'd been given for supper. He had only come to get the top because he thought we'd be unconscious. So it served him right if he was scared, the horrid little sneak. And bad luck to us, too, because now we had to drag him around with us, when he'd probably be looking out for a chance to run away and betray us. For an angry instant I almost wished Olga had flung him into the water, then immediately felt bad for thinking such a thing. Olga had said magic had chosen me because I had 'a fine, strong heart'; little did she know my heart was filled with the darkest things.

Max had taken the lead now. Despite his burden, he was a much stronger swimmer than either of us. Olga was pretty good too, but my inexperience was beginning to tell. My legs felt like lead, my arms felt like they were going to drop off, my breath tore in my chest, but I grimly kept on from pride as much as anything else.

Fortunately, because it was so late, the river was quiet, with very little traffic. And we probably weren't in the water for more than ten or fifteen minutes. But it felt so much longer and so much further. Ashberg is famous for its many bridges, and we had to go under what seemed like an endless parade of them before I finally recognised the great stone shape of the Cargo Bridge looming out of the darkness, with the moored barges clustered thickly under it like chicks around a mother hen.

Nineteen

There were dozens of barges, each with its name and what it carried painted on the side in large letters, like *TOMASINA, Coal*; or *PRETTY LADY, Scrap*; or *SWALLOWTAIL, Groceries*. We avoided the few barges that still had lights shining behind their cabin windows and swam in amongst the boats shrouded in darkness till we came to one which read, *WANDERER, Old Clothes and Goods*. These sorts of barges plied up and down the river and its tributaries, serving as travelling shops for far-flung towns and villages. They not only sold goods but bought them as well, so we had no idea if *Wanderer* had only just arrived in Ashberg with a cargo to unload, or was about to leave Ashberg with new cargo. It did not matter for the moment because it was clearly moored here overnight and, as Max said, if we had to spend time resting in a hold, it was better to be amongst old clothes than coal or metal. Olga held the boy while Max climbed on, then he helped us in; first the boy, then me, then Olga. Once on board, we kept well away from sight of the cabin while we looked for the hatch that would lead to the hold.

Finding it, we opened it and slipped down the ladder one after the other, leaving the hatch a little open so we could see more clearly. It was crowded with things – everything from clothes to clocks, saucepans to saddles, and books to blankets. The air was close and a bit smelly but at least it was warm and dry and, after the drenching we'd had in the river, we were all feeling cold. The child – he'd told Max his name was Tomi – was the only one who was mostly dry, but even he was shivering. I found an old blanket and put it around him as he sat huddled in a corner not looking at anyone while the rest of us quietly found clothes we might change into – not only because our clothes were soaking wet, but because they'd feature in the descriptions the Mancers and the police were sure to put out in their search for us.

Thinking I'd be best off disguised as a boy, I dressed myself in an old blue sailor's jumper with canvas pants, oilskin jacket (I put the locket in the jacket pocket) and scuffed boots while Max appeared in a down-at-heel tweed suit and boots similar to mine. Olga, haughtily refusing to dress in male clothing, scrambled around till she found a faded woollen dress, a coat frayed at the sleeves and some clogs. We stuffed the wet clothes deep within the mountain of old clothes. Discovering a pocketknife, I chopped off my hair to the nape of my neck. Max also hacked at his, then shoved a thoroughly disreputable hat on top so that with the stubble beginning to grow on his chin and upper lip, the fine Court gentleman had quite disappeared and he looked like nothing so much as the kind of street tough one would cross the road to avoid. As to Olga, she refused to touch her hair, tying it up with a piece of string instead. She then made us bundle ours all up and give it to her to throw away or bury later. With a jerk of the head towards the now-sleeping Tomi, she explained, 'In my country wizards use such things as hair and blood and nail parings to bind the most powerful of spells.'

'He's too young to know that kind of spell, surely,' said Max. Olga shook her head grimly. 'We cannot be sure, and better to not take risk.'

Olga was right, I thought. We Ashbergians had lived too long without the experience of magic and so we did not have the instincts born of long understanding. We would certainly need her knowledge if we were to stay free for any length of time.

Now that we were warm and dry and safe for the moment at least, we discussed our next move in low voices. The trouble was that though we all shared the same basic goal – staying alive and free – we each had our own concerns. Max's was to join his father, who, we now gathered, had gone back to Faustina with the Prince, without knowing his son had been arrested; Olga's was to regain safety in Ruvenya; and mine – well, mine was to get the hell out of Ashberg and never return if I could help it. I loved my city, but it didn't love me.

There was nothing there for me any more, and only one person to mourn my going – Maria – but I would get word to her somehow once I was somewhere far, far away. I had lost her the wedding dress, and I could only hope that her innocent involvement in my 'crimes' would not come to light during a Mancer investigation. For investigation there would be, once they discovered we'd flown the coop. The top would have long turned back into a dead leaf, and perhaps might not even be found, so they'd get precious little from that, but they'd be bound to suspect something very unusual had been at work. Even if they weren't sure it was magic, they'd be certain of one thing: a lowly street thief and a foreign werewolf had helped a valuable prisoner to escape and kidnapped one of their own young. They'd want to know why. They'd crosscheck with the police who the prisoner sharing the cell with the Ruvenyan werewolf had been – and sooner or later, they'd come knocking at my father's door.

How furious – and scared – Grizelda and her daughters would be to discover they'd been harbouring a traitor within their very walls! Imagine the gossip in the servants' quarters! Imagine the gossip in the neighbourhood! I couldn't help a grim little smile at the thought that their reputations would be tarnished, and my stepsisters' prospects of making a fine marriage diminished for at least a while, and Babette might as well forget any thoughts of setting her cap at the Prince. They might even be in such disgrace that they'd have to leave the city. It was of some consolation to know that they would suffer, albeit small, for I knew that in the end they'd likely be cleared of any wrongdoing, my father would definitely disown me and I would have no family left at all. I would have to live in exile for the rest of my life and never ever again breathe the air of my native land.

'Are you all right, Selena?' asked Max gently, interrupting Olga as she described the easiest way to get through the Ruvenyan border unseen.

I swallowed. 'Yes, well, not really.'

'Are you afraid?'

'Of course. But right now it is more ... sadness. Because, you see, I don't think that I can ever be at home again in my own city.'

I thought he might ask me what I meant. Instead, he said quietly, his eyes on me, 'I feel the same.'

I said, a little wildly, 'But it's different for you – once you get to Faustina and you see your father, you –'

'I've changed my mind,' he cut in. 'I won't go to Faustina. I think, rather, I will head to – to Almain.'

'Almain? But why?'

'It is safer. They will expect me to go to Faustina and if it is thought that that is what I am doing, then my father will be in great danger. I fear he may even be killed. Better for him if I stay away and he thinks I've just ... disappeared.'

Both Olga and I stared at him. It was Olga who said, 'But Max, your father – no, he cannot accept this, he seek you high and low!'

He shook his head. 'You don't understand. There will be a plausible story. He swallowed. 'A secret mission I'm on, something like that. He will believe what is told to him. Because he can do no other. Please,' he added, seeing the protests forming on our lips. 'I cannot explain. Not yet. But trust me when I say it is so.'

I looked at him. 'Max, do you know what was going to happen to you?'

'I fear it was blanking.'

I gasped and Olga said sharply, 'What does this mean?'

'The process by which a particularly dangerous State criminal has his or her mind remade by powerful spells that blank out his or her former thoughts, memories, and desires, which then leave the space clear for other implantations,' said Max, grimly, as though quoting from a book.

Olga's mouth was open in shock. She said, 'In my country, bad men – they are put to death. Sometimes they are even made to suffer before. It is ugly, yes. But this – this destruction of a soul – this is pure evil.'

It was. I had heard of blanking before, of course – everyone in Ashbergia had. First devised in the years after the Grey Widow's rebellion, it was, as Max had quoted, reserved for only 'particularly dangerous State criminals'. In the early days, it had been used quite a bit. But there hadn't been any blanking for at least the last twenty-five years, since our present Emperor came to the throne. It was said he did not approve of the process, and even after the attempt on his life, he refused to allow it. But if a blanking order had actually been issued against Max, the son of a member of the Mancer Council, no less, it must have been approved by the very highest authority in the land. It must have been approved by the Emperor himself because surely not even the Crown Prince would dare to do such a thing without his authority.

I looked at him and saw he knew what I was thinking, that he was afraid I thought he was truly guilty of some monstrous crime, and it just burst out of me. 'It's the Prince – that wicked man – he has lied to the Mancers, most likely accused you of plotting to kill him and overthrow the Emperor, and that fool of an old man believes what his precious son says. That's why you don't want to go near your father – because you're afraid that he'll be dragged into it as well.'

He stared at me, aghast.

'Oh really, Max, did you think I wouldn't work it out?' I sighed. 'All those hints you've given? It's obvious.'

'Selena, I swear I did not do what –' he began.

'You don't need to tell me,' I interrupted. 'Of course I know it's all lies! Don't forget, I saw what that Prince Charming is really like! I saw a vile, arrogant creep who was full of himself and now I know he's a treacherous, wicked liar as well and if, or rather when, he comes to the throne, God help us all!'

The expression in his eyes darkened. 'Oh, Selena, you don't –'

'Oh no, don't you dare defend him, Max! Why did he do this to you?'

'I can't . . . I can't tell you,' he said, sadly.

'Why not? Is it because of the way you spoke out for me that night? He hated the way you spoke to him, it was plain as the nose on your face! He's supposed to be your old friend but I saw no friendship in his eyes when he looked at you, only cold rage at what he clearly saw as your impertinence. Oh, Max, is it because of me? Because he has cooked up a story about me being a foreign spy, and you being in league with me? I'm sorry if that was what –'

'No,' he said, passionately. 'None of this is your fault – it is mine, I swear it.'

'Yours? What, because you believed that he was truly your friend?'

He swallowed and said nothing, but I saw I'd hit home.

'Stop blaming yourself, Max, stop imagining you could have done better! That creature might call himself a prince but he is nothing but a liar and a coward, and his father must truly be a dotard if he believes him. As to your father, he must be worse than useless but that doesn't surprise me, in my experience fathers are like that, they avert their eyes and run a mile from anything difficult and they would rather protect their precious reputation than their own flesh and blood!' I paused to draw breath and he stared at me as though he'd never seen me before, while Olga looked at us both with a quizzical look on her face. 'And I'm going to help you no matter what it takes,' I went on, passionately. 'It's no good saying I'll be in great danger – I already am. They'll work out we escaped together, so we're already going to be seen as your accomplices no matter what. Don't argue, I know you're important and are used to ordering people about, but my mind is made up, and I've always been told I'm stubborn as a mule and twice as ornery, so don't even try, all right?'

The darkness in his eyes vanished as he laughed. 'All right, little mule.' And the look he gave me then sent a sudden tingle from my head to my toes.

'And I too will help,' said Olga, fiercely. 'For even if they say you are the Devil himself I do not care!'

'You do not need to do this, either of you,' began Max, but we chorused at him to shut up and save his breath for cooling his porridge, which made him laugh again. He admitted that he was quite defeated and that we were all in this together, come what may. And then he told us why he had thought of going to Almain. Max thought that one of his old university teachers, Professor von Munster, an expert on everything to do with the Mancers, might be able to advise on ways of persuading the Mancers to drop the case against him. It seemed like pie in the sky to me, a

143

frail thing indeed to pin all your hopes on, but it was way better than giving up. And at the very least he'd be safer in Almain, especially if his enemies thought he was sure to head to Faustina.

The quickest way of getting to the Almainian border would be on one of the steamers that leave from Silver Harbour. To get to Silver Harbour we'd have to catch a coach from a stop a short distance from the Cargo Bridge. However, as no coaches left before dawn, it seemed safer to stay on the barge a bit longer and rest, with each of us taking turns to watch while the others slept – and before dawn we'd leave the barge and head for the coach stop.

Twenty

I woke with a start into a darkness so deep I could not see my hand in front of my face. For an instant I couldn't remember where I was, and then it all came back. I could hear the others breathing gently around me. In this darkness, I had no idea what time it was. No-one was awake except me – and I remembered with a lurch of the heart that I was supposed to have been on watch, but had drifted off. Yet something had woken me. And in the next instant I realised what it was – something was different. I'd dozed off rocked by the gentle motion of the barge as it bobbed at its mooring on the water. But now, I could feel another sort of motion, and that sound . . .

The hum and clank of an engine – we were moving!

I got to my feet and felt my way towards the ladder that led up to the hatch. Gingerly, I went up the ladder and pushed very quietly at the hatch. And blinked. It wasn't just that I was dazzled, emerging suddenly from deep darkness into light. I was puzzled because I hadn't expected this kind of light; it wasn't the grey light of dawn nor the bright light of morning. No, it was the yellow light of a lantern swinging from a pole on the deck. It was still night – dark night – and yet the barge was moving . . .

'Ah, you're awake.' The voice came from behind and scared me so much I nearly fell off the ladder. I turned to face a man so tall and broad he looked like Giant Ash, the legendary founder of Ashberg, whose statue stood at the Golden Bridge. That wasn't where the resemblance ended, either, for in the wavering light of the lantern his strong-featured face, big hands, and the oilskin jacket and trousers he wore looked as though they'd been carved out of bronze.

'Cup of tea?' said Giant Ash, with a grin that suddenly made the hard face look quite human. 'Just about to make one if you fancy it.'

I was speechless for a moment but managed to stammer, 'Er, yes. Thank you. I'd like that.'

'Good. Up you come, then.'

I hesitated, casting a quick look below. He said calmly, 'Let 'em sleep. Best medicine, sleep, I've always found.'

'Yes,' I said weakly, and came out onto the deck, closing the hatch behind me. He took the lantern off the pole and led me towards the cabin and I meekly followed.

In the light of the lantern I could see that we were steaming down the river between two high banks. There was the huddled shape of houses, and beyond them in the distance, a dark mass of hills. I turned and saw behind me, a good distance away, the bulk of the Cargo Bridge, and much further than that, faintly, the lights on the Golden Bridge.

'Where are you headed?'

'Eventually to the forest lands,' he said steadily. 'Today, well, I hope to put in at Tresholm in a couple of hours and continue on to Marika before midday.' Relief flooded over me. We weren't going out of our way. Tresholm was a small town downriver. It was also one of the stops along the way to Silver Harbour. We'd be able to pick up the coach there.

'When – how long ago did you start?' I asked.

'Fifteen minutes, maybe. Old *Wanderer* isn't very speedy, I'm afraid. Take another fifteen or so before we're out of city limits.'

'It's not usual, is it, to leave in the night?' I said, hazarding a guess.

He shrugged. 'Dawn's less than an hour away. Thought I'd get off good and early before the traffic really starts up.'

We'd reached the cabin. He opened the door and stepped aside to let me through before coming in himself and setting the lantern down on a table.

'Sit down, make yourself comfortable,' he said, waving at an armchair that sat cosily by the side of a wood stove, on which a kettle was bubbling. As he busied himself with making the tea, I looked around me, astonished by what I saw. It wasn't just because of the welcoming snugness of the little cabin. It was because of the shelves lining one of the walls – shelves crammed with books and, judging from their titles, most were not exactly light reading either, but canvassed philosophy, mathematics, astronomy, history. A bargeman with a most surprising taste in literature.

'Here you are, Miss.' He set the tea in front of me and smiled as I registered the obvious and dismaying fact that he had not at all been taken in by my boy-disguise. I also saw what I hadn't realised before. This man might be the size of a mountain, but he was much younger than he'd looked outside in the half-darkness. He'd probably be only slightly older than Max, I thought, in his mid-twenties, maybe. And yet he had the assurance of a man twice his age.

'Thank you.' I sipped at the steaming liquid. It was good, strong and sweet. We sat for a moment in silence. Not an uncomfortable one exactly, but after a while I said, uncertainly, 'When did you –'

'When did I realise you were on board? Oh, about half an hour ago – less. I had gone to the hold to check on something and saw I had a new kind of cargo.'

'Oh. But . . . why?'

'Why what?'

'You find stowaways on your barge and yet you do not –'

'What, scream for help? Call the police? Have you arrested?'

'I suppose so.'

'I've never given anyone up to the police and neither did my father when he was alive and it's not for the sake of a few pilfered old clothes that I'm about to start doing it,' he said. 'Times are hard for many people and you were obviously in need of shelter.' He shrugged. 'As well be my hold as anywhere else.'

I looked at him, bemused, grateful and amazed. Landing on *Wanderer* had really been another kind of magic, I thought, for we couldn't have fallen in better hands if we'd wished for it.

148

'You are . . . you are so very kind,' I stammered. 'Thank you, from the bottom of my heart.'

He waved an embarrassed hand. 'No need to thank me. My hold's hardly a palace.'

'I suppose you . . . you want to know what we . . . why we –'

'You must have your reasons,' he said firmly. 'Up to you if you want to tell me. Don't bother telling me lies, though. I'd rather not know anything at all. Ah,' he added, in a different tone, 'I see we have company.'

I turned just as Max came bursting through the door, his eyes wild, holding an ancient rifle which he trained on Giant Ash.

'I think you'll find that thing's pretty useless,' said Giant Ash calmly, not stirring an inch. Even though he was sitting down, he still made Max, who was hardly small, look frail. 'You couldn't shoot me with it even if you tried. So why don't you sit down with your friend and have a nice cup of tea instead? You look like you could do with one.'

'It's all right, Max,' I said, hurriedly. 'He's a friend.'

Max looked at me, then at the bargeman. Slowly, he put the rifle down and said, harshly, 'Who are you?'

'I could ask you that first. Given you're on *my* boat.'

Max coloured and ran a hand through his hair, looking sheepish. 'I'm sorry. I had a nightmare. Woke up and . . .' He looked across at me. 'Selena was gone. I thought –'

'Quite understandable,' said the bargeman, extending a hand. 'Andel, at your service. Some call me Little Andel.' He grinned.

Max grinned back, and they shook hands. 'And I'm Max.' A pause. 'Some call me Mini Max.'

I groaned loudly.

Andel said, with a twinkle in his eye, 'I have heard your name but I don't think we've been formally introduced, have we, Miss?'

It was my turn to colour. 'I'm sorry. I'm Selena.' Tartly, I added, 'Some call me Ashes, but if you do, I'll not answer for the consequences.'

They both laughed. 'Loud and clear and understood,' said Andel. 'Eh, Max?'

'Sure,' said Max, giving me one of those warm looks that made my insides turn over. Andel saw it too but didn't comment. Instead, he said, 'Now, how's about that cup of tea?'

Within a few minutes, it was as if we'd known him for ages. He didn't ask us questions but talked instead about the weather and the tides and the business of buying and selling old goods up and down the river. *Wanderer* had been in his family for three generations; Andel's father had been born on the boat and so had Andel himself, and 'I expect one day my son will be born here too.'

'Or your daughter,' I couldn't resist interjecting, and he smiled. 'Or my daughter, just as you say.'

Max asked him about the books and Andel said, 'My parents were great ones for education, and, as you must realise, it's not old books that are lacking in the life of a second-hand dealer. They always allowed me my pick from the books they collected to sell and, from as far back as I remember, those are the subjects that interested me.'

'May I?' Max had gone over to the shelf and pulled out a thin leather-bound book. 'I see you've got a copy of *The Laws of Magic*. I heard about it at university.'

'Really?' said Andel, giving Max a sharp look at the mention of university, and no wonder, for the sons of the poor rarely set foot there – and never homeless beggars.

'I never read it, I must admit, but it was a cult book amongst some people,' said Max as he leafed through the pages, not noticing Andel's reaction. 'A bit of a curiosity.'

'Is it a book of spells?' I whispered. If so, Andel was running a very big risk indeed, having it on his boat.

'Oh no, quite the opposite,' said Max. 'It's a philosophical work which tries to prove magic doesn't exist.'

I snorted. 'That's ridiculous! Like trying to prove the sun doesn't shine.'

'And so it doesn't,' said Andel, quietly, 'at night.'

'Yes, but that doesn't prove anyth–' I stopped at the expression on his face. 'You're not telling me you really believe that kind of stuff!'

'I believe the author of this book was on to something,' he said steadily, 'for we have no real proof magic exists. If magic existed, we could solve everything with it. We'd have a perfect world. And I think you'll agree we don't.'

'No, no, it doesn't work like that,' said Max. 'There are laws to magic.'

'Quite. *There are laws*. As this book proves, they are absurd laws that make no sense – because they are just plucked out of the air to describe something that doesn't exist.'

'Look, Andel, magic is banned here, as you well know. There'd be no point doing that if it didn't exist,' I said impatiently. I couldn't understand why anyone could really believe such a crackpot idea; I wanted to yell that I had seen magic with my own eyes but stopped myself in time. Max didn't know that yet either and I didn't want him to find out this way. Instead, I said, 'Why would it only be the Mancers who can wield magic?'

'My point exactly,' he said, with an air of triumph. 'The author of this book doesn't go into that, but it's my opinion that the Mancers are there simply to frighten people into doing what they're told. They're not magicians at all – just secret police with clever mind tricks and subtle forms of torture, that's all. They are enforcers for the Emperor. There to make sure his power is never ever questioned.'

I swallowed and looked at Max.

There was a hard expression in his eyes. He said, 'Some might call that treasonous talk, Andel.'

The big man shrugged. 'And some might call it free-man's talk, Max. Even the Emperor allows people to express an opinion.'

'But, Andel, magic exists elsewhere –' I said quickly.

'That's what we're told,' he said, stubbornly. 'But is it really true?'

I shook my head in disbelief. 'If the Mancers are what you say, how come they arrest people for magical offences? For illegal spells? For shapeshifting?'

'Those types of people – they are just pawns in a great game, randomly selected to prove a point. Oh, I have no doubt that under torture they get them to make confessions just to maintain the tissue of lies.'

'That's monstrous,' Max said sharply. 'Do you really think the Emperor would allow such wicked things to be done to his subjects . . .?' His voice trailed away and I saw in his face that he suddenly remembered the monstrous thing that had been planned for him.

'I think the Emperor is a pawn, too,' said Andel, watching us both. 'I think the Mancers have it all over him. They tell him what they want to tell him and he believes them. Poor man, I think he means well but he's stuck in his traditional ways, and he has evil counsel too, I shouldn't wonder. Why, friend, what's the –'

Max had gone white as a sheet. He stammered, 'No, I can't . . .' and then suddenly he jumped up and ran for the door. I ran after him, and found him on his knees throwing up over the side of the deck, retching and heaving.

'Go away, Selena, leave me alone,' he croaked.

'No, I won't.'

When he'd quietened a little I squatted next to him and put a tentative hand on his shoulder. 'What's the matter, Max?'

'Can't you see? I feel sick,' he said testily. 'I've never . . . been good on boats.'

'Oh come on, Max,' I sighed. 'You know it's what Andel was saying – even now, when you know how they've treated you, you can't bear to have anything bad said against the royal family, can you?'

'He was talking rubbish,' snapped Max, 'and you know it.'

'Rubbish about magic, yes, but not the rest. Max, for God's sake! You've got to face facts. It's no good being loyal to them any more – they're not loyal to you. They were prepared to have you *blanked*!'

He closed his eyes briefly. 'Oh, Selena. You can't imagine how much I wish that it was all a dream.'

'It is a nightmare,' I said, 'but all too real, and you better get used to it if you're going to do anything to change it.'

He looked at me. 'What happened to you to make you so tough, Selena? I am older than you and a man and yet beside you I am a creature of marshmallow and melted butter.'

'It's all too new for you, that's all,' I said softly. 'I have had to get used to it and . . .' And then quite simply, just like that, I was telling him my story, leaving out only, as I had done with Olga, my moon-sister ancestry.

He listened with his eyes on my face and when I finished, he said, 'Oh, my poor, poor Selena.' Then his arms were around me and he was holding me tight. His lips on my hair, he whispered, 'Ever since the very first moment I saw you, I knew that everything had changed –'

It was the echo of my mother's words in the dream and in a nerve-prickling moment I knew that's what she had meant. Everything *had* changed for me when the hazel-tree magic came into my life. It wasn't the Prince I had been meant to meet – it was Max, for it was he whose fate I shared. Everything had led to this moment.

'Oh Max, I have been so alone,' I whispered.

And he said, looking in my eyes and holding me close, 'Selena, my sweet, brave Selena, you will never be alone again. Never, I promise you, whatever happens.' My heart was melting with a singing sweetness, my limbs dissolving with the beauty, the joy – the perfection of a moment I knew I would never forget for as long as I lived.

Twenty-One

By and by he gently released me and helped me to my feet. Taking my hand, he said, smiling, 'That Andel's a discreet sort of fellow, isn't he? But even he must be wondering what we're doing – we *are* guests on his boat, after all.'

'Yes, we are,' I said, smiling back. 'You know, he's a good man, even if he does talk some awful rot.'

He laughed. 'You're right on both counts. I must say I'd like to see his face if he knew what you told me about the hazel-tree magic.'

'Well, he doesn't know and it's better to leave it at that for the moment,' I said firmly. 'He's convinced himself magic doesn't exist because he's never seen it happen. What he can't see with his own eyes he won't believe anyway, and besides, despite that blind spot he's kind and generous and I see absolutely no reason to try and humiliate him with things we know that he doesn't. Agreed?'

He gave me a quizzical look. 'Yes, Miss Selena. Agreed.'

'He didn't ask me why we were on his boat and we don't need to say but I think we shouldn't tell him about the Mancers. It's not that I think he would tell anyone, it's just it would be safer that way – for him. We tell him we are bound for Silver Harbour but nothing more.'

'Yes,' he said. 'But what of the child? We should let him go. We surely cannot take him to Almain with us. It is not right, Selena.'

'We can't let him go, not yet. He would denounce us in a heartbeat,' I said. 'But at Silver Harbour, when we are safely on the boat to Almain, that would be the right time.'

He sighed deeply. 'I suppose you are right, but he is a little boy and he's frightened and missing his parents. I just don't like to –'

'I know you don't, Max,' I said gently. 'But it cannot be helped. You must know that.'

He nodded, sadly.

I hesitated, then quickly said, 'And please don't quarrel with Andel about the other things. I am sure he does not mean those things in a bad way.'

'I know,' he said softly. 'Don't worry.' And putting my hand to his lips, he kissed it, and we walked back to the cabin and went back in.

Andel made no comment on our return, but acted as though we'd taken an unremarkable, quiet stroll. He made no comment either when we told him we'd be getting off at Tresholm and catching the coach to Silver Harbour. He just nodded and said, 'Very well.' He didn't ask why, didn't press us for any explanations; Max was right, he *was* discreet. For a moment I was sorry we couldn't entrust him with our secret because, as well as being discreet, he was also utterly trustworthy. I felt that with every instinct, every nerve. But it was too dangerous for him. He lived his life as a free man, going up and down the river plying his trade, reading his books, and thinking his absurdly radical thoughts, without fear or favour. He was the first person I'd ever met in my life who'd shown not the slightest fear of the Mancers in any way. It was admirable, but it was also wrong, and could easily be his undoing – and I wanted no part in that.

A short time after we came back, Olga and the child surfaced. She had Tomi by the unresisting hand, and he had the dazed and hopeless look of someone who'd woken from a bad dream only to discover it wasn't a dream at all. When he came in and saw Andel, his eyes widened but he said nothing. Olga introduced him as her little brother Tomi, and though he still said nothing, something wild flared in his eyes as she spoke.

It was only when Andel squatted down to his level and said, 'And are you hungry, little man?' that he spoke.

'Yes,' he said, very quietly, his eyes on Olga's face, as though he was afraid she might object. The sight of it gave me a pang I quickly pushed away. Young and scared he might be but he was still my enemy. He might not know that, but I did. And so I had to be on my guard; I couldn't allow my heart to be moved by foolish sentiment that might get us all killed.

'Breakfast coming up for us all, then,' said Andel, cheerfully rattling around in his pantry.

Behind his back, Olga shot Max and me a questioning look. *Have you told him?* her eyes asked, and we quickly shook our heads.

'Andel is kindly putting us ashore at Tresholm,' I said, 'where we can catch the coach to Silver Harbour.'

'So we'd better fill your bellies good and proper because it might be quite a few hours before you eat again,' said Andel. 'What do you fancy?' He lined up several things on the table. 'Now, I've run out of salted pork but I can do you porridge, or eggs, or bread and cheese –'

'But these must be all your supplies, we don't want to eat you out of house and –' Max began, but Olga interrupted him, her green eyes hungrily alight.

'I am thinking hot porridge is good but also fried eggs and creamy cheese on good bread, yes, but how to decide?'

Andel said, with a bright, sidelong glance at her, 'I am thinking now why not we have something of everything, Miss Olga, what think you?' He was gently mocking her accent and she knew it. She coloured and muttered something under her breath which I guessed to be in Ruvenyan, and to be rude.

Andel laughed, and replied with a few words in the same tongue. Olga stared at him and spoke rapidly but he shook his head and returned to our language.

'I only know a little. Never been there, just picked up a few words from a Ruvenyan trader I met once.' He gave her a disarming smile. 'But I'm nowhere near as fluent as you are in our tongue so I shouldn't tease you, I'm sorry. I let my tongue run away with me sometimes.'

'Hmm,' she said, sounding somewhat mollified, but giving him a cool, assessing glance all the same.

Breakfast was as excellent as it had sounded, Andel proving to have quite a light hand with the cooking, and for quite a while there was no talking at all as we all did justice to the copious meal. Even Tomi's pinched, haunted expression was fading and he seemed almost as cheerful as any normal child would be with a good cooked breakfast.

But when Andel got up, wiped his mouth and announced he had to check things to ready for arrival at Tresholm, I saw the hope flare in the boy's eyes and knew at once what he planned to do. So I said, sharply, 'No, Tomi, you must leave Mr Andel alone to do his work in peace.'

'It's all right,' said Andel, 'I don't mind if –'

'He hasn't finished the food on his plate,' I said desperately, 'and Olga doesn't approve of him leaving food. Do you, Olga?'

'What? Oh yes.' Her eyes fixed on Tomi. 'You sit, little man. You finish this food. Look, I even butter this toast for you. You like?'

He nodded miserably, easily defeated by the fear she inspired in him. A little squirm of shame went through me at the sight, and I nearly changed my mind. After all, even if Tomi did tell Andel who he really was, it was highly unlikely – even impossible – that the bargeman would agree to denounce us. But he might well want us to leave the child with him, and that we could not do; not until we were well clear of Silver Harbour and in the stormy international waters where the empire's long arm could not reach us quite so easily.

Twenty-Two

When we docked in Tresholm, it was a little after dawn. Most of the town was still asleep but the docks were already bustling, and the arrival of *Wanderer* attracted no attention at all. Owing to Andel's extraordinary generosity, we were well equipped for the journey before us: he had given us enough coins to pay for second-class seats on the coach, a knapsack filled with a blanket, bread and cheese wrapped in cloth, a bottle of ginger beer, a pocketknife, and a compass. He would have given us much more, only we told him not to, and he insisted that he'd walk us the short distance to the coach station.

Unfortunately, when we got there, we discovered that not only did the next coach to Silver Harbour not leave for another hour, but the waiting room was already full, meaning that even the second-class seats outside would be taken. We'd have to wait for at least another two hours after that and every hour that passed would increase the danger of being discovered.

'Is there any other way of getting to Silver Harbour?' asked Max.

'Not really,' answered Andel. 'Except ... wait a moment. There's no public transport there apart from the coach, but traders do head there all the time and I know quite a few of them. There might be someone who can give you a lift. Come on.'

He led the way through a maze of streets to a shabby little coffee house that was already buzzing with activity. Telling us to wait outside, Andel went in. A short time later, he came out again.

'None of the men in there are leaving for a while, but one of them told me that if we go to the hospital we might just catch a trader in Almainian medicines who's heading back to Silver Harbour within the hour. We'll have to hurry if we're to catch him. It's a good long way away, on the other side of town, right on the road to Silver Harbour.'

The town was beginning to wake, with lights appearing behind windows and carts beginning to rattle through the streets. Andel strode confidently along and we hurried in his wake, with Olga piggybacking Tomi, for otherwise his short legs would hold us up. We didn't speak, but I knew that the tension that was in me was also agitating in everyone's thoughts. Even Andel seemed desperate to get us there in time.

The breath was nearly knocked out of me as I ran straight into Max, who had stopped behind Andel, suddenly.

'What's the matter?' I cried, my heart lurching with fear, at once certain that the Mancers were coming.

Max frowned. 'Not sure, but it looks like an accident up ahead.'

'An accident?' I said, blankly.

'There's an overturned cart and police swarming around, best not to go that way,' Andel said and, motioning to us to follow, doubled back on his tracks and plunged down another street. Now we hurried even more, for this was obviously a longer route to our destination, and I grew increasingly desperate to make it in time.

When we finally reached the hospital the gates stood open and the courtyard was filled with carts and wagons, bringing in patients, discharging supplies, and so on. It was a hospital run by nuns and a number of them flitted about in their black habits and white winged headdresses, looking rather like a busy flock of giant magpies. Andel went over and spoke to one of them, who was chalking numbers on boxes of supplies as they were being loaded into a large covered wagon. She looked at us out of black eyes as beadily bright as a bird's, nodded, and gestured towards one of the other carts.

At that moment, Olga gave a little cry. We turned – and there, coming down the street towards the hospital, was a detachment of police headed in our direction.

'We've got to run,' said Olga, wildly. Andel gripped her shoulder. 'No.' He turned to the nun. 'Sister,' he said calmly, 'your wagon.'

'Of course,' said the nun, instantly, and reaching inside the pocket of her habit, she brought out a small box of chalk. 'Get in and smear this on your faces and hair, even the child's,' she murmured. 'And you, Mister,' she went on, turning to Andel, 'you can help me move these boxes.'

We didn't wait to be told twice but scrambled into the wagon and pulled the canvas flap down behind us.

And there we had a surprise, for it wasn't just boxes the wagon was carrying – there were four or five people in there, who lay unmoving under blankets on straw mattresses. They looked very ill, with wax-like skin stretched tight over their pale, bony faces; their frames like scarecrows with thin grey hair. A couple were asleep while the others gazed at us with dull incurious eyes as Max rapidly crushed the chalk and we did as the nun had told us. Then we huddled in amongst the patients, Olga holding the boy tight to her chest so he couldn't cry out. None of us said a word, but we all thought this desperate stratagem was of no use – that this was the end, that the authorities were on our trail and that we would be found and it would be all up with us.

In those few surreal moments before the courtyard erupted with noise, I heard the murmur of Andel's and the nun's voices, but I couldn't catch what they said. Then Andel's voice rose and to my astonishment I heard him talking with the nun about whether or not it would rain. I could feel the stupid, desperate laughter bubbling in my throat. Well! We'd go to our doom with chalk dust on our faces and hair and inane, pointless chatter about the rain as the last memory of our brief freedom. Some memory!

The sound of heavy footsteps soon followed and I heard the nun's clear voice saying, 'What seems to be the matter, Sergeant?'

'Telegraph from Ashberg,' replied a gruff voice. 'Gang of ruthless bank robbers on the loose.'

Bank robbers! The Mancers must not want people to know prisoners of theirs had escaped, I thought. After all, no-one was supposed to be able to do that.

'Oh dear God,' said the nun, anxiously. 'And it's thought they've come to our quiet little town?'

'Nobody's sure where they've gone, Sister. But every police force has been told to be on alert and to check everywhere. Have you seen any strangers about this morning, Sister?'

'No, I have not. But I've been very busy this morning and would not have noticed.'

'And you, porter?' said the policeman.

Adopting a gruff tone, Andel said, 'I see nobody. But then I weren't looking neither.'

'These people are extremely dangerous,' said the police-man solemnly, 'and must not be approached under any circumstances.'

'Oh my goodness ... My heart fair quails at the thought,' said the nun, faintly.

'You mustn't be afraid, Sister. We are here to protect you. Now, do you mind opening up this wagon just to make sure no-one hid in it while your back was turned?'

We looked at each other. This was it.

But the nun hadn't finished. 'Oh, I can assure you no-one could possibly have snuck in there! We've been here all morning loading on some very sick patients of ours to take to our hospice near Marika for there is nothing more that can be done for them here.'

'What's wrong with them?' he asked.

A pause, then she said something in a whisper that I couldn't hear.

164

But we all heard his reaction. He sounded shaken. 'Oh my God, I'd heard rumours it had returned, but –'

'I'm afraid it's no rumour, Sergeant.'

'And as you know it is very, very contagious,' added Andel, solemnly.

'Yes, yes . . . But I still need to see, Sister. For my report, you understand.'

'Of course, go ahead. But remember, don't get too close.'

The canvas flap flung open and the sergeant's big red face appeared in the opening. He peered in, but not for long. Hurriedly replacing the flap, he said, 'Sister, please get these people to your hospice straightaway. The less time such cases remain in this district, the better.'

'I quite agree, Sergeant,' said the nun, calmly. 'We will do just that.'

'All right, men,' shouted the policeman, his voice fading gradually as he walked away, 'fall in, there's nothing here.' As we sat there quiet as mice we heard their heavy boots as they marched away.

Still, we did not dare to move – not until the flap was moved aside slightly and Andel's face appeared.

'All clear,' he said, smiling. 'But don't get down,' he added, as we made to move. 'Sister Claudia will give you a lift to the next stop for the Silver Harbour coach. It's on her way.'

'How can we possibly thank you both?' I said.

'Don't try, then,' said Andel, flashing a smile.

'Andel . . .' Max began, 'don't think we are what he –'

He held up a hand. 'Stop. Just know this – I have always been on the side of the hunted, never the hunter. I don't want to know why you are hunted, I am just glad I could help a little.'

'It is not a little,' said Olga, solemnly. 'You are good man. Very good man.'

Again, Andel smiled. 'I am glad to hear you say that, Miss Olga.'

Their eyes met and she quickly said, 'You come one day to my country, learn more of our words.'

'I'll look forward to that, Miss Olga,' he said gently. 'Now, I see Sister Claudia looking impatient, so goodbye, and good luck to you all.'

'Goodbye,' we said. I felt strangely touched, and more than a little regretful to be leaving his company, for this was a man whose heart was as big as his size. He reached in, ruffled Tomi's hair and said, 'You look after your sister, then, little man.'

He gave us a final smile and was gone.

'Andel!' Tomi began to yell, but Olga hushed him.

In the next instant Sister Claudia popped her head in at us. 'Please, you must all be quiet, for my patients need rest, and we have a little way ahead of us yet.'

'Sister, we are in your debt,' said Max, 'but we are not bank rob–'

'Pfft,' she snorted, 'as if I would believe such a thing anyway! The very idea! As to debts, light a candle and say a prayer for the sick and wretched of this sad world and your debt will be repaid, my son.' She looked at us with her beady, black eyes and added, 'Now then, I do not know if you heard what I told the sergeant but you must not be anxious as I did not tell the whole truth.'

We must have been looking at her blankly because she smiled and said, 'Then all is well,' before she closed the flap and went away. Moments later, the wagon gave a lurch and we were off.

We looked at each other.

'She said *something* to frighten that policeman off,' said Max, slowly.

'Yes,' I said. 'He certainly didn't want to hang around.'

'She must have told him that it was some dreadful ...' he began, then paused. He glanced at the unmoving patients, most of whom seemed to be dozing. He went pale. 'Oh my God.'

'What?' Olga and I both said.

He leaned forward to us, and murmured, 'The White Death.'

I felt the words lodge like cold needles in my spine as I remembered the stories I'd heard about a terrible wasting illness that slowly drained all the blood from you, turning your hair grey overnight and your skin to wax, making you into the walking dead. I saw the same horror written on the others' faces. Only Tomi looked unmoved. But then Tomi was very young – there was no reason for him to have any knowledge of what it meant.

'But that was wiped out, long ago, in the whole of the empire.'

'No, there were two cases last year,' Max said, bleakly. 'It was hushed up, so there would be no panic.' He read my expression. 'I happened to see it in one of my father's documents. It said that it hadn't spread. The victims were sailors, from –' he looked at Olga '– from your part of the world. They'd only just arrived in Faustina and had no time to infect anyone.'

'Or so it say,' said Olga, with a tremble in her voice. 'Oh my friends, even if we can outrun the hunters still we cannot outrun death itself if we stay amongst these people any longer.'

She made as if to get up. 'Wait, it cannot be like that,' I said. 'Why would the Sister have told us what she did? Remember, she said we must not be anxious.'

'Yes,' said Max, the colour returning to his cheeks. 'And she said she'd told the truth, but not all of it. I think she would have told us to go as soon as the police had left if . . . it was *that*.'

'Perhaps,' said Olga. 'Or maybe this nun she not frightened because she doing holy work and she think the angels will protect her and us just the same.' She shook her head. 'But I know White Death can take holy and unholy and old and young and I am frightened of this thing. I think we go now, me, we should not risk any more.'

I was a little shaken by her vehemence. After all, the disease still existed in Ruvenya and she might even have known people who had fallen victim to it. But then I remembered something else.

'Andel also went along with it,' I said, 'and he is no believer in the automatic protection of angels, I'll be bound. He would never have left us if he truly thought there was any chance these people were sick with – you know what. No, I think Sister Claudia told him the truth beforehand. That's why he played along. He'd never have done it if he thought there was any danger of us falling ill.'

'Especially you and Tomi,' said Max, smiling at Olga. 'He really took to the pair of you, anyone could see that.'

Olga snorted but I noticed the look she gave Tomi. She was starting to get fond of the little boy despite herself, I thought, and if he ever realises that – if he understands she has no intention of hurting him, then she'd have no hold over him and we would be in danger. But I said nothing about this.

Instead I remarked, 'We've got to wait, Olga, we really do, at least until we're well out of this town. Don't you see?'

'Very well,' said Olga, crossly tossing her head. 'As you wish.'

But she moved away to the far side of the wagon with Tomi, as far away as she could from the patients, and glared at them as if she thought the poor wretches might rise up and deliberately breathe sickness all over her and the child. Watching her, I remembered something I'd read once about werewolves fearing sickness – both human and wolf strains – much more than the silver bullet of the bounty hunter. For the rumoured efficacy of silver bullets was just that – a rumour – and hunters could be outrun, while sickness was a very real threat which even the fastest creature might not outrun. They feared it much more than a forest trap or a spell, for though both could be avoided by cunning and care, sickness could not. I knew then not only how brave it was of Olga to stay there when every nerve must be screaming at her to go, but also how much it was the memory of Andel's certainty that kept her there despite it all. Andel, who said he'd always been on the side of the hunted, not the hunter: and who would never have dreamed that, in her case, those words had much more than the usual meaning.

And what of Sister Claudia? She, too, had instinctively taken the side of the hunted against the hunter. She'd shielded strangers she'd never laid eyes on before. Was

169

that due just to her charitable calling, the fact she saw it as her duty to care for the wretched of this sad world? Unlikely, I thought. Her charity and courage were real and came from the heart, just like Andel's. We had been truly blessed, I thought, and for the first time in years, I offered up a silent prayer of thankfulness.

Twenty-Three

Time passed and we fell silent. Sister Claudia might not have looked strong enough to be a capable driver of such a big vehicle, but in fact she was, and the steady slow pace of the horses was very soothing. I could feel my eyelids closing. I will lie down just for a moment, I thought. I'd hardly had any sleep, after all, and I'd been up so early . . .

A voice hissed in my ear, 'Sister, sister.'

Pulled rudely out of a delicious doze, I looked, startled, into a face very close to mine – a face as bony and white as a skull, with brown eyes set deep in their hollows and framed by grey hair like bits of withered moss. Her hands, like claws, were clenched tight. An old, old woman – or maybe just ravaged by the illness, whatever it was, that was eating at her. Though I still believed what I'd told Olga before – that we had nothing to fear from these people – I still couldn't help my skin crawling.

'Sister Claudia's outside. Do you want me to –'

'No. You.' The voice was raw and the words came with an effort.

I looked around wildly. Everyone else seemed to be asleep. 'What is it?' I said.

She unclenched one of her hands. In it lay the compass Andel had given us. She said, weakly, 'It rolled out of your bag, sister.'

'Oh, right.' Max had had the knapsack in his lap, but sleep must have loosened his hold, for it now lay at my feet. I took the compass from her. Her skin felt dry and as insubstantial as rice paper. 'Thank you.'

Now the brown eyes fixed on mine and suddenly I could see a spark of light deep within, like the last embers of a dying fire.

'So few of us left, little sister,' she whispered. 'And you the only young one I have met in such a long time.'

I stared at her. The bottom of my stomach seemed to drop away. I said, feebly, 'I don't understand what you –'

She touched my wrist where the pulse throbbed, her eyes searching my face. 'The moon-blood speaks sweet in you, sister. I hear it.'

I'd known it would happen one day; I'd known I'd meet another of my kind sometime, somewhere, even though I'd not wished for it. I whispered, 'I don't know . . . anything about . . .'

She tried to raise herself up a little, her eyes fixed on my face. 'Do you want to know, little sister?'

I nodded.

She gave a deep sigh. 'Then you must go to Dremda. In the forest.'

I'd never heard of this place. The only place I knew of in the forest lands was my mother's village, Stromsa. But I had never been there.

'How far is it to –'

'That doesn't matter. You must go. You must go to Dremda and speak with Thalia.' She gripped my wrist. 'Little sister, this is not just important for you. It is for us all. Please, you must promise you will go. You must speak with Thalia.'

I was about to explain that I couldn't go to the forest and speak with whoever this Thalia person was – another moon-sister, no doubt – because right now I was bound for Silver Harbour with my friends. But her desperate eyes pleaded so much in that poor ravaged face that I could not bring myself to refuse her.

Quietly, I said, 'Very well, I promise I will go.' *One day*, I added to myself.

She smiled then. It lit up her face so sweetly that for an instant I could clearly see the pretty young girl she had once been. Her thin fingers reached out and stroked my hand very softly like the merest touch of a butterfly's wings, and she whispered, 'Then you will be on the right path, little sister, and have brought peace to my heart.' Then quite suddenly the light went out of her face and I knew she was dead.

Gently, I closed her eyes, and whispered a prayer for the repose of her soul. I could not be sorry she had gone, for she was so very ill, and it seemed merciful to me that she had been taken in a moment of joy and peace. No, I could not regret that. But I was sorry that in my confusion I had not asked her name, or what had brought her to this sad end, dying amongst strangers in a hospice wagon. And I was sorry I had not had time to ask her about my mother. Had she known her long ago? I would never know that now, or anything else about my mother's people.

Unless I did as I had said I would and went to Dremda, wherever that was, and saw this Thalia, whoever she was. Part of me wanted that more than anything. For better or worse, I had to know who I really was. I had to understand what being a moon-sister really meant. I could not turn my back on it till I knew that. But another part of me shrank from it, and knew, too, that this was not the right time. For how could I do it, and help Max? The forest lands were nowhere near Silver Harbour but were, in fact, in the wrong direction. And it was in Almain and the professor that Max had pinned all his hopes. I loved him. I had promised to help and could not turn my back on him now. Yet, I must also keep my promise to the dead woman. Later, I thought, later, when things are resolved, maybe then I'll have time. When things are resolved! Who was I fooling? Max might believe truth and justice would out, but I was not so naive. Truth was as nothing beside power and justice in the hands of the powerful; and against the empire and the Mancers, poor Max had no power at all. But even knowing that, I could not abandon him any more than I could tell him I thought he had no chance.

He woke a short time later. I told him about the woman dying, but I didn't tell him what she'd said or that she'd been a moon-sister. I only said that I had held her hand and that she'd died in peace. It was true enough, but I felt a little guilty when he hugged me tight and whispered, 'That is a great kindness you did for the poor soul.'

'Anyone would have done it,' I muttered. 'It just so happened I was the only one awake.'

'Sister Claudia will want to know of her passing,' he whispered, 'and I will tell her, if you don't mind sitting here.'

'Of course I don't,' I whispered back. He gave me a smile and crawled to the opening in the canvas, undid the flap and slipped out.

But he did not come back for quite a while. I couldn't help but wonder what was happening, as the wagon kept going at the same steady pace. And then it stopped and everyone woke up.

'What is matter?' Olga said sharply.

'Nothing.'

I thought that if she was so frightened of illness, then the knowledge that someone had died would terrify her. It was better to say nothing. The dead woman looked as if she were asleep.

Sister Claudia appeared at the opening with Max behind her. Addressing me and Olga, she said, calmly, 'We are going to have a short stop. I need to check on my patients. You may go out, have a snack and take some fresh air. It's quite safe as long as you keep out of sight,' she added.

'That will be most welcome!' I exclaimed. 'Won't it, Olga?'

'Yes,' said Olga, quickly, and followed me out, as did Tomi (no doubt because he saw I had taken the knapsack with its cargo of sandwiches with me).

It was a grey day outside, overcast with heavy clouds. And we were deep in the countryside. There were fields on the right side of the road with more fields on the left sloping upwards to a patch of woodland in the distance. Close by was a huddle of houses clustered around a little church.

'Let's go for a walk,' I said.

Olga looked at me as though I were mad. 'Didn't you hear what she said – to keep out of sight?'

Max said, quickly, 'I think it's a good idea to be out of . . . earshot.'

Olga shrugged. 'As you wish. Let's go then, Tomi.'

The child suddenly burst into speech. 'No, I am not going!'

It was the first time he had spoken to any of us and we were taken aback. He stood there in the road with his arms folded, glaring at us, his cheeks red, trying to make himself look taller. It was oddly touching.

'You have to come, Tomi,' Max said.

He stared at Max, his bottom lip trembling. And I realised what was wrong. He had misinterpreted our intentions and imagined we were going to lead him into the fields or the woods to kill him.

'Don't worry,' I said gently. 'We are just going for a walk, truly. No-one's going to hurt you.'

Baffled, Max said, 'But whoever said that we –'

'I promise, Tomi,' I cut in. 'We intend you no harm. And as soon as we can let you go, we will. Do you under-stand?' I spoke the words while a part of me was aghast at what I was revealing to the boy.

Tomi's eyes searched my face, then he nodded silently.

We walked a little further down the road away from the village, Tomi now following without protest. Looking over my shoulder, I saw Sister Claudia had clambered down from the wagon and was heading purposefully into the church. She would want the priest to give the last rites over the dead, I thought. All the more reason to make ourselves scarce so I quickly said, 'Tell you what, how about sitting over there, in that nice grassy ditch? It's a good spot to eat our sandwiches.'

No sooner said than done. We sat in the soft long grass, hidden from view by the high banks of the ditch, and started on some of the sandwiches Andel had prepared for us. And then Max, who'd been deep in thought, startled us all by saying, 'Tomi, it is time you knew something. I am innocent, and I will prove it. I know your people, I know the Mancers. I know they are honourable and that they try hard to protect the empire. So I do not blame your people for locking me up because I know they have been told lies.'

Everyone stopped eating and stared. I thought, baffled, after all the Mancers were going to do to him, that's what he thinks? Of course, his father was on the Mancer Council, so he was probably used to thinking of them differently to me, but surely, now … But I said nothing, and neither did Olga, though her mouth hung open.

Tomi whispered, uncertainly, 'But you are bad people.'

'No, Tomi, we are not.'

Tomi jerked his head at Olga and burst out, the words pouring from him in a flood, 'Maybe not you – and … and her –' he gestured at me – 'but that other one – she is … she is a wicked thing! A werewolf. She said she would *eat* me!'

Max took the stunning revelation well. His eyes widened a fraction, then he said to Olga, a little sternly, 'Is this true?'

Olga shrugged and muttered, sulkily, 'I not tell him I eat him, I just say has he heard stories about my people, how they supposed to eat children? He thinks then I will do this. But I will never because I am not –' she glared at Tomi '– *a wicked thing*. I am just werewolf from family Ironheart and never ever we hurt children – *never* – no matter what silly stories you people in empire tell.'

Max said, wonderingly, 'You are an *Ironheart*?'

She drew herself up. 'Indeed. You hear of us?'

'Of course. Yours is the greatest of the Ruvenyan werewolf clans, for your ancestor once saved the life of a Ruvenyan prince who became the most beloved of kings in your land, and ever since then the family Ironheart has been honoured in your country.'

There was a small silence, then Olga said, 'You speak truth.'

I saw he'd touched a real nerve. She was going to help him anyway but now she would feel even more bound to him.

'How you know this?' she said.

'You hear about a lot of things at court,' he said quietly. 'And don't forget, the Empress is from Ruvenya. Not everyone shares the official line on shapeshifters. In fact, there are more than a few people who would like things to change.' He looked at the child. 'Including, I've heard, amongst your people, Tomi.'

'Really?' he said, his eyes wide.

'Really. I would *die* to preserve the honour of the Emperor and the integrity of the empire. And that being so, I would never, *ever* associate with an enemy of the empire – and neither Olga nor Selena are that. That is the absolute truth. Do you believe me?'

Tomi looked at him, searchingly, looked at us, then finally nodded.

'Thank you. So now I am asking you, on your honour as a Mancer, to give us your word that you will not try to escape till we can let you go.'

My eyes met Olga's, but we stayed absolutely silent, as Max and Tomi looked at each other, sizing up one another.

'I give you my word,' said Tomi, softly, and they shook hands, solemnly, and once again I was strangely moved, though the more cynical part of me stood by and laughed. For the bond of a word of honour was one thing, and I understood and valued that myself, for it was the only thing that had kept me from betraying my mother's memory; but who could really believe the word of a Mancer, when lies and deception were part of their stock-in-trade? Well, and there was nothing to be done about it now one way or the other. As to what Max had said about himself, that was dismaying, for it showed he was a long way from accepting the truth about the empire. His attitude to magic and shapeshifters was considerably more liberal than most Faustinians, but he was still a believer in the – what had he called it? – *the honour of the Emperor and the integrity of the empire.* He still clung to that.

He'd said Olga and I were not enemies of the empire; well, I could not speak for Olga, but I had no great love for the empire. For Ashberg and for my home, yes, but for the Emperor and his family and the Mancers – most certainly not.

And it was much more than that. It was the Emperor's ancestor who had slaughtered my mother's kind and made the very name of moon-sister into the badge of a traitor. It was the Emperor who kept up the wicked laws that forced the survivors to hide their true selves, that had sapped my mother's strength and turned a poor old woman into a ravaged husk, that had made me into someone who could not even breathe the truth to the man she loved. No, I had not asked to be an enemy of the empire. But by my very birth I had been branded one in the eyes of the empire – the very empire Max would defend to the death – and though I loved him, I could not reveal my secret. I thought, sadly, of how he could accept illegal magic and werewolves without turning a hair – but moon-sisters? That had to be a bridge too far. And if that was so, then how could anything real exist between us? We were strangers to each other, in truth. Perhaps we only had these feelings for each other because we'd been brought together in such a strange way. It was just the lingering effect of the hazel-tree magic, I told myself. And in time, when that effect faded – what would happen? Perhaps we'd look upon one another with new eyes and not want anything to do with each other.

My gloomy thoughts were interrupted by Sister Claudia hailing us. She hurried towards us, looking anxious.

'The priest in the village told me some worrying news,' she said without preamble. 'The police are out in force not far from here – at the junction between the road to Marika and that to Silver Harbour. I would take you further but I am afraid that –'

'Of course, we understand,' said Max. 'You have done more than enough for us already. We will make our own way to the coach stop.'

'No, no. I'm not afraid for myself but for you. You see, Father Petrus said all the main roads are crawling with police. But there's a path over there,' she said, pointing to the fields on the left. 'That leads through the woodland to a back road which is unlikely to be watched. It will get you to Silver Harbour, too. Now hurry, for Father Petrus will be out with the ointments for the last rites any minute and I think it would be better if he didn't see you, then he can truthfully deny having done so.' Then she made the sign of the cross over us. 'Go with God, my children, and may the angels always protect you.'

'And you too, Sister,' we chorused.

'And take good care of each other, especially the child.'

'Yes, Sister, we will,' said Max, gravely, putting a hand on Tomi's shoulder. 'You can be sure of that.'

'Goodbye, then,' she said, and with a sad little smile and a wave, she hurried back towards the church where a figure in a black cassock was emerging, and we were left alone.

Twenty-Four

'Sister Claudia, she speak of last rites,' hissed Olga, as we gathered up our things to leave. 'What you hiding from me?'

'One of the sick people died,' I said, steadily. 'The woman beside me.'

Olga recoiled. 'Then you might be –'

'No, Olga,' said Max, overhearing. 'None of those sick people had an infectious disease. Sister Claudia told me. They had serious heart problems, cancer, that sort of thing. That poor lady – she had late-stage cancer, only they didn't know quite how close to death she was.' He saw Olga's stubborn expression and snapped, 'For heaven's sake, cancer's not contagious!'

'I know that,' said Olga, 'and if you –'

'Oh, stop wasting time arguing about nothing, the pair of you,' I said, more sharply than was warranted, for I was still oppressed by my earlier thoughts. 'We'll never get anywhere at this rate,' and without waiting for an answer I scrambled out of the ditch and into the field.

'Selena! Wait!' called Max, but I didn't answer. When he caught me up, he said, 'What's the matter, Selena?'

'Nothing, nothing at all.'

'Something's upset you,' he persisted. 'Please tell me.'

'It's nothing,' I said, biting my lip. 'Nothing that can be helped and, anyway, I don't need to tell you everything. You don't.'

He looked as though I'd slapped him.

I went on, harshly, 'You said it wasn't to do with me, what happened to you. Then what was it?'

'I can't tell you,' he said bleakly. 'You must . . . you must trust me on this, please, Selena.'

My throat felt thick. I wanted more than anything to take him in my arms, to hold him close, to say that yes, of course I trusted him; yes, of course I understood, yes, of course it didn't matter, that I would follow him to the ends of the earth if that's what it took. But with the encounter with the moon-sister still fresh in my mind, and the certain knowledge of how his feelings about me would change if he knew my secret, I could not with a whole heart do what I so much longed to do. Instead, I said, tightly, 'I didn't say I don't trust you, only that we do not . . . have to tell each other everything. And you must trust me on that too.'

He sighed and took my hand. 'Fair enough. But you will tell me, won't you, if there is anything – *anything* – I can do?'

I swallowed. Tears pricked at my eyes. 'Of . . . of course.'

'Then I am glad,' he said simply, and kissed my hand. The words as much as the kiss nearly undid my resolve and I am not sure what would have happened next if Olga and Tomi hadn't caught up with us at that very moment.

But they did, and the dangerous moment passed. Max took a complaining Tomi on his back and set off up the hill, with Olga loping on after, while I brought up the rear. We kept to the hedgerow, walking rapidly in single file up the hill towards the woodland. It was all uphill and the path, or rather the faint track, was rough with clods of dirt and I was quite out of breath by the time we finally reached the summit of the hill and plunged into the woods.

We stopped a moment then, much to Olga's impatience, to rest and have a drink of ginger beer. Unlike Max and me, she seemed as fresh as when we'd started. It must have been the werewolf blood in her.

The woods were much bigger and denser than they'd seemed from the road and at times the going was pretty tough. It was hours before we got to the other side, stopping only once, briefly, to finish the rest of the sandwiches and the ginger beer. But what we discovered when we reached the edge of the woods was that there wasn't just one road – if you could dignify the rough tracks not much better than cart-ruts as such – leading out of it, but three, and not one had a signpost.

But we had the compass Andel had given us. Neither Olga nor I was entirely sure of the direction of Silver Harbour, but Max was.

'North,' he said. 'We have to go north. Silver Harbour is probably no more than two or three hours' walk down the northern track,' Max said, confidently, and led the way.

The track was what my Mama used to call a rocking-horse road; it wound up and down, up and down. But at least we didn't have to fight our way through vegetation, like we did in the woods. We passed no other traffic on foot, wheels or horseback, and the country through which we were passing soon changed from patchy woodland to scrubby heathland with precious little sign of habitation. The day stayed grim and grey without the threatened rain materialising. An hour passed. Two hours. Three hours. Four hours. And still no sign of Silver Harbour. The track was getting narrower and heading into woodland again when Olga stopped and said, firmly, 'We go wrong way.'

'No,' said Max, sliding Tomi off his back and pulling out the compass. 'Look at this. See, we're still going north, heading in the right direction. We just haven't gone far enough yet.'

Olga shook her head. 'I think you make mistake, Max. Maybe you think of direction of Silver Harbour from road where Sister Claudia leave us and not from top of hill.'

'I most certainly did not,' he said crossly. 'What kind of fool do you take me for?'

Olga raised an eyebrow but said nothing.

'Look, I factored all that in when I took the compass bearing. It's north we should be going. It's just further than I thought.'

'Very well,' I said, placatingly, 'but if we don't get to Silver Harbour soon, we're going to have to stop for the night somewhere. It'll be dark in a couple of hours and there's no moon so we won't be able to keep going.'

'We'll be in Silver Harbour long before nightfall,' said Max crossly, and strode off down the track with Tomi on his back. Olga and I looked at each other and shrugged. There was nothing else to do but follow him. After all, we were hardly going to retrace our steps at this stage; the junction of the three roads lay way back in the distance, hours back, and this road had to end somewhere . . .

It did, an hour later, but not at Silver Harbour. Not in a town or village or even a hamlet, but at an isolated farm. There were a series of outbuildings clustered around a small farmhouse made of pearl-grey timber, with a sloping shingled roof pulled down around its eaves like a hat, as well as a vegetable garden and small orchard on one side, and a barn full of hay. Smoke was rising from the farm-house chimney, but no-one was to be seen.

Max said, helplessly, 'I don't understand how it happened. I really don't. North should definitely have led us to Silver Harbour.'

Olga and I looked at each other and said nothing. There was no need to rub it in now.

'I'm sorry,' he went on. 'Truly sorry. We're quite lost and it's all my fault.'

'It's not as bad as all that,' I said. 'We're all exhausted and we can at least get some shelter here in their barn or something. Maybe they can even sell us some food. We've still got that money Andel gave us. And they can tell us where we are, too.'

All at once Tomi, who had been standing silently looking around him, burst out with, 'I don't like it here.'

'What do you mean, Tomi?' Max said.

'There is . . . a funny smell,' the boy said, uneasily.

We sniffed. I couldn't smell anything out of the ordinary, nothing one wouldn't expect. Max couldn't either, and more to the point, neither could Olga, and a werewolf's sense of smell is much more acute than a human's.

'There is only the smell of smoke and hay and the smell of animals,' she said. Her nostrils flared, and her eyes lit up. 'Oh, and something like stew cooking inside. All good smells. You are from city,' she added, kindly. 'You are not used to country smells, that is all.'

'No,' said Tomi, stubbornly, 'There *is* a funny smell.'

'It's that or sleep in the open, Tomi,' I said. 'You don't want that, do you?'

He swallowed and shook his head. He didn't say anything more but kept very close to Max as we walked in through the gate and up the path that led to the house.

Max knocked on the door. No answer. He knocked again and still there was no answer. Trying the door, the handle turned easily, and we walked into a most cheerful, big room with a table laid for four, and a cookpot bubbling away on an old-fashioned wood stove, a fire burning merrily beneath it. I could feel my mouth watering and I know I wasn't the only one. Even Tomi had considerably brightened up. There was no talk of 'funny smells' now, not surprisingly, as the smell coming from that cookpot could in no way be considered peculiar, only rich and meaty and almost unbearably appetising.

There was more food on the sideboard: bread, cheese and jam, a jug of milk and one of ginger beer. There were pictures on the walls, colourful rugs on the floor, and bedrolls and blankets were neatly stacked on a shelf along one wall. Everything spoke of a busy family life, and of ordinary activities only just interrupted; but there was nobody there, not a soul. Where were the householders?

We went to look in the outbuildings. The barn was full of hay but empty of people. In the stables, two horses and a cow looked up from their mangers and regarded us incuriously, but there were still no people to be seen. We even looked in the henhouse, where the drowsy chickens rustled on their perches. But when we went around the back of the house, we saw a meadow sloping down to a stream. On the other side of it were fields full of some kind of late crop stretching as far as the eye could see.

Max said, with a relief we all shared, 'Ah, that's what it must be, the men have been working in the fields and the lady of the house has gone to fetch them in for dinner.'

'Then we'll wait inside for them to come back. I'm sure they won't mind,' I said firmly, and no-one made any protest at all, for it was getting darker and colder, and the thought of that bright, warm house was very tempting indeed.

Twenty-Five

We waited and waited. The night drew closer and closer to the windows, and still the householders did not return. All the while the warmth of the fire seeped into our tired limbs while the appetising smell of stew tortured our nostrils and made our bellies rumble.

At one point, Max said we should go and see if we could see the people coming, but when he opened the door, such a cold wind blew in, and the night was so pitch-black, that he closed it again in a hurry. Then the rain that had threatened all day began to fall, and fall with a vengeance, pounding at the shutters and the roof, while the wind howled. We sat in the cosy, warm kitchen, knowing that we could not go out again into that foul night. We all knew, by this time, that there was no family living here. The table had been laid for four *because there were four of us*. We were in an enchanted place. What we were yet to know was whether the enchantment was good or bad.

It was hard to believe in its being bad, though. Not in this cosy, warm atmosphere, with the food smelling so good. I could certainly not feel any evil intent here. But who said that evil magic must *look* evil?

Tomi's instinct as a Mancer hadn't trusted this place at first. But that instinct was trained to sniff out illegal magic, and illegal magic wasn't the same as evil magic. It could be good, like the magic of the hazel tree. Or bad, like the magic of a curse. One had to know who had made the enchantment to know for sure whether it was good or bad. I'd known the hazel-tree magic was good because it was my mother's. But I had no idea who had brought us here, for we *had* been brought here. There was no doubt of that, I thought. Max was probably right; going north *should* have brought us to Silver Harbour. And yet it had not. But how could that be?

It had been a very overcast day, I thought. Impossible to get a bearing from the sun. So Max had had to rely on the compass. The compass, which had definitely pointed north. We'd all seen it. The answer was so absurdly simple, yet so stunning a thought, that I gasped out loud.

'The compass. It's the compass!'

'What?' said Max.

'We didn't go north, Max. We went . . . in some other direction. East, I think.'

'East! But that's going inland, towards the forest lands, not towards the coast at all!'

I swallowed. 'Yes.'

'It's impossible,' he said, sharply. 'I can read a compass, you know. And it was definitely pointing –'

'North, I know. It wasn't your fault.' I took a deep breath. 'You see, I think the compass had a spell on it.'

Olga's mouth dropped open. 'Surely you do not say *Andel* –'

'No, no, it wasn't Andel, of course not. It was that lady who died. She – she had it in her hand when I woke up.'

Three pairs of eyes stared at me. 'What are you talking about?' said Max, confused.

'You see, she was a m– that is, she was a witch,' I corrected, hastily, nobody seeming to notice my slip.

'She *told* you that?' said Olga, warily.

'Not in so many words, but – yes, now I come to think of it, that's what she meant.'

'But why would she put a spell on this?' Max said, taking the compass from the bag and staring at it as though it would give him a clue.

'She must have known that we were in trouble,' I improvised, rapidly. 'She wanted to help us, wanted us to be safe.' With a little tremor, I remembered her last words, *Then you will be on the right path, little sister . . .* 'She must have thought Silver Harbour *wouldn't* be safe so she put a spell on the compass to bring us here instead.'

Tomi's eyes bulged. He jumped up from his chair and yelled, 'Oh, we are doomed! We are in the house of a wicked witch and she will turn us all into frogs and I will never, ever see my home or my mother and father again!' He burst into loud, frightened sobs.

We all moved towards him, but it was Olga who reached him first. She put a hand on his shoulder. 'Don't be afraid, little man. Don't be afraid.'

'Don't touch me! I hate you, I hate you all! I wish I had never seen you in my whole life! Oh I don't want to be a frog; I hate frogs, I hate them, horrible, slimy things they are!' He was screaming hysterically by this time.

'It's all right, Tomi, it's all right,' said Olga, gently, as she knelt down beside him and put an arm around him. She held him till his screams died down and his sobs quietened, till he hardly even struggled against her. Then she stroked his hair and said, firmly, 'You will *not* be a frog, Tomi, I swear it. Not a frog, nor a toad, nor anything but Tomi, not while I am here, for no wicked witch or wizard get past werewolf, that I promise you!'

I had no idea if that was true – but she was the only one of us here who had a good deal of experience of magic, so it rang true, and it certainly helped to calm the little boy.

He looked miserable and hung his head. 'I . . . I am so ashamed.'

'Of what, Tomi?' whispered Olga.

'I am a Mancer. Nothing should frighten me.'

Poor little Tomi, I thought. His world had turned upside down and he was still trying to live up to something he only half understood.

'Listen to me, Tomi,' Max said gently. 'A very great Mancer once said to my father that is only those without honour who claim to know neither fear nor shame.'

Tomi looked at him. 'Is that really true?'

'It is the absolute truth,' said Max, steadily, and as he did I saw the expression in the boy's eyes change and soften. I knew that the young man had once again found the right words to appeal to and comfort that fierce little heart.

After that, somehow, it felt all right to help ourselves to the stew and the bread and the other good things that had been left out for us. We took the lead, and after watching us cautiously, Tomi soon joined in and ate heartily. Nothing happened to us, of course, other than our bellies becoming pleasantly full. Then we found some board games in a chest by the door and spent a pleasant hour or two playing snakes and ladders before Tomi fell asleep in a bedroll by the stove.

We talked then for quite a while about what had happened. Olga and Max asked a few questions about the dying woman, which I answered as best I could. The moon-sister hadn't said in so many words to tell no-one about Dremda and Thalia, though I knew she had chosen a moment when everyone else was asleep. Moreover, she had not trusted to persuasion only; with the compass spell, she had ensured we would have a night of respite: safe, warm and well-fed. And I was sure it had killed her. The effort of the spell must have drained the very last of her forces, so even the small time that was left to her had been cut brutally short. I owed it to her to do what I had promised. But I couldn't reveal the real reason why she'd so desperately wanted us off our course; and so I had to improvise and embroider on my theme of 'the witch' wanting to protect us.

Fortunately enough, both Olga and Max seemed to accept this. After all, there was no real reason not to. We had indeed been lucky with the kindness of strangers so far. And a secret witch would be even more likely to want to protect fugitives from the authorities than a bargeman and a nun. We discussed why she'd brought us to this particular spot and decided that this house, with its spirit of kindly magic, must once have been hers. Why she would leave such a welcoming place for the hospital in Tresholm, though, was a mystery; but perhaps she'd had no choice or been driven out. Or perhaps this place was not quite what it seemed. Remembering how the hazel tree's magic had faded after a few hours, I wondered if this one was similar. Was that what all moon-sister magic was like – temporary? Would we wake in the morning to find ourselves in the ruins of a broken-down, old house where the moon-sister might once have lived? Still, even if the glamour faded, we'd have had a few precious hours of comfort and safety.

'Though we might have been taken out of our way, it was for the best,' Max said. 'After all, we'd been told the road to Silver Harbour was being watched; so why not Silver Harbour itself? We might have been caught there.

'What's more,' he said, cheerfully, 'we could still get to Almain this way, overland. It's a much longer way, granted, than going by boat, and there'd be a nerve-racking bit when you crossed from Ashbergia into Faustine lands proper, for the border of Almain and the empire meet there; but it is just a far-flung area of remote villages – not any place where Mancers might be likely to lurk.'

There was just one problem: what to do with Tomi now that we couldn't leave him at Silver Harbour as planned. Of course, we'd have to let him go somewhere before we entered Almain. Quite where and when, though, we had no idea. He had to be absolutely safe where we left him and we had to be sure that he could be reunited soon with his family. There was no way now that any of us would have it otherwise. For he had stopped being 'the Mancer brat' or even 'the child' and had become a real person to all of us – even me. He was Tomi, our companion for better or worse, and that made things both easier and harder.

Twenty-Six

I am in a forest. It is not a dark forest but green and gold with sunlight filtering through leaves. The grass is lush and there are clumps of flowers growing at the foot of trees. It is a beautiful place, peaceful and quiet but for the rustling of leaves and water nearby. Drawn to the sound, I walk towards it and find a waterfall gushing out over a shelf of rocks into a sparkling pool. The water looks so good I cup my hands to drink it and as I do so, I feel a tap on my shoulder.

I turn – it is not my mother this time, but a young girl. I do not know her name and yet I recognise her at once, though she looks very different from when I last saw her. It is the moon-sister from the wagon.

She is smiling. For an instant we look at each other, then she turns and walks rapidly towards the waterfall, while I am rooted to the spot, watching her. She does not hesitate at the water's edge but walks right in, through the veil of water, and vanishes, and I am left alone in a dazzle of sunlight that is pouring onto my face.

I opened my eyes to a beautiful morning, a sky rinsed a clear blue by last night's rain, to find myself alone, lying curled up in a soft, dry tangle of straw, bracken and fern, under a roof long fallen in and open to the sky, held up only by a frail wooden skeleton of walls. Everything else was gone: the room, the furniture, the food, the outbuildings and all the animals. I'd been right. It had been a temporary glamour.

As rested as if I had been in a feather bed all night, I got up in search of the others and found them not far off, in the wildly overgrown orchard, picking apples from an old tree. Tomi, riding on Max's shoulders, plucked fruit from the higher branches. I watched them for a moment thinking what a peaceful scene it looked. I do not know if it was indeed the moon-sister's home, or more likely, some kind of safe house she knew from back in the old days, between the forest lands and the road to Ashberg. Whatever it once was, there was still a kindly spirit hovering, and I felt that nothing bad could touch us while we were in its warm, gentle, and oddly timeless hold. 'Thank you, sister,' I whispered to the air. 'Thank you for taking care of us,' and then I went to join the others.

The apples were delicious, the flesh a meltingly snow-white, the skin rosy and fragrant. They made a perfect breakfast, washed down with fresh, clear water from the stream below the ruins of the house.

'It's odd, but it's almost as perfect here this morning as it was last night,' said Max and we all knew what he meant.

Even Tomi, who confessed that he'd dreamed he was a frog sitting on a lily pad, but in the dream he didn't mind so much because, as he said, 'I could jump so very high, like this!' And he jumped around in a pretty good imitation of a frog, and we all laughed. This was the first time, I thought, the very first time, I had ever heard him laugh.

By and by, we packed some more apples into our knapsack, filled the empty ginger beer bottle with water, and set off. We followed the stream up, and followed the sun, too, for Max wasn't sure he wanted to trust to the compass any more (though I was sure that the spell on the compass had faded like last night's magic and that it would point true, especially now we were doing what the moon-sister wanted us to do).

At first we were in open country but soon we entered the woods. This wasn't the forest proper, just its outskirts. The stream became a little brook, then a rivulet, which then turned into a spring bubbling from a rock, where we stopped to drink. At first, we had seen no-one, but just a short way into the woods, we began to pass people: woodcutters, charcoal-burners, herb-gatherers, a rabbit-hunter who sold us one of the skinned rabbits hanging from a pole over his shoulder. He looked surprised when we told him we wanted to go to the forest and told us that if we walked briskly in a certain direction, we should reach a hamlet called Smutny by nightfall, on the very edge of the deep forest. He told us he hadn't been that way in a long while but believed it was possible we might find some form of shelter there. But why didn't we go instead in the other direction, which would be easier going and lead to the main road, not to mention one or two comfortable inns?

We thanked him but said we had to go this way.

He shook his head and said, 'Well then, I'll be wishing you luck.' Then he very kindly gave us some dried, salted mushrooms, telling us that if we soaked them in a little water, they would make a fine sauce for the rabbit. He was a nice man – the only person we met that day who was anything like what you might call nice, or even civil. The other passers-by seemed surprised to be greeted with Max's cheerful 'Good morning', and looked at him warily before scuttling away, so that soon he stopped doing it.

'I thought that country people were supposed to be much friendlier than city folk,' he complained, when we stopped for a quick lunch of apples and water.

'Oh no,' I said. 'That's a city idea. We're used to strangers, they're not. They probably take you for an escaped lunatic to be got away from as quickly as possible.'

'Well, thanks very much,' said Max, indignantly, when we all burst out laughing.

We kept walking and time passed uneventfully. Tomi grew tired and had to be carried again. Because we'd only had more apples and water for lunch, so as not to stop for too long, the thought of a roast rabbit dinner with mushroom sauce was beginning to seriously disturb my thoughts well before the shadows of afternoon had begun to lengthen, so that by the time we were within sight of Smutny, I was absolutely ravenous. And I wasn't the only one.

Smutny was a miserable sort of hamlet of about a dozen houses in various states of disrepair, and the welcome was about as warm as you might expect. In fact most people simply refused to talk to us at all. At last we were rather grudgingly sold some bread by the village headman, a wizened old fellow with sly blue eyes, who told us that we could spend the night in the village barn – a crumbling affair which smelt of mouldy hay – and gather some wood for a fire (both of which had to be paid for with the last of Andel's coins). But when Max tentatively asked him if he knew of anyone who might guide us to the border, or any maps to consult, he was flatly refused, with the door slammed in his face.

These were the forest lands. My mother's country. When I was little, she used to tell me such jolly stories about her village, Stromsa; about mushroom-gathering and berry hunts, feasts of roast boar and deer around the fire, and of course the tradition of giving honey, cream and roses to girls on their sixteenth birthday. It had seemed so beautiful and I had always wondered why on earth she had never wanted to go back. Now I thought I understood. She had painted a rosy glow over things because she had needed something to hold on to. Life in Ashberg had proved disappointing; but life in this region was hard, and hearts harder still. For my poor mother, there was no going back, and nowhere she could truly be at home, except in golden stories of once upon a time.

Yet maybe I was making too much of it. Smutny wasn't Stromsa, after all. I had no idea where exactly my mother's village lay in relation to this place, and it was no use asking these people, they seemed to think any bit of information was too precious to let out of their mouths, certainly not without a coin in return.

Twenty-Seven

I woke out of an uneasy sleep knowing at once that something was wrong. I lifted my head cautiously out of the straw. Everything was quiet and dark. It was the middle of the night and the waxing moon only faintly lit things so I could see, to one side, the soundly sleeping shapes of Max and Tomi, the little boy huddled up close to the young man. To the other, Olga was not lying asleep but had her back to me, she was over by our things and . . .

I realised it wasn't Olga at all! The shape and size were all wrong. Without even stopping to think I crept quietly to where the intruder was rummaging through our things. He was so intent on what he was doing that he didn't notice me until I was nearly upon him; then with a strangled gasp, he leapt forwards with surprising speed, making a dive for the ladder that led up to the hayloft. He scrambled down with me in hot pursuit and before he even managed to get halfway across the floor below, I had knocked him to the ground.

The wizened old man with the sly blue eyes looked up at me fearfully. I'd disliked him yesterday on sight; this certainly didn't improve that impression.

'I can explain,' he quavered.

'You'd better. What have you done to Olga – to my friend?'

'Nothing, I swear it,' he stammered. 'I saw the girl go a little while ago.'

'Go? Go where?'

'Into the forest,' he said, promptly.

I remembered the green glow of longing in Olga's eyes, as she had finished sucking on the last of the roast rabbit, and knew at once why she'd gone into the forest in the middle of the night. The rabbit had been delicious but not quite enough for four people, especially not for a werewolf who could hunt.

'That doesn't explain what you were doing rattling around in our things.'

'I was just looking,' he said, sulkily.

'What were you looking for?'

He shot me a sly glance. 'Nothing.'

'Give me what you took.'

'I took nothing,' he protested.

But I slipped a hand into the inner pocket of his greasy coat and took out first the compass, and then something small, hard and shiny.

'My locket!' I said, without stopping to think. The compass had been in the knapsack he'd been rifling through, but not the locket. That had been in my jacket pocket. He must have taken it before he'd even started going through the bag. I saw the amusement in his eyes.

Yesterday, he hadn't seen through my boy-disguise; but now he knew I was a girl. My skin crawled at the thought of those hands on me. I wanted to hit him; but stopped myself in time. Instead, I said, menacingly, 'Why did you take these?'

'To sell, of course. Why do you think?'

His voice had a mocking edge now and it riled me.

'You miserable thief,' I said, furiously, losing my temper now, and shaking him like a rat. 'So help me God I'll teach you a lesson you won't forget.'

I saw the fear was back in his eyes. 'Please,' he said, 'please, Miss.' The mocking tone was quite gone from his voice. 'I am sorry, I am very sorry. I am poor, I just –'

'We gave you all our money already, you disgusting object,' I hissed. 'We are homeless strangers – guests in your village. I was always told that the people of the forest were so hospitable. And yet look at you – look at this place! What is wrong with you people?'

He laughed bitterly. '*What is wrong with you people?*' he mimicked. 'Why, my lady, would you ask the dead that question, too?'

I released my hold on him. 'What?'

'We are dead,' he said and sat up, painfully. He turned his pale gaze on me. It was no longer sly, but bleak. 'Or we may as well be. Our villages are emptying, our women don't bear children, our crops fail, our animals don't thrive and our streams are drying up. Some say we are cursed.'

I remembered how the rabbit-man had tried to tell us not to come here.

'Cursed? Why?' I whispered.

He shrugged. 'Some say the heart of the forest is dying,' he said. 'Nobody knows why.' He shot one of those ugly glances at me. 'But you're from the city – from Ashberg – why do you care?'

'My mother was from the forest,' I said. 'From Stromsa.'

His eyes narrowed. 'Was? She is dead?'

I nodded, sadly.

'What was her name?'

'Jana,' I said. 'Jana Lubosdera.' I watched him carefully to see if he knew my mother's secret, but all I saw was a flash of recognition of the name, nothing more.

'You are old Lubos' granddaughter?' he said.

'Yes. I never met him or my grandmother. You – you know them?'

'*Knew* them,' he corrected. 'They're both long dead. Well, well, I heard old Lubos' daughter married a rich man from Ashberg.'

'She did.'

'They didn't like the match, but she wouldn't be told. Well, well! What are you doing, rich man's daughter, dressed in rags and sleeping in a barn?' he said, the mocking tone back in his voice, but this time it only made me sad.

I said, gently, 'It's a long story and I don't want to tell it to you.'

'Oh, like that, is it? I think I can guess. Your mother's dead, your pa's remarried and the new wife doesn't like you. Am I right?'

I said nothing but he must have got his answer from my face, for he said, 'I see. And now you have come back here to try and see if there's a welcome for you in Stromsa. Well, I'm sorry, my girl, but you'll be disappointed.'

I looked at his wizened face, curdled with misfortune, bitterness and malice, and marvelled at how the face of the moon-sister, all ravaged by illness and most likely more tragedy than he had ever known, could nevertheless be filled with a sweetness of spirit, a beauty of soul that he could not come close to. He'd said he might as well be dead, but the dead I knew – my mother and the moon-sister – were far more alive than he was. And suddenly, despite everything, I was filled with a queasy pity for him. On an impulse, I held out the compass to him. 'Take it.'

His jaw dropped and his eyes widened.

'Take it,' I repeated. 'It's the only thing of value we have, take it and go. Leave us in peace.'

'But . . . why?'

'Because you need it more than we do, for you have lost your way,' I said, quietly, and shoving it into his unresisting hand, I turned on my heel and headed back to the ladder.

Before I could reach it, he came after me and said, wonderingly, 'Who – who are you?'

'I told you.'

'What do you want?'

'Nothing. Just for you to go away.'

He looked disturbed. 'But I cannot just . . . you must want payment for the compass.'

'You were ready to steal it,' I said. 'Why the scruple now?'

'This is different.'

I was going to tell him to begone when a thought came into my head. I turned. 'Very well, there *is* something you can give me in return.'

He looked sideways at me. 'I can't give you too much for it. It's not the newest of compasses, and see, there's a nick here where it —'

'Spare me,' I snapped. 'I'm not interested in bargaining. I want you to tell me how to get to Dremda.'

He nearly dropped the compass. 'What?'

'Simple question, I would have thought.'

'Why do you want to go to —'

'It's my business,' I said crisply.

'Dremda is about a day's walk from here.'

'Is it on the way to the border?'

'No, the Dremda track does branch out from that road but —'

'Is there a signpost?'

He laughed. 'A signpost! Where do you think you are — Ashberg? Of course there's none.'

'How will I know it, then?'

'I heard that there used to be two silver birches at the entrance to the track. They're probably dead by now though.'

'How far is the turning?'

'Not for quite a long way. If you leave first thing, you won't reach the Dremda track before evening, I'd say. But I warn you, it will take you a long way out of your way, for it is a dead end. You'd have to go back on your tracks to get back to the border road. It would delay you at least a day, maybe more, if —'

'If what?'

'Nobody's been there in a long, long while,' he said. 'The track is very overgrown so it's easy to get lost. And there'll be wild beasts, I'll be bound.' His eyes glinted. 'I don't know what myths you learned at your mother's knee, but there's nothing left there. Nothing. It's dead, like everything else. If I were you, I wouldn't bother.'

'But you're not me,' I said, tartly. 'So thank you, but I don't need your advice. Oh, and by the way, you know my friend Olga – the one you saw going into the forest?'

He shrugged. 'Yes. So what?'

'She was hunting,' I said.

He laughed. 'She won't have any luck. There's no game any more.'

'Maybe not for a human,' I said calmly.

'What?'

'She's a werewolf.'

His face lost all colour. He didn't protest their existence as a city person might have done. He was from the forest lands, the heart of wolf country, where the werewolf memory was very close, and he knew at once I was telling the truth.

'So if you don't want me to tell her how I found you sneaking around,' I went on, 'if you don't want me to tell her how you came by that compass, you will not breathe a word of what I have asked you to anyone. This is what you will do: you will tell my friends you found out about my mother coming from the forest land and that you then felt bad about taking our money and that you decided to give it all back to us, plus some food for the journey tomorrow. And that I was so touched by this I gave you the compass in return.'

He looked at me. His chin wobbled. 'You are the Devil,' he said, between bloodless lips.

I smiled thinly. 'Do you agree? Or do you not?'

'Very well,' he said, between gritted teeth. 'I agree.'

'Go and get it now,' I said. 'The money and the food. I will say you came to me tonight and offered it.'

He shot me a hard look, but nodded. He scurried off and was back very quickly with the coins and a greasy parcel of stale bread and dried meat. I could have told him it wasn't good enough, but I was feeling oppressed by the whole thing now, so I just took it all without comment, and said, 'Now go away and leave us alone. If you keep your promise, no harm will come to you.'

He gave me a glance in which fear and hatred mingled. He took a step back, then another. 'I want you all – I want you all to be gone first thing tomorrow morning. And never come back,' he added, over his shoulder, as he scurried away.

'You will not see us for dust, dear sir,' I called after him, and clambered back up to the hayloft where Max and Tomi were still sleeping soundly. I felt a strange mixture of elation and sadness. Yes, I'd seen off the old thief, and ensured at least some supplies for the next day; but his revelations had disturbed me deeply.

No sooner was I settled again in the hay when I heard Olga's soft footfalls below. I quickly closed my eyes and breathed softly, pretending to sleep. She was rummaging about for a while longer before silence descended again and I heard her soft, sleeping breath. I lay awake for a long time, thinking over things and by the time I finally fell asleep, not long before dawn, I had made my decision.

Twenty-Eight

My story about the old man's change of heart went down perfectly well with the others.

'It was all right to rip off strangers from the city as far as he was concerned; but forest folk – that's a different matter,' I said. 'He felt ashamed of doing it and even insisted on giving us directions for our journey today. I was quite touched and that's why I gave him the compass. I hope you don't mind, Max.'

'Not at all. Didn't really trust that thing any more,' said Max, cheerfully. 'You did exactly the right thing, Selena.'

He smiled warmly at me, and I felt bad, because he might not trust the compass, but he did trust me and I'd told him a lie. I had to, because he could not know what I intended to do tonight.

Olga didn't seem to be suspicious either. Of course, she'd been out hunting when the old man had come so she could hardly say one way or the other what had occurred. Not that she had found anything worth having – the old man had been right about game being scarce – so she was glad to see the dried meat and bread too, and didn't ask any questions.

We set off from an eerily quiet Smutny. No-one had come out to watch us go, though we still had the feeling of watching eyes behind twitching curtains, as we followed the track deeper into the forest. The path was reasonably clear and we made good headway, but the further we went in, the more I noticed how quiet – how unnaturally quiet – the forest was. No-one passed us. We passed no villages, though once or twice at the beginning we noticed tracks which most likely led to villages. It wasn't just humans who were missing in this place. There was no rustle of animals in the undergrowth. No birds sang. There wasn't even a ruffle of wind in the leaves or the flutter of a butterfly's wings. But it wasn't only the silence. A couple of times we went over what had clearly once been little streams but were now just dry beds of pebbles. And though the leaves of the trees had turned to the autumnal colours of the season, there were no brave reds or bright yellows amongst them, only browns. Worse still, the needles of the evergreen trees were scattered with sickly yellows and browns, and there was little of the strong piney smell you might have expected. It was hard to escape the memory of the old man's words. The forest was dying, from the inside.

We didn't talk much but hurried along; none of us liked being there, and Tomi was clearly very ill at ease, sticking to Max even more than usual. I wondered if, in his case, the general feeling of eeriness was combined with an instinctive revulsion against this kind of country that had

210

once been the redoubt of those the Mancers had destroyed and banned. This was my mother's country, the country of the moon-sisters, enemies of the state and a threat to everything the Mancers stood for. He probably knew only the barest details of these things because he was so young; but it would still speak in his blood.

The shadows of late afternoon were lengthening into twilight by the time we passed the overgrown and tangled path which led to Dremda. I'd been keeping an eye out all day but somehow it was still unexpected. The old man had been right. Two very tall silver birches had once stood at the entrance of the path. They didn't stand any more, but had half-fallen sideways across it, their roots showing, their topmost branches tangled with other trees. There was something sad and pitiful about them, as if they weren't merely dead trees but giant sentinels slaughtered in battle.

I couldn't dwell on it, not now. I had to turn my back on the path and keep going with the others to the border. But I did not want to go too far or I would never find my way back. So when we reached a small clearing about half an hour later, I suggested we stop for the night.

There was no argument; everyone was tired and hungry, and a little cold. We made a fire and toasted the leftover bread from lunch on sticks and chewed on the rest of the meat. Max and Olga talked while Tomi slept and I sat brooding, thinking of what I had to do that night. They talked about how much further it might be to the border, whether there'd be any village along the way where we might stop and buy some more supplies, and what we'd do once we did get to the border. Max noticed my preoccupation and asked me gently if I was all right. I said I was just too tired to think straight and, if he didn't mind, I'd as soon go to sleep.

I was ashamed of how kind he was to me when I was lying to him. He put his coat over me as I lay curled up in front of the fire with my eyes closed, pretending to sleep. He sat there long after Olga went to sleep, feeding the fire, prodding and poking it for quite a long time, apparently deep in thought.

By the time I woke up sweating from a nightmare of ghostly, giant guards marching relentlessly towards us through the forest, I found he had at last dropped off to sleep. The new moon had long set and the night sky was filled with masses of cold, burning stars. They and the red embers of the dying fire were the only light in the black night.

As I got to my feet knowing it was now or never, for it must have been past midnight already, I felt terribly uneasy. What on earth was I doing? I was safe here, amongst friends, and on my way to freedom. The old man was most likely right – there was probably nothing for me at Dremda. But it wasn't just a question of my promise to the moon-sister, Mama would have wanted me to do this. I couldn't leave her country without understanding what I was – *who* I was. I quickly made myself a rudimentary torch with a strip of cloth torn from my sleeve and tied around a stick. I put the end of it in the fire to set it alight, slipped the coat off my shoulders and put it gently over Max. Oh Max, I thought, if only I could explain! But I couldn't. Yet I must tell him something, or he would come looking for me, if I wasn't back by morning. I took a piece of charcoal from the fire and I wrote these words on the greasy paper that had been wrapped around our food: *Going to my mother's people. Don't wait for me. I'll catch you up.*

My eyes pricked with tears. I wanted to write, 'I love you, Max,' but was afraid that if I did, I wouldn't be strong enough to leave. Instead, I took the heart-shaped locket from my pocket and left it on the paper, hoping he would understand and forgive me. In the light of the burning torch, I took one last look at him, Olga and little Tomi. Then I left the camp swiftly, without another glance behind me.

Everything looked different at night. The forest that had seemed merely sad and eerie in the day seemed much more sinister: the silence that hung over it was no longer of a dead place, but of an alien one. Like our departure from Smutny, it felt as though unseen eyes were watching me, eyes just beyond the small pool of light cast by my torch – eyes that bore me no goodwill. As I hurried down the track towards the path to Dremda, I tried to tell myself it was all fancy and that I had nothing to be afraid of in this empty place. Besides, I might be a stranger but I had moon-sister blood; the dying woman in the wagon had told me I must go to Dremda and she wouldn't have sent me there if it was dangerous. But still the sense of danger nagged at me, and every shadow seemed menacing as I hurried along with my heart in my mouth and the sweat pouring cold out of me.

I reached the silver birches. In the starlight they gleamed with an unearthly glow, which made them look just like the ghostly beings in my nightmare, only they weren't marching anywhere but lying quietly in the very same places I'd seen them in that day.

Telling myself to stop being a baby, I took a deep breath and plunged under their tangled branches. Almost immediately, my torch went out. I threw it aside and fought my way past some brambles and clinging vines to the overgrown path that lay beyond. On and on I went round more brambles, through long grass and tangled bushes. While all the time, unerringly, there was the faint path gleaming in the starlight, and somehow, as I kept on, the going seemed easier, the bush less dense and the brambles less cruel. Then I heard the sound of water faintly in the distance and my heart leapt, though I did not yet know why.

I hurried along, the path changing as the bush melted away and the brambles disappeared until, after a time, I found I was walking on a broad track. And though it was the darkest time of night, I knew it was not far to dawn. The sound of water was getting louder and then – I heard my mother's voice, mingled with the sound of water, and I ran. I ran as fast as I could, round one corner, then another and another until I suddenly stopped and stared.

For there was the place in my dream – the place where I'd seen my mother and the moon-sister from the wagon. There was the waterfall, falling over rocks into a pool surrounded by trees. Only – only it had changed. Oh, so much! The trees were bare, skeletal. There was only a trickle of sluggish water going over dull, black rocks. The pool was practically empty, with only a few puddles of muddy water . . .

With a cry, I ran towards it and knelt by the pool. I closed my eyes, waiting for the tap on the shoulder, for my mother, or the moon-sister, to speak to me. But nobody spoke, nothing happened. I opened my eyes and looked at the muddy water. I cupped some in my palm, like I had done in my dream, and lifted it to my lips – and saw that it was squirming with things. Insects, frog-spawn and God knows what else. With a cry of disgust, I flung it from me, and got to my feet.

'See Thalia,' the moon-sister had said. But where was she? There was no-one here and no sign that anyone had been here for a very long time. I was suddenly beside myself with disappointment and a wild unfocussed anger.

I shouted, 'Why have I been brought here? What do you want with me? If you are here, show yourself, Thalia!'

My voice rang and echoed in that dismal place, bouncing off the rocks. But nothing and nobody answered. I shouted my challenge again, quieter this time, but still defiant. This time, as the echoes died away, even the trickling water grew silent as if my shouts had frightened it into stillness. In the next moment, the black rocks cracked wide open, and something like a huge bat came flying out, straight for me.

I didn't even have time to scream, let alone run, before the thing was on me, knocking me backwards. And then it came to land quietly by me, and to my utter astonishment I saw clearly what it was. Not a giant bat, not a bird or an animal – or a monster of any sort. No, nothing like that. *But a large book loosely bound in black cloth.*

Twenty-Nine

Whatever I'd expected, this certainly wasn't it. Sitting up, I stared at the book half-expecting it would turn into something else, or start talking to me, or – I don't know what! But it stayed mute and still, just within reach. Gingerly, I put out a hand to touch its cover. As I did so, words suddenly appeared on it as though by an unseen hand, words written in a hurried scrawl of spidery silver script: *The Book of Thalia, Oracles of the Moon.*

So it wasn't a person I was meant to see, but a book! And oracle meant a kind of fortune-telling, didn't it? Was that what the moon-sister had meant by 'speaking with Thalia'? Cautiously, I picked up the book. It was nowhere near as heavy as I'd thought it would be.

I settled it on my lap and, with my heart beating fast, opened it. The first page was blank but as soon as I touched it, words appeared in the same spidery script.

What is the question you wish to ask?

'What?' I said, dismayed. 'I can have only one?'

Yes.

There were so many questions I wanted to ask. So many things I wanted to know – about my mother, my family, what it really meant to be a moon-sister, my happiness, my fate ... And yet the first thing that came unbidden to my lips was none of these things.

'Why am I here?' I whispered.

The silvery script blinked a few times, like a signal-lamp going on and off, then went out and the page was blank again. I turned it. On the next page words winked into sight.

Because this is the time.

I wanted to say, 'Time for what?' But I remembered I could only ask one question. I thought a moment, and said, 'I don't understand.'

As I'd hoped, more words appeared.

You are the last. The last child of the blood. The last, come at last.

I thought of what the old man in Smutny had told me. And of what the dying moon-sister had said: 'There are so few of us left, little sister, and you the only young one I have met in such a long time.'

'That's why the forest lands are dying,' I said, aloud. 'Why they say there is a curse on this land – because the moon-sisters are dying out. And worse still, the forest people have forgotten the moon-sisters even existed, so they don't even know why it's happening.'

Yes, said the book, and I could almost hear the sad sigh in the simple word.

'But what can I ...' I began, then remembering the protocol, went on, hastily, 'I have heard a curse can be broken, if the right way is found.'

I turned the page. Instead of a blank page, there was a shimmering surface as clear as a pool of pure water. And in it I saw not my face, but a scene reflected as if in a mirror. I looked into a huge, grand room of golden pillars and marble floors and crystal chandeliers. It was crowded with people in fine clothes, but I could see above the heads of the crowd to a raised platform at one end, with three thrones on it: a big one in the middle, and a smaller one on either side. There was a person sitting on each of the thrones and I recognised them at once to be the Emperor, the Empress and Crown Prince Leopold.

'I don't see why you are showing me this,' I mumbled.

Something appeared on the shimmering surface like a patch of foggy breath on a mirror, and then a single word appeared, written in a shaky hand: *Watch*.

I did as I was told and looked at the imperial family's faces. I thought that the Emperor looked old and weary, and the Empress was still beautiful, though her eyes were a little sad. But Leopold looked just the same as when I'd first seen him dancing in his sky-blue uniform at the ball: dashing, handsome and entirely, arrogantly sure of himself. I watched as courtiers, ambassadors, advisers and even a Mancer or two swirled around the imperial family, bowing and fawning over them. At one point, I caught a glimpse of someone else I recognised: Count Otto, talking with some other courtiers. With a pang, I saw that he looked both drawn and anxious. Perhaps I'd been too cynical in assuming all fathers were like mine, perhaps he really was missing Max and didn't believe the lies they'd told him.

'I want to . . .' I began, and then stopped. The hair prickled coldly on my neck, for I had suddenly seen someone else I knew. Someone I knew very well indeed. For that someone was myself . . . yet changed.

I hadn't seen my mirror-self because I – she – it? – had been hidden by a pillar. Now my mirror-twin had stepped out of hiding and revealed herself in a magnificent dress of silver and white brocade. On her glossy head was a silver tiara that shone like the new moon and in her hand she carried a silver fan. It wasn't those things that I found so alien, so changed, but the fact that she had a look of serene calm such as I had never worn – a look of perfect understanding, as if she knew precisely the purpose of her existence. Suddenly, as if I was there in her mind, I *knew*. I knew what deadly weapon the silver fan concealed, in its hollow stem. I knew what mission she was on – a mission of death. She had come to kill the Prince!

The scene vanished and words appeared. Sharp, hard words that bore into my mind.

The shadow will only be lifted if the last daughter of Serafina spills the blood of the last son of Karl.

A picture then appeared. Not a scene, but an old portrait of a woman. Though she was not in the first flush of youth, she was still beautiful, with large, dark eyes and lips slightly open in an enigmatic smile. Her raven hair had a strange silver streak in it. Her dress was of the fashion of a hundred years ago, on top of which she wore a pearl-grey cloak with a hood.

Karl had this painted as a gift, said the book. *A gift for his beloved Serafina before he betrayed her by delivering her to her enemies.*

So this was what it was all about! Revenge for Serafina the moon-sister whose rebellion against Karl the Great a century ago had brought disaster to the moon-sisters and put all magic in the hands of the Mancers. Instinctively, I'd never believed that the story of Serafina, the Grey Widow, was quite as imperial propaganda had told us. But was the rest of it, too, a lie? 'I want to know if what they say is true – if she did mount a rebellion against him.'

Yes, said the book, as the page turned. *That part is true. But our people were suffering. She did what she thought was right.*

Big deal, I thought. How could she have possibly expected that the Emperor would take it well? She must have known her ill-judged revolt was likely to bring disaster not just on herself but on the thousands of others she'd rallied to her standard. She'd brought a dreadful punishment not just on herself but on all her people. Why would I want to avenge someone like that? Even more, why would I want to avenge someone I'd never met, someone from long ago?

Yes, it was true that ever since her defeat the empire had maintained the cruel laws that made my kind fugitives and outcasts; and yes, I had no love whatsoever for the imperial family, but I did not want to kill any of them, not even creepy, arrogant Leopold. I was not some nemesis, nor some ruthless figure of ancient justice. I was just an ordinary girl.

I said, sharply, 'This has nothing to do with me. I am not Serafina's daughter, I am *Jana's.* And my mother, though a moon-sister, did not carry old hatreds. Never. She was beautiful, loving and kind. All she ever wanted was my happiness.' I turned the page. 'No, I will not do it.'

It is your destiny, came the reply.

'I don't believe in destiny,' I said harshly.

Only you can save them and there is so little time.

'I'm sorry,' I snapped. 'I'm sorry for all the people of the forest, but they are strangers to me and I to them and . . .'

I broke off, for a scene had suddenly flickered into view on the page. It was of a small room. The curtains were drawn, the room dark, but I could just about make out overturned chairs and a table, and what looked like a bundle of rags on the floor. Then my breath caught in my throat for the door opened to reveal Prince Leopold. Carrying a lamp, he headed straight for the bundle of rags. And as the light from his lamp shone on the scene I saw that it wasn't a bundle of rags he was standing over but *someone* – Max! – lying dead or dying on the floor.

Max's face was still and grey as waxwork. There was blood coming out of his mouth and his eyes were fixed and glassy. My heart shrank and withered at the sight and a dreadful, dreadful cold invaded every cell in my body.

And then Leopold turned and looked straight at me, smiling the most horrible smile I had ever seen. I could not look away. I saw his lips move and realised that, of course, he wasn't looking at me but at someone else coming into the room.

I could only see the newcomer from behind as he approached the Prince. Wrapped in a long overcoat, he wore a hat that shadowed his face and carried himself in a way that was oddly familiar. The shadows in the corner of the room moved and a figure in a black cloak emerged. As it approached the other two men, I knew, with a stunning shock, just why I had that odd sense of familiarity. *The two cloaked figures were the men I'd seen secretly meeting in the cemetery in Ashberg.*

Suddenly, the scene vanished only to be replaced by a string of words piling hectically onto the page.

He is in terrible danger. Unless you do what you must, he will most surely die. His enemies will never rest till he is dead, for only then can they feel truly safe.

I couldn't bear it. Forgetting the rules, I screamed, 'Why, *why* does Leopold hate Max so? What secret does he know that is so dangerous? And those other men – his accomplices – *who* are they? How have they made the Emperor believe Max is a traitor?'

The page went blank and the book began to close.

I tried to calm myself and stammered, 'Please, I'm sorry. I'm very sorry. I will do it. Please help me.'

The book flew open again. *The last reserves of power in this place will be given for your task. But if that is so then you must promise not to falter, no matter what happens, no matter what you learn. You must not tell anyone, or he will die, there is nothing more certain.*

'I promise,' I said, hastily. 'But I do not know how I can get into the palace to –'

The power of Dremda will help you, but only to a point – you will have to use only your wits to get into the palace itself.

Well, thanks very much, I thought, sourly. 'Please tell me what I must do next.'

Break a twig from the hazel tree closest to the water and put it in your pocket. Drink one scoop of water from the pool. Take Thalia and climb to the top of the black rocks and tap your foot three times.

I was about to ask why but thought better of it. Instead, I put the book down and went to the hazel tree closest to the water – a rather twisted and withered-looking thing – broke off a twig, and put it in my pocket. Then I knelt down beside the pool and, grimacing, scooped up some muddy water and drank it, trying not to gag as I felt slimy things go down my throat. I picked up *The Book of Thalia* – now closed – put it under my arm and began to climb up the black rocks. It was quite a scramble, especially as I was handicapped by the book, but I managed it and reached the top quickly enough.

I took a deep breath. Then I tapped my foot once, twice, three times. At once my ears filled with a horrific shrieking till my head felt as though it might explode. The book flew out of my hands. The rocks collapsed under me as if made of sand and I fell headlong into complete darkness.

Thirty

I hurtled blindly through the darkness like a rag doll, with the shrieking in my ears accompanied by a low, rushing rumble like distant thunder. I was beyond fear, beyond questions, beyond even my own body – plunged into a nether world of violent sensation that seemed endless.

And then, quite suddenly, the shrieking stopped, though the rumble continued. Light punched painfully under my eyelids, and I opened my eyes. For a moment my brain could not make sense of what my eyes were seeing. I was lying on my back in a long, narrow space, a red light flashing. And under me was that rumble, that rushing . . .

In the next moment I knew I was moving, or rather the place I was in was moving, and in a heartbeat I knew where I was.

I was lying in a train corridor. I sat up, holding my aching head. The train was rushing through the country-side. It was just on dawn, the red light of morning flashing in and out of the windows. Beyond that, I had no idea.

'What do you think you are doing?'

Startled, I looked up at the owner of the stern voice. A maroon uniform with gold buttons. A jowly face under a peaked cap. A train attendant.

Trying to gather my scattered wits, I said, hastily, 'I . . . was, er, on my way to . . . to the, er, washroom and I fell over. Bumped my head.'

'You should stay in your seat when the train's in a long tunnel. It's safer that way,' said the man, sharply.

A tunnel! That explained the darkness and the shrieking, which must have been the whistle of the train as it raced through the tunnel.

Scrambling to my feet, I said, humbly, 'I'll make sure to keep that in mind next time. Um, can you please tell me how far it is to our destination?'

'Faustina is about an hour away, sonny,' he said, raising an eyebrow.

He'd called me *sonny*, I thought, confused for an instant before I remembered I was still wearing boy's clothes.

I gave a sickly grin. 'Oh, right. Thank you, sir. I'll be off to the washroom, then.'

I turned and started down the corridor, but he called out, sharply, 'Hey, washroom's the other way. The way you're headed, you'll end up in first class, and if you've got a first-class ticket, sonny, I'll eat my hat in mustard sauce.'

Your silly hat's quite safe from the mustard sauce, I felt like saying, but ducked my head and scuttled off as fast as I could in the direction he'd indicated.

Reaching the washroom, which was fortunately vacant, I went in and locked the door. I sat on the lavatory lid for a moment, breathing deeply. I splashed my face with water from the washstand and dried myself with a thin towel. I looked at myself in the mirror. I was pale, my eyes were a little bloodshot and my head ached. But my memory and reasoning were intact.

I remembered I'd been on the rocks at Dremda, not long before dawn, before I had been brutally thrust through space and time. Now I was on a train, racing through the dawn to the imperial capital – to Faustina. I did not know for sure if this was the same day I'd left Dremda, but I thought it most likely was. What kind of massive power had there still been at Dremda to do this? Thalia had said it was the last reserve of power. If that was so, I could only imagine what that power must have once been long ago, when the moon-sisters were as important a magical order as the Mancers! It was a thought both awe-inspiring and sad – for now that power was reduced to, well, to *me*, in a train heading to Faustina.

Me, the reluctant assassin. The thought should have been frightening and bitter, but somehow it was not. Something had changed in me between Dremda and here. Maybe it was the water I'd drunk at the moon-sisters' pool. Maybe it was the hazel twig in my pocket. But most likely it was simply the certain knowledge, in the deepest part of me, that this was the only way Max would be safe from Leopold. While the Prince lived, Max would be in danger – and our friends, too. Only I could save them. It was simply as stark as that and I'd accepted that this was my fate. It didn't matter to me that Thalia's deepest aim in revealing this to me must have been to save the forest lands, and not just Max and my friends. What mattered was *my* aim. And it would be true – straight at the black heart of the wicked prince.

What would happen to me afterwards, I did not know. I hoped I would be able to get away, hoped that there might somehow be a life together for Max and me, somewhere. Yet I knew the likely outcome was far darker.

I did not want to think about it, not now, for if I did, fear and sadness would grow in me and I couldn't allow it. I could not even think too much about the one I loved, could not allow myself to imagine what he might be thinking right now, having woken up and found my note. Could not allow myself to dwell on the fact that he might imagine I'd had cold feet about him, had betrayed him, did not want to help him. Could not think of the others, either, and what they might feel. The only thing I had to remember were those terrible scenes that would come true if I did not act. I had to steel myself and become a warrior. I remembered my mirror-twin and the expression on her face, that strange calm. I did not feel like that, not yet, not by a long way. I did not know how long it would take; but it would. It *must*.

I felt in my pocket for the hazel twig. It had been a withered stick when I'd first broken it off, but it had become suppler, greener, as if the sap of life was running through it again. An image came unbidden into my mind then, of the first magic hazel twig I'd held back home in Ashberg, and tears suddenly came to my eyes. Despite all my resolve, my memory jumped to that moment on Andel's barge when, folded in Max's arms, I had understood what the hazel-tree magic had brought me: an end to loneliness, the beginning of love, and the sharing of two fates – Max's and mine.

That had been my mother's magic, because all she had wanted was my happiness after years of pain. But the intertwining of my fate and Max's had led to the *second* hazel twig, whose magic was far sterner and was not of happiness, but of sacrifice. I was sure it was not the result my mother had intended; but it had turned out as such. And so it had to be.

Eavesdropping on people's conversations in the corridors, I soon learned that not only was it the same day I'd left Dremda, but that the train I was on was the overnight express from Ashberg. I spent the rest of the journey skulking between compartments and the washroom, just in the unlikely and unfortunate case there'd be someone on the train who might know my family and recognise me. It seemed unlikely given the fact I looked like a ragamuffin, but I could not take any chances.

Nothing happened and when the train, draped in a thick scarf of steam, finally pulled in at Faustina Central Station, I was one of the first to jump off and saunter away through the bustling crowds.

I had never been to Faustina in my whole life. I had only ever seen pictures of it and, of course, heard my stepmother's endless stories of how much more elegant and grand and wonderful Faustina was compared to Ashberg. I'd always shut my ears to her nonsense but now that I was here in the midst of the great city, it was hard not to be impressed. Even Central Station was enough to take one's breath away; with its enormous, echoing marble hall; its soaring, glittering glass-domed roof and gilt fretwork; its hordes of people and rows of massive trains coming in from all parts of the empire and abroad.

But that was nothing compared to the wide boulevards lined with grand government buildings, charming mansions and beautiful shops, including a stately department store so big that it was like a hundred Ashberg shops put together. There were a good many parks and gardens, too, much more showy and grand than those of Ashberg. It was only when I came through the largest of these parks and emerged into a sweeping avenue and saw the golden gates of the Imperial Palace that I was really struck dumb.

For there, behind the golden grilles, behind the sentries in their boxes, was my target: a vast sprawling building, beside which Ashberg Castle looked like a mere country cottage. Built from massive blocks of white stone, it boasted marble pillars in reds and greys and hundreds of decorated windows, while all around it stretched acres of gravelled paths and formal gardens with fountains and statues.

There were knots of tourists gawking through the closed gates and I crossed the road to go and gawk with them and eavesdrop on their conversations. They were Faustinians from the countryside by the sound of them. All of us in the empire learn Faustinian as schoolchildren – our own languages are only spoken at home – and though their country accent wasn't quite what I was used to, I easily understood everything they said.

One man said, 'Look, the flag's flying. They're in.'

'And the Crown Prince,' replied his friend, 'is obviously back from Ashberg – look, there's his standard up there.'

There on the roof, fluttering in the breeze, were the imperial standard and Prince Leopold's flag that incorporated the arms of Ashberg.

The first tourist mused, 'I wonder why he is back so soon? Maybe Ashberg wasn't to his liking.'

I pricked my ears up at that, but all his friend said was, 'I heard a rumour that his father the Emperor had been taken very ill so he had to return. But there's been nothing in the papers about it, so I don't know how true that is.'

Not true at all, I thought. It was weird to be so close to the place I'd seen in Thalia's book and my heart beat fast at the thought that very soon I must go through those gates and carry out my task. And to do that I'd have to use my wits. There was no way I could get in through those gates as an ordinary person. And I could not bust my way in; the unmoving sentries might look like giant toys in their plumed hats, red uniforms and boxes but I knew that they were very far from harmless and that any would-be intruder would soon find themselves dead. And Thalia had told me that I couldn't use magic. Somehow I had to contrive to be *invited* in through those gates as a guest. If the image I'd seen in *The Book of Thalia* reflected the future faithfully, I would have to be every inch the fine lady.

I left the palace and went back towards the busy centre of town. There was so much traffic, both wheeled and on horseback, and the streets were so wide that it seemed like you'd be risking your life just to cross the road. And it was so noisy! Chatter and church bells and street sellers' shouts combined with the clank of machines and the rumble and clatter of vehicles, creating a cacophony that set my ears ringing. Of course, we had those noises in Ashberg too, but nowhere near this level. There were so many smells, too – horrid ones from the stink of drains to the smog of coal fires; and good ones, like the mouth-watering smells coming from bakeries and roast-meat stalls . . .

I had no money, for I'd left the few coins we had with the others. But I did have the twig. And though Thalia had said its magic could not be used for getting into the palace, she had not forbidden other uses, or why tell me to bring it at all? I put my hand in my pocket. The twig felt warm and tingly. I could feel the bumps of new buds, though there were still no leaves yet. Perhaps it would work anyway, I thought. Keeping my hand in my pocket, I scraped off a bud with a fingernail, and holding it in my closed palm, silently visualised a coin. At once, the bud moved and swelled, changing in texture and weight. I opened my hand and found not one, but several coins – good silver pieces, not copper nothings either.

I couldn't help feeling pleasure at the sight, not just because I'd now be able to buy a hot pork bun and a cup of coffee and plenty more besides; it was also because, unlike before, I felt in control of the magic. It was a bittersweet pleasure because I knew full well the magic was obeying me for its own reasons – or rather, Dremda's reasons – for I had to survive in Faustina till I could carry out my mission.

Funny how the human mind can find frivolous things to fasten onto to distract it from dark things! It is shameful to relate but I confess that as I sat in the bakery swilling the hot fragrant coffee and munching the delicious pork bun, I began to feel a little excited at the prospect of what

I might do with the magic twig. It would only last for a short while, probably no more than a few days, as Thalia had said there was very little time. But while I had it, before I had to face the moment of reckoning, I thought I might as well take pleasure in what I could, for it would stop me from being afraid.

Thirty-One

🌙

I had to find somewhere to stay and as it would be a good deal easier for a respectable young woman to impress a landlord than a ragged boy, I needed to return to the appurtenances of my gender. But I had to do it discreetly, in stages. I most certainly could not walk into some fine shop and buy good clothes, not to start with anyway. A small, unfashionable shop was called for first, perhaps even a second-hand dealer. There were more than a few of these in Ashberg in the poorer districts, and I assumed it was the same in Faustina.

I walked around for quite a while till I found, in a back-street that was considerably more shabby than the wide boulevards of the town centre, a crammed little shop whose window was filled with the sorts of clothes once-genteel people pawned when they were down on their luck. It was the kind of place where the shopkeepers are so used to stories of hardship that they don't ask questions at all. I went in and, for three or four silver coins, bought a plain grey woollen dress, a shawl of a slightly darker grey, a simple black bonnet, and a small black velvet handbag with drawstrings. I explained it was all for my sister, who was not very well, to the indifferent shop assistant who wrapped it all up in brown paper.

Now to find a place where I might change without attracting attention. I walked around for a bit before accidentally hitting on a solution: the deserted gatehouse of a quiet graveyard. I could see the caretaker raking leaves on the path some distance away, and hoped he'd be occupied enough to give me time to change.

Scrambling out of the coat and shirt (I had no time to change the trousers), I quickly flung on the dress and shawl and shoved my hair up under the bonnet so that it would look like it was in a bun. I couldn't do anything right now about the clumsy manlike boots, but the dress would cover them and I hoped no-one would wonder at my odd gait. I just had time to wrap the coat and shirt back in the brown paper when the caretaker turned up and asked me, with a little frown, what I was doing in his gatehouse.

'I was just looking for you to ask if there was anywhere nearby where I could buy flowers to put on my uncle's grave,' I said, smiling sadly at him.

He told me he didn't sell flowers but that there was an old woman nearby who did. He then asked for my uncle's name but I pretended not to hear, just thanked him for his help and left, with my parcel under my arm.

I found the right sort of place in a pleasant little district not far from the city markets, an area of little coffee houses, modest restaurants and a great many small hotels and boarding houses of all sorts. I chose a place for students because they offered much shorter stays – you could pay day by day there whereas in the other places it was for the week or even the month.

Nobody asked me questions. The owner, a big blowsy woman, hardly even looked up from the novel she was reading. She just took my money and pointed me up the stairs to a tiny attic room. It was cold and dusty with a lumpy, narrow bed and a dressing table with a cracked mirror as the only furniture. But all I cared for was that the door locked with a bolt so I could have my privacy. Sitting on the bed, I unwrapped the parcel and took out the twig from the coat pocket. There were more buds on it now, and one of them had unfurled into a leaf.

Gently, I picked the leaf. I held it in my palm then gently closed my finger over it. If a simple bud had given me a fistful of silver then maybe a leaf would give me the gold I needed for my next transformation. I closed my eyes and visualised a purse of gold, enough to set me up with all the needs of a fine lady. But when I opened my eyes and my hand, I saw instead a slip of paper, with a name and address written on it: *Finasera, 25 Wilhelm Street*.

It meant nothing to me, but by now I knew I could not take anything for granted. Poking a hole in the thin cover of the mattress, I slipped the twig inside where it would be completely hidden from sight, and drew the covers over it again. I put the parcel in the drawer of the dressing table, picked up my bag, and went out, closing the door firmly behind me.

I didn't want to ask the blowsy woman for directions to the address I'd been given – she had been thankfully incurious and I wanted it to stay that way – so I walked to the markets and asked one of the stallholders, a butcher's assistant, if he knew where Wilhelm Street was.

'A fair walk from here,' he said, and gave me directions.

The day had turned from chilly to grim and it looked like it might start to rain at any moment by the time I got to Wilhelm Street and realised that the place I'd been sent to was in the heart of the financial district and, further, that number 25 was a bank! In fact it was a branch of the Bank of Ashberg.

Now I had to go in and ask for – who was it again? Finasera, whoever that was. Not a native Faustinian by the look of the name, it was more like a surname from my country, at least from the forest lands, though not quite right because … I suddenly realised what I should have seen before if I'd had my wits about me: 'Finasera' was actually an anagram of 'Serafina'! Then, I thought, it was unlikely I had to ask for someone by that name, rather, that was the name I should give.

Shaking my head wryly over the tricky impudence of the thing, I went inside. The bank was quite small, with only a couple of tellers at desks behind screens, a few customers lined up before them. I joined one of the queues and waited for my turn, not knowing quite what I would ask for until the moment I stood in front of the grey-haired teller. He had ink-stained fingers and wore spectacles and a fussy cravat. 'Good morning, Mademoiselle. How may I help you?'

'I've come to make a withdrawal,' I said, trying to keep my voice steady. 'The name is Finasera.'

'Very good, Mademoiselle,' the man said, without surprise. I noticed he had a slight Ashbergian accent himself. 'Please wait a moment.' He pulled a fat ledger out from under his desk and started leafing through it. 'Finasera, Finasera – not here . . . not there . . . Mademoiselle, I don't think that it is this bank where you –'

'And I'm quite sure,' I said. 'I don't think you've looked well enough.'

He looked up at me with his faded, disapproving blue eyes. He frowned, pursing his lips. And then quite suddenly I saw the expression in his eyes change. He went pale and whispered, 'Fina . . . Fina . . . sera – I recall seeing the name somewhere, someplace . . .'

I had a bad feeling in the pit of my stomach. His eyes were still fixed on me and I was sure that he had grasped the significance of the name. He was from my country after all. What would he do now, call for help? Get me thrown out? Call for the police?

He did none of these things. Instead, he ran his finger down one of the pages of the ledger and said, 'Ah, yes, here it is. Finasera. Deposit made a few years ago, in trust for you, Mademoiselle. Forgive my inattention, I missed it previously.'

'That's all right,' I said blankly. 'I . . . I quite understand.'

'Would you like to withdraw it all, Mademoiselle, or only partially?' The teller's voice was steady now but his fingers less so.

'Er, all, please.'

'Very good, Mademoiselle. Will you wait a moment, please?'

'Certainly,' I said, though I felt less than certain. He got up and disappeared out the back. I waited there in a perfect fever of anxiety, wondering what was going to happen and whether I should make a run for it while I still could. Fortunately, I'd been the last in the queue with no-one behind me. The other teller was busy with his customers so no-one took any notice of me. I could see the open ledger from where I was, upside down, but I could plainly see there was no deposit in Finasera's name written there. It was odd and just as I had decided I had to leave, back came my teller, carrying a fat white envelope. No longer pale but red and sweating, he pushed the envelope across the desk to me.

'That's all I could . . . that's all of it, Mademoiselle,' he caught himself, smoothly.

'Thank you,' I said, putting the envelope into my reticule. Even without opening it I could see that it was stuffed with banknotes. 'You have been most helpful.'

'Only doing my job, Mademoiselle,' he said, mechanically. There were red spots in his cheeks and a strange look in his eyes, as if he could hardly believe what had just happened. I could hardly believe it myself – I could hardly take in the enormity of the fact that a respectable, elderly teller had made up an imaginary deposit and *stolen* money from his own bank for me.

I said, gently, 'You are from Ashberg, sir, like me.'

'No, Mademoiselle,' he said, very quietly. 'I am from a much smaller place. You probably have never heard of it. Its name is Smutny.'

We looked at each other. And suddenly in those faded blue eyes behind the spectacles, I caught a faint resemblance to someone I'd met.

'I've heard of it, but never been,' I said. 'Do you still have family there?'

'A brother, Mademoiselle,' he said. 'My elder brother. We don't get on. Haven't seen each other in years.'

No, you wouldn't, I thought, remembering the bitter old jackal of a man back in that decaying village. He and his brother were like chalk and cheese.

I said, softly, 'Sometimes our nearest are not always our dearest.'

He nodded with a sad smile. Then as a customer approached, the teller said, quickly, 'If that will be all, Mademoiselle, I wish you good day.' His voice dropped and he added, 'And good luck.'

'Thank you, sir,' I said. 'And I hope that all will be well for you and that there is no –'

'Very good, then, Mademoiselle,' he interrupted me, with a fixed, artificial smile, and I knew then that I should go, that he would not welcome further effusions.

As I walked out of the bank, I felt a strange mixture of elation and anxiety. Thanks to the old man's brave presence of mind, I now had plenty of money – real money. There was no danger of its withering into dead leaves. Oh, the hazel-tree magic had worked in a wonderful way indeed this time!

And yet anxiety nagged at me. Not for myself so much, but for the teller. Eventually, it would be discovered that the money was missing. How long would it be before suspicion fell on him? And if it did, it wasn't just his career that would be ruined, it was his very life. He would go to prison at the very least. And for what? Not for me, a random stranger, but for a *memory*; for the honour of the forest lands, and a name from long ago. For Serafina, the rebel who had raised the moon-sisters' standard against the ruler of the very city in which he now lived. And yet he could have no idea what I planned. Not only that, he hadn't wanted to know. It was both very moving and very confusing. How strange and unexpected people were!

On the way back to the boarding house, I bought a large piece of roast chicken, a cake, a bottle of ginger ale, and a couple of newspapers. Safely bolted in my room, I had my meal and counted the money. There was more than enough to see me set up very comfortably. I then combed the newspapers for the details of any upcoming palace functions. Remembering the picture I'd seen in *The Book of Thalia*, I thought it shouldn't be a ball or a dinner or a garden party or anything of that sort, but something more businesslike as there'd been diplomats, officials and councillors at the event I'd seen.

There were several events of that kind but I finally settled on one which would be held in four days' time. It was to be a general audience, a meet-and-greet affair involving diplomats from minor countries, provincial officials and businesspeople from far-flung regions. What was perfect about it, though, was that unlike many of the other functions, you could actually apply to be part of the guest list by presenting your credentials to the Palace Protocol Office which would then issue you with a ticket.

I'd need a useful cover story to present myself as hailing from a place obscure enough that I could say just about anything I wanted. And it was while I was skimming the rest of the newspaper that I happened upon the perfect thing. Yet, at first sight it hardly seemed like that, for it was an advertisement for a herbal elixir 'made from the finest mountain plants and mixed with the essence of ground Green River pearls from the fabled eastern land of Pandong, refined into a truly miraculous elixir that will cure all your ills'.

In an old geography book of Mama's, one of the few I'd rescued from Grizelda's rubbish heap, there had been a short article about Pandong. It had mentioned that a hundred years before, some merchants from Faustina had settled in Pandong's capital, Menglu, to trade in just those Green River pearls. Eventually, so many families moved there that their quarter was nicknamed 'Little Faustina'. It was an exotic story but it was also an obscure community that was hardly known at all.

I would be one of those people. Pacing around the room, I built up the story in my mind. I would be Miss Maria Tarneleit (the surname pinched from another advertisement), only child of an elderly, respected Menglu businessman who had been sent by his community to pay his respects to the palace but who had died before he could finish his journey, which had been continued by his daughter. Before going to the Palace Protocol Office to secure my ticket, I would prepare the following: a quaint but dignified letter from the merchants of 'Little Faustina', introducing Mr Tarneleit and his daughter and asking the Emperor for an audience; a heart-rending note from the sick father, tasking his daughter to continue his mission; a reference in foreign-inflected Faustinian from the Chief Court Adviser of the King of Pandong, vouching for the Tarneleits.

'Hmm,' I said, thinking aloud, 'a most useful addition would be some Green River pearls to present as a gift, but that might be easier said than done.'

Before that, though, I would have to engage in a complete makeover – go to the public baths and have myself scrubbed, perfumed and primped within an inch of my life. Then I'd buy some better clothes. That would all have to be done before I found a suitable hotel to establish myself as a young woman of means.

But right now I badly needed a nap. My head was spinning, my eyes felt grainy and my limbs heavy. Exhaustion and tension had caught up with me with a vengeance. Putting the envelope of money under my thin pillow, I lay down and almost instantly fell asleep.

Thirty-Two

I am back in the forest. It is very dark, I can hardly see the path, but there is a light in the distance. I know I must walk towards that light or I will be lost. There are eyes watching me – unfriendly eyes – and if I take one step off the path I'll be doomed. Then I hear a sound. It is faint but unmistakeable – the sound of someone weeping in the darkness, off the path. Someone weeping inconsolably. The sound lodges in my heart like an arrow and more than anything I want to step off the path and comfort the weeper, but I cannot because if I take one step off that path all will be lost.

So I keep walking. But the sound does not stop; it does not get fainter. In fact, it gets louder and louder and louder the more I go along. It tears at my heart. I put my hands over my ears and keep going. And then I stop. Someone has emerged from the darkness and is standing directly in my path. It is the weeper, and I know now why I was so stricken. My heart knew what my head did not. It is my mother and she is standing in my path, weeping, holding out her cupped *hands to me. In them lies the still body of a dead bird, a little finch, and under its body are the ashes of dead leaves. She weeps and weeps and her grief is so painful to me that I cry out her name and run towards her. But just as I am about to reach her, it is as though a wall of glass has come down between us. I cannot touch her, I cannot get any closer to her, and though I see her lips move, I cannot hear what she says. Then her form begins to waver – like smoke, like mist – and in a moment she has faded away, gone from sight, and I am left alone.*

The dream ended as I woke with a jolt. My face was wet with tears, my heart racing. For a little while I could do nothing but lie there, so strong was the impression the dream had left behind. Every other time my mother had come to me in a dream, it had been to make me strong; to give me patience, to help me and to comfort me. This time it was she who had needed comforting and I was powerless to provide it. Not because I didn't understand, *but because I did.*

She had never intended for her gift to do anything but bring me happiness – to bring about an end to my ordeal, to bring me a chance of escape, of love, of making a new life for myself. And it had given me that chance. But she did not want me on *this* path, and just as I was powerless to comfort her, she was powerless to stop me. It was my choice.

'I'm so sorry, Mama,' I whispered. 'I'm so sorry but I have given my word and if I break it everyone I care about in this life will die.'

There was no sound apart from my own whisper in the air, no feeling of her presence at all. My mother was not there with me and I was seized with grief at the thought she might never be again. For a moment my resolve faltered – and then into my mind clear as day came the memory of the scene in Thalia's book of Max lying dead on the floor and I knew that while there was any chance that might come true, I could do nothing other than what I had sworn to do. And nothing could stop me, not even my mother. I loved her dearly but she was in the afterlife. She was in no danger any more. She was out of harm's reach. Not like my sweetheart. Not like my friends.

It was strange but I felt even stronger now. I'd been tested and had passed the test. Nothing could touch me now, nothing would deflect me from doing what I must.

The public baths were fairly quiet and, after a hot soak followed by a cold rinse, I was soon ensconced in a private cubicle where my hair was washed and trimmed, my fringe curled, and a long switch of hair of the same colour was attached securely to the back of my head. My nails were cut and polished, my skin rubbed with sweet oil, my face lightly powdered, my lips reddened. No questions were asked, either; bathhouse attendants were famously discreet, and the sight of a crisp handful of banknotes was answer enough to any curiosity.

After that I went to scout for a hotel suitable for the daughter of a foreign merchant, that is, one of great comfort but not princely luxury. The Hotel Bella suited the bill perfectly: a pretty building situated in the centre of town but in a quiet street, and a short hansom-cab ride from the palace precinct. I did not go in to ask for a room, for first I had to be properly attired for that.

Instead, I went back to the boarding house and took the twig out from inside the mattress. There were two more leaves on it now. I carefully picked them and put them in my bag, then wrapped the twig in some brown paper and shoved it down the front of my dress. The rest of the parcel I hid under my shawl and then I went out, closing the door behind me without regret. I would not go back there. I dumped the shirt and coat in a pile of rubbish in a back alley some distance away and then headed for the big department store I'd seen when I'd first arrived. In a large place like that, with crowds of shoppers and shop assistants running around, I'd be less likely to stand out as an object of curiosity than in some fashionable boutique.

That proved to be the case and I was soon the proud owner of a very pretty dress in pale green wool, a cream-coloured coat, a selection of fine underclothes and stockings, an elegant green hat, dark green leather gloves, a lace-trimmed umbrella and a smart pair of cream-coloured boots. Not only that, but I was ushered politely into the plush fitting rooms to put on my new clothes, with the old ones wrapped in paper and put in a large travelling bag I had also bought (the twig I transferred to my new coat pocket). I'd told the shop assistants that I'd just arrived from a far-flung place and, though I had a good deal of money, I did not possess any fashionable clothes. My clodhopper boots and plain dress were rather less than 'unfashionable' but any suspicions the shop assistants might have had as to

246

my *bona fides* were soon allayed by the sight of my money. What a smooth path money gives us!

After that I selected a nightgown, a dressing gown, slippers, and a case of what they called 'necessaries', which included a brush, comb, mirror and a flannel as well as nail scissors, cosmetics, a little bottle of perfume and creams. I got the shop assistants to wrap it all up and instructed them to have it delivered to Miss Maria Tarneleit at the Hotel Bella. That would establish my identity in the eyes of both the store and the hotel.

Well pleased with myself, I hurried to the hotel, where I soon obtained a room, signing myself in under my new name, putting 'Menglu' in the 'From' section of the hotel form. I told them my luggage would be following on shortly, and explained that my lack of a maid or other personal servant was due to the fact that it was not the custom in Menglu to pay for the fare of a servant when travelling to foreign parts, but rather to hire one upon arrival. The receptionist clearly thought such 'customs' were penny-pinching and uncivilised, but only delicately suggested that if I liked, suitable people could be recommended. I thanked him and said that I would not need anyone till the next day.

'Very good, Miss,' he said. 'And will you be requiring dinner?'

'Yes, I would, but in my room,' I replied.

He then called a porter to accompany me to my new quarters.

It was a large room on the first floor, its walls papered with a pretty pattern of cream and blue roses, its polished floors set with pale blue rugs, its window curtained with blue velvet. And there was everything in it that one could possibly want: a four-poster bed covered by a blue velvet bedspread; a down quilt and pillows; a small washstand complete with blue-patterned china jug and bowl (the actual washroom, with its beautiful deep bath, was just down the hall); a dressing table; an armchair; a wardrobe; a lockable roll-top writing desk and chair.

But there was no time to admire it – I had to go shopping. Hiding the twig deep in the locked roll-top desk, I put on my hat, coat and gloves, and stepped back into the chilly day. My first stop was at a stationer's where I bought elegant, thick writing paper and envelopes, a sheet of the best-quality art paper, white tissue paper, a fine pen, brown and black ink, some red sealing wax and a decorative stamp with an elaborate design of interlaced dragon heads and tails.

I then called in at a haberdasher's and bought some thin red and black silk ribbons. At a milliner's I bought a single, delicate red silk flower, shaped like a lotus bloom, and a satin bag of the sort you use to store bonnets flat. Then I went into a bookshop, hoping I might find a useful book about Pandong. I only found a thin guidebook about the region, which not only took in Pandong but several of its neighbouring countries as well. And in a book on gemstones, I found a long entry on Green River pearls, so I bought that too. The more I knew about my supposed home, the better.

After that, I looked in at a shop that specialised in hiring out evening wear – an unheard-of novelty in Ashberg. Not here, where the middle-class aspired to live like great lords but couldn't always manage the cost so had to settle for merely appearing so. I looked through the rows of dresses till I found one that resembled the dress I'd seen in Thalia's mirror, though not identical, and certainly not as magnificent. But remembering the experience with Maria's dress, I thought I could rely on magic to improve it. I booked the dress for three days hence, also booking a silver tiara and a gauzy silver scarf that would do well as a wrap.

On my way back, in a street right near the hotel, I happened across a small jewellery shop, which had some Green River pearls set into drop earrings in its window display. I went in, bought a pair, and as the jeweller put them in a little box for me, I said, emphasising my Ashbergian accent and thus my provincial ignorance, 'These are an unusual sort of pearls, what are they?'

'Green River pearls, Miss,' said the jeweller. 'Freshwater pearls from far away. Cheaper than the sea variety as a gemstone but not all that easy to get because people use them in medicines, you see, and so the apothecaries usually snap them up.'

So perhaps an apothecary would be a better person to ask where a supply might be had, I thought, and was going to ask the jeweller where I might find one, when I noticed something in one of his display cabinets. It was a selection of miniature jewelled weapons: a tiny silver revolver with a mother-of-pearl inlay; a delicate gold swordstick, and a fine dagger set in a chased silver scabbard that strangely resembled a closed silver fan.

Catching my breath, I said, demurely, 'Oh, that's so pretty! How much is it?'

The jeweller named a price much higher than the earrings. I paid up, and he wrapped it and the pearl earrings without surprise.

'I hope you will have no cause to use this, Miss,' he said, 'but you are right to make sure of your protection, that is what I always tell the ladies. Too many criminals around these days and you can't always wait for the police to come to your aid.'

I murmured something vague, thanked him and left the shop with my purchases. My heart was beating wildly at the thought of what I carried in the jeweller's neat box. For the first time I thought of what it would be like to plunge that delicate, deadly thing into another human being's heart. Would I truly be able to do it? Could I really look into his eyes and then stab him to death? I pushed the weak thoughts away; of course I could do it – would do it. While Prince Leopold lived, Max was in mortal danger. That was the long and short of it.

A few doors down, I saw an apothecary's shop and, remembering what the jeweller had said, went in. I bought an ounce of the expensive Green River pearl powder and, while the apothecary ladled it into a twist of paper, I asked him where he bought his pearls to make the powder.

'They come in on the ships every so often,' he said, 'but there isn't one due for a while. And I strongly recommend that you don't make your own powder. It's a real art, Miss.'

With a nervous little smile, I assured him I had no such intention, thanked him and went out with the pricey, useless powder in my bag. Oh well, I thought, I'd have to do without the pearls. I'd have to think of some other gift to bring . . .

I spent the rest of the day forging the necessary papers with many flourishes of ink and quaint phrasing, deliberately making a vague reference to a gift I'd been entrusted with. Once the ink was dry, I put the 'merchants' letter' and the 'letter from my father' in the envelopes, finishing them off with the dragon-stamped seal. The fabricated letter of introduction from the Pandong Court Adviser, which I had drawn up on the art paper, I rolled like a scroll, tying it with the red and black silk ribbons, with the lotus flower looped into them. I was very pleased with my handiwork, for it all looked very impressive. Carefully, I wrapped them individually in tissue paper and slid them into the satin bonnet bag. I then put it into the locked desk along with the silver dagger, still in its presentation box. Just as I finished, the porter knocked on the door to deliver the rest of my purchases from the store. After he'd gone, I sat down with my new books and read them attentively, and more than once. By the time I'd finally decided that it was all stuck in my head, the gas lamps in the street outside had come on and the waiter was bringing up my dinner tray.

Dinner was simple but good: spinach soup, roast chicken and vegetables, followed by a lemon mousse. Yet, though I'd been hungry, it had little savour for me and I left most of it untouched. As I had started my meal, an image had suddenly come to me of the previous night's dinner around the campfire in the forest. The food had been poor and the accommodation worse but now it seemed like a lost piece of heaven for we'd all been together. Now alone, the enormity of what I was doing weighed on me. The excitement brought on by my hectic activity, the sense of accomplishment for using my wits, and the feelings of rightness that had sustained me for so many hours, had finally ebbed away, leaving me drained, exhausted and utterly numb.

Thirty-Three

I was ready early the next morning for my mission to the Palace Protocol Office and was just about to go when I noticed that my handbag seemed heavier than before. And it was no wonder, for instead of the paper twist of powder I had left in it overnight, was a little ivory casket of the most delicate workmanship – and full of small, perfect pearls, more beautiful than the ones that hung from my ears, with a shimmering pale-green lustre that took one's breath away.

It was a wonderful surprise, but also puzzling. How had it happened? And then I noticed a hazel leaf on the bottom of the bag – a little curled and starting to brown, but still whole. Now I suddenly remembered I'd put two leaves in it yesterday when I'd left the boarding house. One of them must have locked onto the twist of pearl powder and transformed it. But I hadn't asked for it, had I? I thought back to yesterday, when I'd been planning my strategy, and remembered how I'd mused aloud how useful it would be to have Green River pearls. But it hadn't been a direct wish ... Perhaps, I thought, the presence of the pearl powder on top of the leaf had given it extra power.

I couldn't help smiling at the sheer elegance of it. Olga had said once that you didn't choose the best magic, it chose you. Now I understood what she meant. It wasn't one-size-fits-all magic; it was different for each person. It fit like a glove to a hand; no, better still, like skin on bones. It picked up little vibrations from one's being – subtle undercurrents, half-conscious thoughts and feelings – and expressed them in an unexpected, yet perfectly judged way. It was astonishing, exciting, and frightening, too. Accepting the way the magic worked was like starting to tell a story aloud when you didn't know the ending. You had to learn to trust it, to have faith and to understand that the story itself would find its own expression through you, that the shroud of darkness would clear as the words came out of your mouth. Or you'd be lost. And in my case, that was much more than mere metaphor. It was a matter of life and death.

The Palace Protocol Office was a short distance from the gates of the palace in a little colonnaded building guarded by policemen in shiny black caps and dark-green uniforms. I stated my assumed name and business, and was ushered into the waiting room. I didn't have to wait long before being called into an office where a man with a round bald head and wearing a smart suit and blue cravat sat at a big black desk. A shelf full of books sat behind him, a large oil portrait of the imperial family prominent on the same wall. On his desk a small brass nameplate read: *Officer P.S. Hedde.*

'Now then, Miss Tarneleit,' the man's stony grey eyes surveyed me expressionlessly, 'I understand you are a merchant's daughter from Pandong and that you seek a place at the general audience in three days' time. You have cut it a little fine, haven't you?'

'I'm sorry, sir,' I said quickly, 'but I was much delayed on my journey –' I dabbed at my eyes '– owing to my father's untimely death, and I only arrived in Faustina yesterday. I have a letter, if you –'

'No, no. Just show me your official documents,' Officer Hedde said, impatiently.

I handed them to him. He read the letter from the Menglu merchants with an expressionless face, but the Court Adviser's letter seemed to interest him more. He looked at the seal carefully and, I thought, suspiciously. In a panic, scared he would work out they were forged, I felt I had to do something.

I took out the casket from my handbag, put it on the desk in front of him and said, 'This is the gift, sir, that my father was bringing. A gift from all the merchants of Menglu, in most respectful tribute to the imperial family.'

I glanced up at the portrait as I spoke, thinking that the painter must have been some fawning court toady, for the expression painted in Prince Leopold's eyes was so much sweeter and warmer than the eyes of the real person. Imperial propaganda, of course, I thought.

The man's eyes widened a little as he opened the casket and saw the pearls. 'I have never seen such fine specimens,' he said, picking one up between thumb and forefinger and examining it minutely. 'They seem truly flawless.'

'They are, sir,' I said, eagerly, 'of a quality that is rarely found even in Pandong and never here. They come from a new field discovered only a couple of years ago by –'

'Yes, yes,' he said, waving an impatient hand. 'Save that for the audience. Now I regret to inform you that the Emperor will not be there, for he is unwell, but you can present your gift to the Crown Prince.'

'Yes, of course, sir,' I said, inwardly rejoicing, for it seemed like fate had played into my hands and I should not have to kill Leopold in front of his father.

Officer Hedde took a sheet of paper out from a desk drawer. It looked like some kind of official form.

'Your full name and address, please. Address here, too.' He wrote down what I told him, then stamped, signed and dated the form. He handed it to me and said, 'Down the hall, second door on your right, they will give you an official ticket in return for this.'

'Thank you very much, sir,' I gabbled, picking it up with my documents and the casket, pretending not to notice that Officer Hedde still held the pearl he'd examined. I'd seen the covetous expression in his eyes when he'd looked at it. Leaving it with him was a small price to pay for having my path smoothed. And hopefully the pearl would keep its magicked form long enough for my purposes.

'Very well, very well,' he said, officiously shuffling papers on his desk as if I was interrupting him in some important task. Smiling to myself, I said goodbye and went out.

The clerk in the ticket office scarcely glanced at the details on the form – Officer Hedde's signature and stamp were clearly enough. Taking a card from a box on his desk, he filled in my name, then put the card in an envelope and handed it to me.

'In here you will find the ticket in your name, and other details,' he said, and went on to recite mechanically, 'You are to arrive at the gates at least an hour before the stated time to be processed and instructed on the correct protocol for the audience. This ticket is valid only for the person named, for one entry only and only for this audience on the stated day.'

I thanked him and left. It had been much easier than I'd thought. But then everything had been since I arrived here, with it all falling into place in the most unexpectedly appropriate ways. My luck would last till the end, I thought, as I walked away from the office. Dremda would have ensured that.

'Oof!'

I'd been so lost in my thoughts that I hadn't noticed the girl coming towards me or she I, for she, too, had been walking along with her head bent. We both saw stars.

'Sorry,' we both said at once, and then looked at each other.

The shock of recognition was so great that for an instant I couldn't speak. But if I was shocked, she seemed absolutely terrified, rooted to the spot as if turned to stone. Her eyes like dark holes in her chalk-pale face, the envelope she'd been clutching dropped unregarded to the ground as she stared dumbly at me.

I found my voice, and grabbed her by the arm. 'What are *you* doing here?'

She swallowed and quavered, 'Are you ... are you a g– a *ghost*?'

'What are you talking about?'

'They said you were dead,' whispered Babette. 'That you'd drowned in the river trying to escape from prison ... that you'd escaped with a gang of hardened criminals who tried to kill a warder ... And Mother ... Mother said it was a mercy you died.'

'She did, did she?' My mind was whirring. I dug my fingers into her arm and she winced. 'You haven't answered my question,' I growled. 'Why are you here?'

'Father's been taken very ill. Mother brought him here – the doctors are better.'

'What?' My stomach lurched. 'What are you talking about?'

'He's in a coma. And it's *your* fault, because it was such a shock when he heard about you that he was struck down with apoplexy. Mother and Odette and I, we knew all along you were bad – evil – but he wouldn't believe it, not till *they* told him. Thank God at least nobody else knows. They said it was not our fault, and that nobody need know.' She shot me a scared glance and said, trying to sound defiant, 'And if you don't let go of my arm at once, I'll scream for the police.'

'I wouldn't do that if I were you,' I said calmly, and took a deep breath. Reaching into my bag, I pulled out the leaf. This was going to be a gamble but I had to take it, I had to trust my instinct. Her eyes followed my every movement. 'They didn't tell you the whole truth about me, you see. I'm not just a thief, Babette; not just an ordinary criminal. I'm a witch. And I'm very good at it. *That's* how I escaped them.'

From white, she turned grey. Her hands shook. 'I . . . I don't believe you.'

'Well, you'd better, dear sis. You'd better believe that I'm a very powerful witch indeed and if I want to I could turn you into a frog or a worm or' – I remembered one of Babette's pet hates – 'a spider, or anything at all, just with one word. Watch!' And I breathed on the leaf and said, 'Be a spider,' hoping that it would work.

Instantly, the leaf twisted in on itself and suddenly there, on my hand, sat a spider – a big, brown ugly spider with hairy legs and wicked little eyes.

'How do you like my friend, then?' I said, moving the spider closer to her.

She was transfixed by horror, her eyes bulging. She moaned, 'No, please – don't . . . don't let it touch me. I'm sorry . . . I'm –'

'You listen carefully, Babette, because I will say this only once. You will turn around and walk away and you will not breathe a word about having seen me to a living soul. If you do, I will know. And if I find out you have broken your word, I will hunt you down wherever you are. I will turn you into a spider for ever – a thing everyone will hate on sight and you will have to spend the rest of your miserable life in hiding.' Deliberately, I dropped the spider on the ground and stamped on it. 'Just like this one. Do you understand?'

She looked as if she'd be sick. But I had no pity for her. For years she, her sister and her mother had made my life a bleak misery and at last the tables were turned and I could now pay her back a little for what I'd suffered.

'I asked you a question, Babette,' I said, sharply.

She flinched. 'I ... I understand,' she said in a very small voice. 'I ... I promise I will not say anything to anybody.'

'Good.' I released my grip on her arm. 'Now go. And remember what I said.'

'I will,' she quavered and then backed away a couple of paces before quickly turning around and scuttling off as if the Devil himself were after her.

Now it was all over, I began to feel a bit trembly. I was lucky it was silly, gullible Babette I'd run into, I thought, and not her sister or mother. They'd have been much harder nuts to crack. And though it had been a dark pleasure to see how terrified Babette was of me, it had been no pleasure at all to learn of my father's condition. He had not been a real parent to me for years, but he was still my father. Babette had said it was my fault, and though I rejected her words, it still stung. I did not like to think of him so ill and I did not want him to die. But there was nothing I could do; nothing that would ever make it better between us.

In a way, meeting Babette had been a blessing in disguise as I had learned other things important to my mission. First, that either the Mancers had not found out about my involvement with magic, or that they were keeping it quiet for their own reasons. I thought it was probably the former reason, as otherwise, surely, they'd have questioned my family who would have been under suspicion too ... and they clearly weren't. So I had that card up my sleeve.

Second, they had said I'd *drowned*. Telling my father that would have ensured he wouldn't go looking for me nor ask awkward questions, for the Ash River was notoriously deep and treacherous and full of the bodies of people who'd drowned, never to be found. Not that I thought it particularly likely he'd have stuck his neck out anyway – not for me, who he'd neglected for years. But Prince Leopold and his accomplices weren't to know that, and they wouldn't want to take any chances.

Clearly, they didn't want anyone to know the truth about the man they were hunting. Olga and I didn't matter, not really. They didn't care about either of us except that we might learn the truth from Max. The Prince and his friends could have no idea that the thieving servant girl had any connection with the Champainian lady who had rejected the Prince at the ball. As to Olga, well, a foreign werewolf was just vermin. Even Tomi was of no importance to them, Mancer child or not. For Max had said that he believed the Mancers had been deceived too ...

Deep in thought, I was about to walk away when I noticed the letter Babette had dropped still lying on the ground. I picked it up and saw to my astonishment that it was addressed, in the brown ink my stepmother favoured, to Count Otto von Gildenstein. What on earth was Grizelda doing, writing to Max's father?

Then a stunning thought struck me – here was an undreamed-of opportunity. Max had been so worried about his father. And I remembered the sadness on the Count's face in that scene in Thalia's mirror. He might not know of his son's true fate but he was uneasy, I knew that instinctively. I could set his mind at rest. What was more, he was on the Mancer Council. I could even plant a subtle suggestion about the way they'd been used and I could easily do that without jeopardising my task. Indeed, it could only help to protect Max and my friends.

I wouldn't say who I really was, of course. He'd only met me once, as Mademoiselle Camille St Clair, but I could make sure I looked nothing like that. I could dress up in those clothes I'd bought from the pawnshop and say I was a maid in the employ of Lady Grizelda, tasked to deliver the letter personally and privately into his hands. And once I was in his presence, I could see how the land lay. If it felt right, I could tell him his son was safe for now and warn him of the situation. If it didn't, I'd keep mum, and there'd be no harm done.

First, I had to know what the letter contained.

On the way back to the hotel, I passed one of those street stalls that sells gags and jokes and disguises, and on impulse stopped and bought a pair of plain glass spectacles. Back in the privacy of my hotel room, I locked the door and sat down to read the letter. It had my father's seal with an address in the city.

Dear Count Otto,

I hope this letter will come as a pleasant surprise. I have recently arrived in Faustina with my daughters, for the sake of my husband's health. Sir Claus is not well but I am confident he will be better soon, with the good care of Faustina doctors. However, I imagine we will be making our home in Faustina for quite some time to come. In a week from now, I will be hosting a small, informal dinner in our new home and it would be my fondest wish, and that of my daughters, that you and your son might see fit to attend. I dare to hope that the good memories you held of the last time we met, and the warm sympathy we shared, will induce you to grant this wish and honour us with your presence.

With sincere regards and salutations from,
Lady Grizelda dez Mestmor

I shook my head. It was so like Grizelda to be thinking of her social position and her daughters' marriage prospects at a time like this, when her husband lay at death's door. It was all so cold-blooded and calculating. And that bit about 'the warm sympathy we shared' – that was sheer flirtation. Did she think there could be something between her and Count Otto? In any case, though it disgusted me, it mattered little. Nothing would surprise me about my stepmother. What did matter was the fact that she mentioned Max. And I could use that, simply by adding a line to the letter.

I uncorked my bottle of brown ink, dipped the pen in it and, imitating Grizelda's flowing script, wrote:

Postscript: If you would be so kind as to give the bearer of this letter an indication of you and your son's intentions, I would be most grateful.

That would give me the perfect and natural opportunity to put the question I needed to ask. Well, dear stepmother, I thought, smiling to myself as I re-addressed a new envelope, for the first time in my life I feel grateful towards you, even if you won't ever know it.

Thirty-Four

While I waited for the ink to dry, I changed into the grey woollen dress and the shawl from the pawnshop, powdered my face till it looked pasty, then put on the spectacles, and tied the bonnet unbecomingly close to my face. Looking at myself in the mirror, I was certain there was no question now of the Count recognising the fine lady from the ball in this mousy creature.

I took the twig out from the desk and found that another leaf had unfurled. I picked it and put it in my bag, replacing the twig in the desk along with the casket of pearls and the forged documents. Once the ink had thoroughly dried, I folded the letter, slipped it into the envelope, and sealed it with a blob of red sealing wax. I didn't put it in my bag, for I did not want to run the risk that the magic might somehow interfere with it. Drawing on my gloves, I unlocked my door and looked out into the corridor. I thought that if anyone saw me, I'd just say I had come for an interview as a maid for Miss Tarneleit.

But in the event there was nobody, so I set off down the back stairs the hotel staff used. Though I encountered a couple of staff members on the way, they barely glanced at me, and I reached the ground floor and slipped out of the service entrance with no problem at all.

I was back at the Palace Protocol Office in hardly any time. Nobody recognised me and, after I stated my business, the same policeman ushered me in, the same clerk took my new name – I called myself Tilda Smit, a suitably innocuous and common sort of name – and the same official I'd seen as the incarnation of a Menglu merchant's daughter sat across the desk and looked at me with disfavour but not recognition.

'Count Otto is an important man, and is very busy,' snapped Officer Hedde. 'Give me the letter, Miss Smit, and I will see it gets safely into his hands.'

I gave a nervous laugh, the kind that suited a Miss Tilda Smit. 'I'm very sorry, honourable sir, but my mistress was very insistent.' I made my accent thick and slow, and saw the impatience on his face.

'Your mistress being this Lady Grizelda?'

'Yes, sir, Lady Grizelda dez Mestmor, wife of one of the richest and most important Ashbergian nobles, Sir Claus dez Mestmor, and a personal friend of the Count's, as I explained to your clerk.'

Officer Hedde frowned. 'I have not heard of these people.'

'I am sure, sir, that if you look in *The Golden Dictionary*, you will find the name "dez Mestmor" has great honour,' I said, primly, having noticed it on his bookshelf. It was a book that listed all the noble families in the empire, and something of their ancestral history. My father had it in his own library.

He grunted and, as I'd hoped, reached over to his shelf and pulled out the book. He opened it and leafed through the pages.

'Hmm ... Arden ... Ashberg – here we are ...' He ran his finger down the column of names. 'Yes, I see, dez Mestmor. Let me see ... "One of the oldest families of Ashberg with an unblemished record of service to the empire" ... um, blah blah, "one of the biggest fortunes in Ashberg ... present holder of the title: Sir Claus dez Mestmor". Let me see, two marriages "first to Jana Lubosdera, one issue, a daughter; second to Grizelda Krasenstein, widow of the late Officer Sigmund Krasenstein of Faustina." Why didn't you tell me your mistress was Officer Krasenstein's widow instead of gabbling about provincial nobility I've never heard of! Officer Krasenstein was a colleague of mine and much respected in this office.'

'I'm ... I'm sorry, sir,' I said, taken aback. 'I didn't know.'

'Oh, well,' said Officer Hedde, in a noticeably softened tone, 'I suppose, coming from sleepy, little Ashberg, Miss Smit, you can't be expected to know much of what happens in this great city. Is this your first time here?'

'Yes, sir, this is my first time. And I can't believe my eyes, sir! I'd seen pictures but it's not the same! Oh, it's like being in a dream, it's all so amazing –'

'Yes, yes,' he said, holding up a hand to stop my gabbling. 'Quite overwhelming for a little provincial, I'm sure. After all, you are in the centre of things now, not

267

stuck in some obscure little backwater. Quite a relief for your mistress, too, I imagine.'

'Oh yes, sir,' I said eagerly, while inwardly amused by his patronising stupidity, and at the thought that for all her airs and graces, my stepmother had just been the widow of some obscure little pen-pusher in this office. 'My mistress is thrilled to be back in her native city.'

'Quite. Now, then, let me find out if there is any possibility that Count Otto might be able to see you today. Briefly, mind. Like I told you, he is very busy.'

And he got up, went to the door and called out, 'Messenger! Come here!'

They were the longest ten minutes of my life, as I sat in Officer Hedde's office waiting for the messenger to come back. And it wasn't just that I was on tenterhooks. It was also that Officer Hedde clearly saw it as his duty to instruct an ignorant little provincial on the history, customs, manners and wonders of the imperial capital to make me understand just how lucky I was to be here. Torn between boredom, anxiety and indignation, I almost wished I really did have the power I'd told Babette I did and could turn the pompous old fraud into a toad or something. As it was, I just had to sit tight and smile eagerly and ooh and aah.

Finally, my ordeal ended. The messenger came back with good news: Count Otto had agreed to give me a few moments of his time and I was to be taken to him at once.

I bid a fawning goodbye to Officer Hedde and followed the messenger out of the office towards the palace. We did not go in through the main gates, but down a side street into the entrance of a building that stood apart from the palace proper, separated by a locked gate. This, the messenger informed me, housed the offices of the senior advisers and palace staff.

The place was like a rabbit warren, with corridors leading off here and there and rows of closed doors. The messenger led me down one corridor and up another, then up some stairs and finally to a door down the end of the next corridor. He knocked twice, then the deep voice of Count Otto said, 'Come in.'

It was quite a big room, with a window that gave out onto a courtyard. Simply furnished, it was obviously a working space and not a place to impress. The walls were lined with shelves crammed with books and papers, and tall wooden filing cabinets. The only decorations were the usual portrait of the imperial family on one wall and a plain carriage-clock on the stone mantelpiece. A fire burned in the gate. Count Otto himself sat at a leather-topped desk covered with papers, writing busily. He looked up at me, but without recognition.

I thought, with a pang, that he didn't look well. There were dark circles under his eyes and a tension in his lips that suggested some gnawing anxiety.

'This is Miss Smit, my lord,' the messenger announced.

'Please take a chair, Miss Smit,' the Count said, quietly. 'I won't be a moment. And you can leave us alone now, George.'

The messenger bowed and withdrew, closing the door behind him.

For a moment all was silent apart from the ticking of the clock and the scratching of Count Otto's pen on paper. And the rapid beating of my heart, though I didn't suppose he could hear that. My hands were shaking a little and I tried to keep them still. Finally, he finished writing, folded the letter, and put it to one side. He looked up again, and this time he smiled – a tired smile, of a man ground down under some burden.

'I'm sorry to have kept you waiting, Miss Smit.' He spoke as though his mind was elsewhere. 'Now, I understand you have something to give me?'

'Yes, my lord,' I said. 'This letter, from my mistress, the Lady Grizelda dez Mestmor, she was most insistent you receive it personally.' I handed it to him.

'Such a pleasant surprise,' he murmured as he slit open the envelope with a paper knife and extracted the letter. Watching him as he scanned what was written inside, I thought of what he'd been like when I'd met him in the corridors of Ashberg Castle. Big, confident and exuding power. Now he seemed fretful, a little shrunken, and hunched, as if he'd aged years – not days – since I'd last seen him. Something was wrong and I knew what it was.

He looked up again. 'I am very sorry to learn of your master's illness,' he said. 'He seemed like a good man.'

'Thank you, my lord. He was – is. It was very sudden, his illness. Quite a shock to everybody.' To my horror, I could feel tears pricking at my eyes. 'But we hope he will be better soon.'

'Amen to that,' he said gently. 'Your mistress has done the right thing bringing him to Faustina. We have the best doctors in the world. Please tell her that if there is anything I can do to help, I will do so without hesitation.'

'Thank you, my lord, I'll be sure and tell her.'

'It is really most kind of your mistress to invite me. I have fond memories of meeting her, her charming daughters, and your master, of course. Good food and very good company – an exemplary household.'

Ha, I thought, without letting my feelings show on my face.

'Unfortunately, though I should very much like to accept her invitation, I am afraid that may not be possible right now. Later, perhaps.' He made as if to hand me back the letter.

I said, quickly, 'My lord, if I may, I know my mistress will be greatly disappointed.'

'I'm sorry, Miss Smit. I really am, but I have too much on my mind at the moment. Too much work. Perhaps later, as I said. I should very much like to call on her one of these days.'

'If I may be so bold, my lord,' I said, desperately, 'might you perhaps nominate a date when you and your son might be able to honour us with your presence? I know it would mean so much to my mistress.'

'I'm afraid I can't be sure,' he said. 'And as to my son, he's away. I don't know when . . . he'll be back. Perhaps we should wait till he is home.'

There was no doubt in my mind any more. The expression in his eyes as he spoke was fear, naked fear. And it decided me.

'Is he abroad, my lord?'

'Yes. No. Yes ... He's on important business.' His hands were shaking now as he pushed the letter across to me. 'Now if you don't mind, Miss Smit, I have a good deal of work to attend to, and –'

I took a deep breath. 'Don't be afraid, Count Otto,' I said, very quietly. 'He's safe.'

For an instant he stared at me as though turned to stone. Then he got up slowly and in a terrible voice, he said, 'What did you say?'

I stammered, 'Max ... your son ... he is quite safe and well, my lord. I swear it.'

He sat down again, heavily. He had gone very pale. 'What ... how – who are you ...?'

'I am a friend, my lord – a friend of your son.'

'What? He doesn't know a Miss Smit – what are you –' He was babbling, and I interrupted him gently.

'No, my lord, I'm not Miss Smit. She doesn't exist. The letter – I stole it so I could get to you and tell you – to set your mind at rest.'

'That is ... very kind of you,' he said, mechanically. There was a little colour starting to come back to his cheeks. 'Tell me ... tell me where he is that I may go to him and –'

'I can't tell you where he is, my lord, only that he is safe and on his way to right the terrible wrong that was done to him.'

'Oh my God ...' He covered his face with his hands.

'They told you he'd been sent on some secret mission or something like that, is that right?'

He looked up and stared at me. 'Y– yes.'

'But you didn't believe it.'

'I tried to but it just didn't add up. I am usually briefed about such things. I felt uneasy –' he broke off. 'What really happened? Please. You can't hide it from me, not now.'

'What really happened,' I said, 'was that your son was dragged off in the dead of night and secretly locked in a Mancer prison. They were going to have him blanked and, if he hadn't escaped, then, well, he'd pretty much be a zombie now.'

His eyes flashed, and he stood up. 'No, I can't believe that! I can't! It's just not possible. The Mancers would never dare touch a hair on the head of my son, I'm certain of it – certain! I'm *on* the Mancer Council, for God's sake! And how, if he really was in a Mancer prison, could he have possibly escaped? It's never been done before.'

'Thankfully, a way was found, my lord,' I said, discreetly. 'As to the rest, well, Max believes it wasn't an official Mancer operation – he believes it was done on the sly by rogue elements.'

'What? Who?'

'Think, my lord,' I said. 'Think.'

'I can't,' he said. 'I don't understand.' But I had seen the expression that flashed in his eyes and I knew that he understood, that he had already suspected the truth.

'A blanking order can only be authorised at the very highest levels. A rogue Mancer could certainly not do it, not even the General Secretary of the Mancers can do it. You know that, my lord.'

'You are surely not saying that the Emperor –'

'No. I do not think it was the Emperor. He has been as deceived as the Mancers. Count Otto, I know it was Prince Leopold who forged his father's signature on the order and that it is *he* who is behind it all.'

There was a dead silence.

Then he said, slowly, 'It can't be. The Crown Prince and my son – they are best friends. Close as ... brothers ... since childhood.'

I saw the knotting of his hands as he wrung them together. He was protesting, I thought, but it was no real surprise to him.

After a time, he said, 'Why? It makes no sense. What has Max done to deserve –'

'It's not what he's done, sir. It's what he *knows*.'

He jerked his head up and stared at me. 'Whatever do you mean?'

'Max knows something about Leopold – a secret so big and dangerous that the Prince is willing to kill him for it and to take the most enormous risks, like counterfeiting his father's signature on a blanking order.'

'Max – Max told you this?' he quavered.

'No, I worked it out for myself. But I know that's why he was worried for you. He'd hoped you'd believe the fairytale they told you about a secret mission and that you wouldn't ask awkward questions.'

'Why, in God's name, would he think that?'

'Because he was afraid that if you got even an inkling of the truth, you'd be in great danger too. That's why he didn't try to get back here, and why he hasn't tried to contact you.'

He swallowed, running a nerveless hand through his hair. 'But he has changed his mind as he sent you here.'

'No, my lord, he did not send me and he doesn't know I'm here. I just thought you needed to know.'

'Thank you,' he said. 'Thank you so much. I can't tell you how important this is to me. Oh, my poor son.'

'He is very brave, my lord,' I said. 'Brave and loyal and steadfast and true ...' My throat thickened, for I'd had a sudden image of Max and all at once I missed him so much it was like a dagger thrust in my heart. 'He is a real hero. A true prince of the heart, not like Leopold who is a prince only in name.'

He winced and I thought I'd gone too far. Then he looked at me shrewdly and said, 'You love him, don't you?'

I swallowed. 'Yes, I do. I love him very much. And he ... he feels the same.'

'I can see why,' he said. 'You are the most unusual person I have ever met. And still I do not know your name.'

'That is not important, my lord,' I said. 'What matters is that I am a friend of your son.'

'And of mine too, now, I hope,' he said, getting up. He walked around his desk and held out his hand. 'May I hope for that?'

'It would be an honour, my lord,' I said, and we shook hands. It felt like such a solemn moment, and yet like such a joyful one, too. The tears in my eyes were now as much of gladness as of sadness, for I no longer felt so alone.

'Well, my dear friend, I think we cannot let things go on as they have. We need to help my son.'

I thought of telling him what I planned to do but two things stopped me: one, I was not sure if the shock Count Otto had already received would be stronger than the loyalty of a lifetime dedicated to the Emperor and his family; and two, I remembered the warning Thalia had given me at Dremda. I could not tell anyone about my mission, no matter what happened. But I had to say something. 'Yes, but what can we do? What do you suggest?'

'I think we need to know what we are up against,' he said. 'And for that we need some answers. We need to know what secret Leopold is hiding. I think I may have just the idea as to how we might be able to trick it out of him. Listen . . .'

Thirty-Five

His plan was bold but simple. Leopold would be asked to come that very day, in lieu of his ill father, to an urgent meeting at a hunting lodge Count Otto owned in the woods on the outskirts of the city. He'd be told that he was to meet an important representative of a foreign power, who had insisted on the meeting being kept strictly private. Leopold would then be taken to a room where one of Count Otto's most trusted servants, a man called Bastien, would play the part of the mysterious emissary, while Count Otto and I would be concealed behind a panel in the same room. Bastien would be briefed with a set of questions which were designed to flush out Leopold's secret without appearing to do so. What would happen afterwards, the Count said – whether we simply used the information as leverage over Leopold to ensure Max's safety, or revealed it to the world – would depend on what secret the Prince was concealing.

When I asked, Count Otto said that Leopold was unlikely to be suspicious about the meeting because, since his return to Faustina and the illness of his father, he'd had to deal with quite a few matters that the Emperor would normally have handled personally. 'Besides,' he had said, with an ironic air, 'he adores intrigue and thinks he has me thoroughly fooled, so why should he fear me in any way?'

This is how it was to be done: I was to go to the hunting lodge at once in Count Otto's carriage with a message for Bastien, and then I was to wait there. Count Otto, meanwhile, would go to Leopold's quarters and brief him in person about the meeting (less risky than sending a message). All going well, they would be at the lodge within an hour or two. As soon as they arrived, I would conceal myself in the meeting room, to be joined by Count Otto shortly after Leopold was introduced to 'the emissary' who'd be waiting in the drawing room. Both would be taken to the meeting room when we were out of sight. It all depended on ifs and buts and a good sense of timing. But there was a hardness to Count Otto now, a steely purpose in his eyes, that made me feel that this plan would work. The man of action and power was back, I thought, and Leopold had made a formidable enemy. But he didn't know it, not yet, and therein lay our chance.

But as I sat in the Count's carriage a few minutes later, it had suddenly become more than a chance to learn Leopold's secret. Why shouldn't I kill him today at the meeting? The audience had always been a big risk, with all those people. But it had been a risk I'd been willing to take as I'd thought there was no other way of getting to the Prince. Now there was another way, I felt I had to take it.

I had to retrieve my weapon from the hotel and bring it with me. I would not tell the Count I had it, of course. Nor would I tell him of my intentions. I'd take them all by surprise and it would be done before they even knew what was happening.

I asked the driver to stop near the Hotel Bella, telling him I wanted to be sure we weren't being followed, and ran all the way to the hotel, where I got to my room without attracting attention. I unlocked the desk, tore open the box, and threw the dagger in my bag. Then I slipped out again and was back in the carriage in no time.

Alone in the carriage, I took out the dagger from my bag and looked at it. The scabbard, with its fine chasings, gleamed in the dimness of the carriage like a silver shaft of moonlight. I took off a glove and carefully drew the blade out. Made of fine tempered steel, with a silver hilt, it was a beautiful piece of workmanship. And wickedly sharp, as I learned to my cost when the knife slipped a little in my hands and nicked a finger, drawing blood. Sucking the finger to stop the bleeding, I awkwardly replaced the blade in its scabbard and was about to put it back in the bag when I suddenly remembered that I still had a leaf in there. I could not risk it touching the dagger for any length of time. Because, if I was right about how the magic worked, it might somehow pick up on my half-buried qualms and pull the rug out from under me by changing the dagger in some unexpected and unwelcome way at the wrong moment.

I could not hide the knife in my clothes, for it might drop out at any moment, so instead I withdrew the leaf from my bag and tucked it securely under the cuff of my sleeve. I put the dagger back in the bag, padding it out a little with strips torn from the hem of my petticoat. I wrapped my bleeding finger with another strip of cloth and put my black gloves back on, then sat for the rest of the journey with the bag on my lap, nervous as anything, but glad for it would all be over soon.

Once we'd left the city boundaries, it was only about ten minutes before we reached the hunting lodge. We weren't far from the bustling streets of Faustina, but we might as well have been in another world, I thought, as the carriage drew up in front of a large, but simple, two-storey house made of weathered pine. There were a few outbuildings scattered around: a stable, a henhouse, a shed – all set in the middle of a deep, green wood. The air was fresh and clean, and all was quiet, with only the occasional birdsong breaking the silence. There was not a soul in sight and, for an instant, I felt uneasy.

The driver smiled at me and said, 'I expect the servants are having a nap – they'd not be expecting anyone,' then marched up to the front door and knocked. Moments later, a servant came to the door, a small hard-looking man with a face that looked as though it had been carved out of rock. The driver told him I had been sent by Count Otto, that I had a message for Bastien, and that I was to be afforded every comfort while I waited. Then he tipped his hat at me and went off back to Faustina to pick up the Count and the Prince.

The servant silently ushered me into the house to a sitting room where a fire burned brightly. I took off my bonnet and gloves and looked around. It was a cosy, welcoming room, with good armchairs, a fine rug, and a portrait above the fireplace that was not of the imperial family but Count Otto's own. There was Max, aged about eleven or twelve, standing next to a younger-looking Count Otto behind an armchair on which sat a dark-haired woman of a delicate, almost frail, beauty. This must be Max's mother, I thought. Startled, I realised something I should have noticed before. Max had never spoken of her to me – not once. He had spoken of his father but not of his mother. And the Count had not mentioned her either, which probably meant that she was not there any longer; that, like me, Max was motherless.

But on Andel's boat, I'd told him about my mother's death and what had happened after. He had hugged me and comforted me. And yet he had not said a word about his own loss at a time when, surely, it would have been natural to tell me. It was strange and a little disturbing. But there must be an explanation, I thought. Perhaps he had not been close to his mother. Or perhaps she had died a long time ago and it no longer affected him. Or he had simply not wanted to intrude on my own grief and troubles. But none of it seemed particularly plausible when I thought of the Max I knew.

'Good day, Miss,' said a voice behind me. I turned to face a tall man dressed all in black, with greying hair cropped short and steady green eyes. 'My name is Bastien. Will you please come with me?'

Still clutching the bag under my shawl, I followed him to another room. It was a small, pleasant dining room with a window looking out across the woods. Its panelled walls were plain except for the fact that halfway up they were painted with a faded, but still pretty, frieze in a pattern of flowers and leaves, and here, too, was a fire burning in the grate. The table was set for one, and there was a sideboard on which reposed platters of cold meat, cheese, fruit and bread. There was also a carafe of what looked like freshly made lemonade.

'Count Otto thought you might be in need of refreshment while you wait,' said Bastien. He closed the door behind him, and added, 'As this is the room where the meeting is to be held, I am also to show you where you must conceal yourself when the time comes.'

He pressed a spot in the wall closest to the sideboard, and the panel instantly slid across to reveal an opening.

'To close it again, you just need to push the lever inside. You also use it to get out again. Watch.' He stepped into the opening, and touched a lever set into the wall inside. At once, the panel began to close. He pushed the lever again and the door opened. 'Is that clear, Miss?'

'Yes. But is there a way to see what's going on in this room from there?'

'Of course. Take one of those stools over there and I will show you.'

I obeyed and stepped into the opening with him. Beyond was a dusty space about as big as a fairly large wardrobe, certainly enough to conceal two people. Bastien took the stool and placed it against the wall.

'Climb up here, Miss,' he said. 'See the raised knot of wood to your right, there? Press it.'

I did, and the knot of wood slid up to reveal a hole about the size of a small plum. It was closed off at one end by some gold-coloured glass.

'Put your eye to it, Miss,' Bastien instructed.

I did, and saw that though the scene outside was bathed in yellow light, I could see clearly into the room.

'From the outside it just looks like part of the frieze, like the coloured heart of a large daisy. Nobody has ever spotted it.'

'It's so clever,' I said in genuine admiration.

Bastien shrugged but looked pleased. He ushered me back into the dining room, closed the panel, and said, 'Now, Miss, if that is all clear to you, I will leave you here in peace to enjoy your meal. I will be back in a short while.'

And he went out, closing the door behind him. I experimented a couple more times opening and closing the secret panel, and looking out through the peephole before sitting down to a very hearty meal, suddenly as hungry as a wolf and as thirsty as a desert.

Time passed. Bastien came back and cleared the table while I went back to the sitting room. I tried to read for a while but the books on Count Otto's shelf were not very interesting and even if they had been, I doubt I would have been able to concentrate. It wasn't just my nervous tension. In the warmth of the sitting room, my heavy meal was making me feel a little sleepy, though I tried hard to fight it. I opened a window, breathed in the fresh, cool air, and paced up and down the room, trying not to think too much. But nothing seemed to work. And then, just as I thought I would have to give in and lie down on the sofa for a few moments, the door opened and Bastien came in.

'The carriage is approaching the house,' he said. 'It's time.'

He looked quite different, dressed in smart travelling clothes: a grey suit under a silk-lined grey coat that made him look every inch the diplomat. From his hand dangled a black silk mask. He saw me glance at it and smiled.

'Count Otto's idea. A mysterious foreign emissary should want to conceal his identity till he is face-to-face and alone with the one he has come to see.'

I smiled back. Count Otto was no fool. Hiding my bag under my shawl, I quickly followed Bastien back into the dining room, now set for two, but much more elegantly than it had been for me, with silver cutlery, crystal glasses and a vase of flowers atop a snowy white tablecloth. I only just had time to glance at it before Bastien pressed the panel to let me into my hiding place. He handed me a handkerchief.

'It's dusty in there, Miss, and you must not make a sound. Now, please relax. The Count will join you shortly.'

The panel closed, and I was left alone in the dark.

Thirty-Six

I felt my way to the stool and climbed on. I found the knot of wood, slid it open and looked into the empty room. Minutes passed. It was very close in the space and dusty, too. I could feel my nose starting to tickle. I buried it in the handkerchief to stop myself from sneezing, and peered out, wishing desperately that Count Otto would hurry up.

Then I saw the door open and someone step into the room. But it wasn't Count Otto. It was Prince Leopold. I hadn't seen him in the flesh since that fateful night of the ball but he looked just the same: tall, handsome and elegant. There was a noticeable stain on the front of his white shirt, like a splash of wine or sauce. Perhaps he'd been at table when the Count called, and had not had time to change. My mind ran wildly. I'd thought about this moment so much but now that he was actually here my heart was racing so much I felt sick. And where was the Count? He should have been here first.

Leopold seemed quite relaxed. He went to the window and stood looking out for a moment. Then he turned around and pulled out something from his pocket. And my heart nearly stopped, for I realised two things: first, that the thing he held was a revolver; second, that the stain on his shirt wasn't sauce or wine at all – *it was blood, fresh blood* . . .

In a quick, sudden movement, he drew the curtains, abruptly cutting out the sunlight, and sat down at the table, moving the chair slightly so that he faced the door. His face was still and perfectly calm. A shiver ran down my spine. The hairs on the back of my neck prickled.

Something terrible must have happened to the Count. I pictured him shot to death, lying in his own blood in the carriage while the Prince calmly went on his way to the supposed meeting. He must have guessed it was a trap, I thought. But instead of hiding he'd decided to come here to see who it was that the Count had so wanted him to meet. It was a bold move but then just about everything Leopold had done was. Evil, yes, but bold. He was a gambler; cool-headed, quick-witted and infinitely dangerous. But why would he have done it? Why would he murder his father's chief adviser in cold blood? Was it because he'd suspected he was being led into a trap? And then the answer came to me – the Count must have guessed his secret and shown it on the way here . . . and Leopold had assumed he'd got it from Max. He probably thought Max was the mysterious visitor he was being brought to meet . . . and had come to turn the tables on him!

Where were the others? Bastien? The servant? The driver? I could only assume that they were lying dead somewhere while the Prince sat here calmly. I felt very cold. This was my fault. Max had said his father would be in mortal danger if he knew and he'd been right.

And now I knew why. There could only be one reason why Leopold would do the things he'd done. The secret he was hiding was no ordinary crime, but a crime which, if discovered, could send him to the scaffold even if he was the Emperor's son. And that was because he was striking at the heart of the empire. He hadn't wanted to wait for the throne to pass to him in due course. *He'd been plotting to overthrow his own father* – to kill him and seize the throne for himself. Somehow, Max must have found out and Leopold knew he had to act at once if he was to stop his secret from ever being discovered. And so Max had ended up in a Mancer prison.

It all made sense now. How I wished I had understood earlier! But the time for wishes was long past. The time for plans had gone, too. Now there was only one thing I could do. I slid the dagger out of my bag and eased the blade from the scabbard. And then I pushed the lever.

Nothing happened. I pushed the lever again. Still, the panel wouldn't open. Panicked now, I pressed again. Nothing. The lever must have jammed or somehow become stuck. I put my eye to the peephole and nearly fell back off the stool. For there was an eye looking back at me, blue, turned green by the yellow glass.

'Well, well,' said Leopold, lightly, 'are there rats in the wainscoting, I wonder. What do you think?'

For a moment I thought he was addressing me. Then another voice answered, in the same light tones, 'There's always a rat, I've found, Your Royal Highness.'

I did not need to look through the glass to know who it was. Bastien! He must have been working for the Prince all along! He must have helped to kill the Count and the others. And it was he who must have jammed the mechanism, who had trapped me here like a rat to be killed at leisure. I was doomed. All I could do was to go down fighting.

I held the knife to my chest, the point facing out, with both hands clenched tightly over the hilt, and waited. But the panel didn't open. And when it didn't, I knew that they had no intention of letting me out. Not yet. I was to be held there, helpless, till I had seen and heard everything they wanted me to.

I could have chosen not to look, not to listen. I could have chosen to stay there slumped in the dark. But I had to see, I had to know. I looked through the glass and saw the Prince and Bastien sitting at the table, calmly quaffing some wine. They'd lit a lamp, which cast a pool of light over the scene. I could only see Bastien from behind, half in shadow. He still had that stupid cloak on, which in the shifting shadows looked black.

But that wasn't the only thing that caused the breath to stick in my throat. There was another man in the room, standing by the window and looking out through a chink in the curtains. He was tall and burly, in a dark overcoat and hat. He carried himself in such a way that you knew at once this man was the most dangerous of the lot. I'd seen him at the cemetery, in Thalia's mirror, and now. But there was something else, something that nagged at my benumbed brain, some half-formed sense of familiarity, of . . .

And then he turned. Time seemed to stop as I saw clearly who he was, and everything I'd thought I understood dissolved. I was suddenly in a world of such monstrous deceit and treachery that for a moment I felt as though I were going mad. A wicked son plotting against his own father; an evil father willing to destroy his own son for power.

Max's father stood regarding the others, a frown creasing his brow.

'You'd better be right this time,' he snapped. 'It's all very well saying your spies saw someone answering his description arrive at the river port this morning; but any amount of times you'd told us he'd been spotted, and every time, it was a false alarm.'

'My dear Otto, there's no question of my being wrong this time,' said Bastien, calmly.

This was no servant, that much was clear. This was someone who felt himself to be absolutely the Count's equal.

'He's been clever, I admit, but sooner or later, given his character, he was bound to make a mistake. That's what this girl gave us – his weakness. This is the only way it could have been done.' He held up something that looked like a small bag, no bigger than something you'd use to keep a pair of earrings in. 'A strand of hair from her bonnet, a piece of her bloodstained glove and the lock of his hair you gave me.'

In a heartbeat I knew who he was. Or, rather, *what* he was. I thought of Olga gathering up my and Max's hair after we'd chopped it off on the barge. She had said it had to be destroyed for in her country such things as hair and blood were used by wizards to bind powerful spells. Ignorant, gullible fool that I was, I'd left my bonnet and my gloves in the sitting room. And Bastien had known how to use them because he was *a Mancer*.

The rogue who had deceived his fellows. Or had he? What if he was acting with the full, secret authority of the order? His manner certainly did not suggest a low-level Mancer, but one used to dealing as an equal with an important courtier, a member of the Mancer Council . . .

Fretfully, Prince Leopold said, 'Why should he come? *I* wouldn't.'

Bastien shrugged. 'No, *you* wouldn't. But he's not like you. And he's in love. The danger spell will bring him, there is nothing surer.'

I wanted to believe he was bluffing. I wanted to believe that there was no possibility that the spies were right and Max was at the river port on the way to Almain, not on his way here. I wanted to believe it because if what Bastien said was true, there could only be one explanation – that Max had been trying desperately to find me, that he had somehow followed my trail to Faustina. I wanted to believe so much, but I didn't . . . there was a dreadful certainty in me that Bastien was telling the truth.

I banged on the panel, cursing, but they did nothing. Uninterested, they didn't even look up. I was simply bait to be kept waiting till I had served my purpose. They didn't know who I was and they didn't care. They just knew I loved Max and he loved me, that he was brave and would not think twice about facing terrible danger to help the one he loved. And *I* told them that. *I* had given them the means to trap him. It was the bitterest thought of all – that our love was what would put the noose around his neck.

'Then all will be well, and nothing more can stand in our way,' the Prince said, his eyes bright.

'Only if you do what I told you to do, for you have already caused us a good deal of needless trouble,' Bastien snapped.

'But, Master, I *had* to kill the driver. He might have let something slip and we can't afford that,' the Prince said sulkily.

Count Otto and Bastien looked at each other in exasperation. Even if the Prince was the symbolic heart of the plot, it was clear that they were the prime movers in this vile affair, I thought, not Leopold. Whatever he might imagine, he was a puppet and they were pulling his strings. And Bastien wasn't even bothering to hide his contempt.

The Prince had called him 'Master', I thought, so Bastien must be a top-ranking Mancer. That seemingly unimportant fact gave me the first ray of hope. *That*, I thought, was why Prince Leopold and Count Otto had gone to Ashberg. Only there, with their Mancer connection, could they be sure that Max would be destroyed, no questions asked; which must mean they most certainly did *not* have the backing of the Mancer Council. If only I could get word to them somehow . . .

If only the power of Dremda would help me. But its last reserves of power had been used to get me here and, even if it had not, there was no guarantee that it would help. For the Mancers are the moon-sisters' hereditary enemies and there is nothing in common between them. The magic of the moon-sisters and the magic of the Mancers

291

are opposites – indeed, they are opposing forces. Why would it matter to Dremda if the Prince overthrew his father to rule the empire? One Emperor was very much like another – all bad, that is. The prophecy had said that 'the shadow would only be lifted when the last daughter of Serafina spilled the blood of the last son of Karl'. The shadow was likely the power of the Mancers. In Dremda terms, my mission had not just been about avenging Serafina's death; it was also about destroying the power of the Mancers, which guaranteed the power of the empire. And so warning them about a traitor in their midst hardly figured in that.

Besides, I'd left my hazel twig in my desk at the hotel. And then I remembered the leaf I'd picked that morning, which I'd tucked under my sleeve cuff on the way here. I extracted the leaf and held it in my hand. Suddenly, a thought came to me that was so unexpected and extraordinary that it was like a blinding shaft of light in the pure darkness of a cave.

Yes, the Mancers and the moon-sisters are enemies – but it hadn't always been so. Yes, their magics are opposites but once, a long time ago, before Serafina's rebellion, they had co-existed peacefully. And that meant that maybe, just *maybe*, they could do so again. At least, just this once.

I had to evoke both Mancer and moon-sister. And, ironically, it was Bastien who had shown me how. I had no idea if it would work but I had to try.

I picked up the handkerchief Bastien had given me – that had touched his skin. I rubbed the leaf with it, and it twisted, its edges curling, as if it was about to wither.

Quickly, I picked up the dagger and, with it, nicked my finger. Drops of blood fell on the leaf and it went black, curling up even faster. And just as I had begun to think it had died, to think I had wasted my one shot, the leaf gave a sudden shiver, a silver shimmer, and there in my hand was a mirror, like a small version of the one in Thalia's book.

In it I could see a chamber, within which a group of men sat around a table, the crest on the wall behind them bearing a snake and two wands. The man at the head of the table was older than the others, greyer, hunched and a little frail, yet there was a chill power to him that instantly commanded respect. Though I had never seen him before, I knew who he was: the General Secretary of the Mancers. They were all so still, their eyes all fixed on one point: at me. I knew they could see me – I could see it in their shocked faces. They knew what I was – the past rising up before them, the magic they thought was destroyed. I was the ghost of the vanished moon-sisters, and for a moment they could not move or speak, so total was their dismay. And I knew I only had that sliver of a moment before they would shut me out.

I murmured, desperately, 'You are my enemy, as I am yours; but we have a common enemy now, and so I beg you to listen.' There was an uproar in the chamber. The General Secretary held up a hand for silence and I heard his cold, precise voice in my head: 'It is said an enemy's enemy may be an ally, if not a friend. So speak, moon-sister, and we will hear.'

I swallowed down a rising tide of bile and whispered, 'A Master of Ashberg has betrayed his vows and joined with Prince Leopold and Count Otto von Gildenstein to overthrow the Emperor and destroy my friends in the process. For the sake of your honour, I beg you to act. Ah!' I screamed as the mirror melted in my hand, turning into a hot silver lump which promptly vanished, leaving a fiery red mark painfully branded on my flesh. Outside, in the room, there were yells, screams and loud crashing noises. The wall panel opened, the lamplight flooded in and I was roughly hauled out.

Thirty-Seven

Count Otto was shouting hoarsely in my face, incoherent words I couldn't make head nor tail of. Something had happened to him: his face was bruised, his clothes torn. Leopold lay slumped at one end of the room, moaning and holding his head. The room looked as though a gale had been raging through it: the table and chairs were over-turned amongst shattered plates and crockery that'd been bent out of shape.

'Stop it, Otto.'

It was Bastien's voice, a little shaky but still commanding. He got up from the tangle of chairs and came towards me. He, too, looked as though he'd been in a brawl: there was a bruise on his face that was going to turn into a beauty of a black eye. He grabbed my hand, turned it over and recoiled.

'It can't be true,' he whispered.

'What can't?' Count Otto yelled.

In answer, Bastien held up his other hand. There, branded in his palm, was a mark identical to mine.

Blankly, he said, 'She took my power. She used it. Mine and hers.'

'What are you talking about?' shouted the Count.

'She must be a witch,' Bastien stammered. 'But that spell – whatever it was – I have never seen anything like it. I have never *heard* of anything like it. It's never been done. Never. Never . . . How could she possibly have known to –'

The Count's eyes flashed as he cut Bastien off in mid-sentence. 'She's a *witch*, and I sent her to you, and you said *nothing*?'

Bastien shook his head dazedly. 'I didn't see it. I didn't see it at all. Even when I used her hair – her blood – I felt . . . *nothing*. She seemed just an ordinary girl; a gullible, lovesick little fool who had walked into your trap, that's all.'

The Count's voice stung like a whip, his eyes were icy chips. 'Devil take it, Master, how could that be? Your job is to hunt witches. You know all the signs. How did you miss it?'

'He didn't,' I said, finding my voice at last – my voice, along with my strength and my pride, 'because there were no signs. How could there be? I am not the kind of poor, pathetic specimen he is used to dealing with. The power of Dremda is in me for I am a moon-sister.'

There was dead silence. Both the Count and Bastien stared at me as though I had sprouted two heads and a forked tail.

'She's lying, she has to be,' the Prince said petulantly, looking the worst of them all, his face weirdly twisted out of shape. 'The moon-sisters died out a hundred years ago. They don't exist, except in the pages of history books.'

I smiled and looked him right in the eyes. 'Wrong, *Your Royal Highness*. We were just in hiding, waiting for the right time.'

I reached behind me and picked up Prince Leopold's revolver which was lying on the ground. I cocked it and advanced upon him. He took a step back, then another, his eyes wild.

'Help me, help me! Do something! She's going to *kill me*!'

But the other two didn't move.

With the wild new clarity that sang in my veins like moonlight, I knew that the magic I'd created was so powerful that not only had it used up all of Bastien's power, it held the pair of them as though they were flies in a web. I could do anything I wanted and they could do nothing but watch, helplessly.

I'd backed the Prince into a corner he couldn't escape. He was weeping now, the tears rolling down his face, his skin so grey and pasty that it looked like melting wax, his eyes fixed on me in abject terror. There was no pity in me, only a fierce joy as I raised the gun and –

'Selena, no! Stop!'

And there was Max, suddenly beside me. He was – alone, pale and travel-stained. There was an expression in his eyes that struck my very heart.

But I couldn't allow it to weaken my resolve. Keeping a wary eye on the dumbstruck Prince, I said, harshly, 'It's too late, Max. This is how it must end.'

'Oh Selena,' he whispered. 'Please, if ever you cared for me, don't do this.' And he took a step closer to the shaking, terrified, moaning Leopold.

I swallowed hard. 'You don't understand. Stand aside, Max.'

'No, I will not. Not until you tell me why.'

'You need to ask that? After all he's done to you?'

His eyes flicked to Prince Leopold, then back to me. He hadn't even glanced in his father's direction or in the Mancer's. It was as though only the three of us existed.

'Yes,' Max said, steadily, 'I do.' He paused. 'Because I don't think you're doing it for me, Selena.' His voice was full of a terrible sorrow and it cut me to the quick.

'It was for you!' I cried. 'To keep you safe. You and our friends.'

'Is that what you heard at Dremda?' he said, and for a moment I thought I hadn't heard him right.

'You know . . . *about Dremda?*'

'Yes,' he said and looked at me. 'Olga told me she'd seen the old man coming out of the barn in Smutny. We remembered how he'd changed so suddenly so we went back there and he told us what you'd asked him. And then I knew.'

'Knew what?'

'Why our compass had been changed. What the old lady in the wagon was. Why you had gone to Dremda.'

My throat was constricting. I stared at him and said, numbly, 'How . . .?'

'Because it was once the sacred place for the moon-sisters. I've read a good deal, you know, Selena. A good deal about the . . . the history of the empire. I knew then what your secret was – I knew you were a moon-sister.'

I looked at his face and saw that there was no horror, nor fear or judgement in his eyes, only love and acceptance. 'Then you understand that I must keep my promise.'

'What promise, Selena? For pity's sake, what is it?'

I whispered, 'The shadow will only be lifted if the last daughter of Serafina spills the blood of the last son of Karl,' and I raised the gun, my finger on the trigger.

Max cried out, 'If that is true, then it is *my* blood you must spill, Selena!'

I stared at him, my finger trembling on the gun. 'What do you . . . what do you mean . . .?'

But before he could speak, Leopold yelled, the terror in his face replaced by a wicked glee, 'You fool, he's the Prince – the *real* Prince! We got a spell to change places. *He*'s the last son of Karl, moon-sister, the very last one – not me!'

A red mist appeared in front of my eyes and blackness raged in my heart. With an inarticulate cry, I rushed at Leopold, my finger on the trigger. Before I could stop, Max threw himself across my path in front of the spitting gun. He fell to the floor, red blood seeping through his shirt just over his heart.

Leopold, laughing hysterically, screamed, 'You killed him! Idiot, you killed him!'

Then the room erupted with noise as a crowd of people rushed in: men in Mancer masks and cloaks, others in the uniform of the special forces, and my friends – Andel, tall as a giant with Tomi perched on his shoulders, and Olga with her hair flying and her eyes flashing.

I hardly even noticed as the gun dropped from my nerveless hand and I sank to the floor beside the dying young man I'd known as Maximilian von Gildenstein. The world shrank down to just him and me and the terrible thing I'd done. I'd murdered the love of my life for the sake of a faith that cared nothing for us, but only about the ghosts of a dead past.

His eyes were closed and his breathing had become shallow. He was so white it was as though all the blood had already left his body. But then he opened his eyes and whispered, 'I'm sorry, Selena. I'm so, so sorry.'

I ripped at my petticoat, pulling off strips and wadding his wound to try and stop the bleeding. My hands worked without my even being aware of it, my whole being suspended and unreal. My lips so stiff and my throat so raw I could hardly speak; the tears which were running down my face half-blinded me. 'Don't, my love. Please, don't.'

'I wanted to tell you so much,' he said. 'But I couldn't. I could tell no-one till I had found a way to break the spell I'd so stupidly agreed to. You see, what I'd done – it had already put everyone and everything I cared about in so much danger. And all for what? For my own selfish whim, in the end. Oh, I told myself it was for the highest purpose. That I needed to know what my people really felt. But inside, it was all about me. Because when you are the Prince, everyone sees that, first. First *and* last. I wanted to know what it was like to be seen for myself. In the old days, I could have just gone incognito. But these days – our faces are on every public building, in every newspaper and magazine. Someone would have recognised me. And then my friend – Max – he and his father came up with 'his brilliant and risky plan . . . for us to change places in a ay that no-one would ever guess.'

'Of course they did,' I said, bleakly, 'it was their great rtunity.'

'It was *my* fault, Selena. *I* cast aside my duty. When they proposed that we use Mancer magic to literally change our faces, I could have said no. It's forbidden magic. *I* could have refused to break the law. *I* should have seen that my poor, weak friend was consumed with jealousy and that his father was consumed with ambition. *I* should have foreseen the danger. Instead, *I* allowed myself to be tempted.'

'Because you are not superhuman,' I said, my voice breaking, 'but only human.'

He looked up at me. There was a wondering expression in his eyes. 'Then you . . . you forgive me? You don't hate me for what I did? For what I am – the Emperor's son?'

'Never,' I said. 'Never. How could I? I love you, prince or not, Max or Leo, it makes no difference. Only that it is you and I wish I was dying in your place. I cannot bear what I have done to you and –'

He had taken my hand and kissed it and, crying, I could speak no longer. The others had begun crowding around us and I was vaguely aware of them but it was as though they were behind glass, my love and I alone in these last precious, dreadful moments as he held my hand and closed his eyes . . .

A voice spoke quietly behind me, cold and precise. 'May I sit by you, Selena dez Mestmor?'

I turned my head and saw a cloaked old man. A little hunched, he appeared grey and frail yet his eyes were not old and the aura that came from him was not frail in the least.

I whispered, 'Yes, General Secretary.'

301

He knelt down beside us, a little creakingly, and said, 'Put your hand on his wound.' He added, a little ironically, 'The one with the brand on it.'

I did as he said, and then he laid his hand on mine. It was leathery and dry as a snake's and, instinctively repelled, I wanted to jerk my own hand away. He looked me in the eye and I knew he knew exactly what I was feeling but all he said was, 'Are you ready to do this?'

I nodded mutely, every one of my nerves strained to keep my hand where it was.

He smiled a thin smile, but a real one nevertheless. 'Then, Selena dez Mestmor, together let us save our Prince's life.'

He closed his eyes and murmured some incantation. His hand twitched and gripped mine harder, and a flutter of panic rose in me as I felt his mind lock onto mine, but I managed to keep my nerves and my hand steady. Though my eyes were open, I could see a vision before me.

It was of Dremda, not as it was when I saw it – sad and broken and neglected – but as it had been in my dreams. It was beautiful: the green-lit forest, the tumbling waterfall and the sparkling pool. But that wasn't all that was beautiful about it, for my mother stood there smiling at me. Her face shifted and I could see the old moon-sister's features; then it shifted into the lovely face of the woman I never knew, Serafina.

My mother's face appeared again, smiling at me with so much tenderness and so much love. She reached out to me and I felt her touch on my forehead. Warmth flooded through me, rushing through every vein, every cell, every pore, my whole being aglow with it. It flowed through me and melded with the crackling energy of the General Secretary into a vast healing power that flowed into my beloved's body – into the true Prince's failing life force.

His face had begun to change, the features realigning. It was almost too much for me, almost too frightening, but I held on. I locked my power with the Mancer's, making it even stronger; I could see the General Secretary getting tired, even afraid. There was sweat on his brow, his grey face even greyer, while a band of steel constricted around my own heart, tighter and tighter.

And then my beloved opened his eyes. And I saw that though his face was no longer the one I had known – no longer the borrowed face of Maximilian von Gildenstein, but the face that had stared out at me from those official portraits and newspapers – the eyes were the same as the ones I'd fallen in love with. Clear, grey-blue, and warm. Those official portraits hadn't told a lie. They'd told the truth, if only I'd seen it. The spell had broken. This was the true Prince. And my true love.

He smiled and held out his arms to me and I was in them, breathing in the living scent of him, laughing and crying. His lips were on my hair and he murmured, 'Will you stay with me always, Selena? Will you, my love?'

'Yes!' I cried, 'Yes, yes! Oh yes, my darling . . . my love.'

I was still shy about using his name, for it was hard to call him Leo, not Max. He smiled again, knowing what I felt, and said, 'When I was a child, I always preferred to be called by my second name. It seemed to me so much more exciting than Leopold. You can call me that if you like.'

'And what is it?' I asked, laughing.

'It is Ash, in honour of Giant Ash from your own country, Selena,' he said quietly.

My scalp prickled and my breath caught. 'It is a good name, Ash, my love,' I said, as steadily as I could. He kissed me. 'Yes. Yes, it is.'

And then he looked beyond me at the General Secretary, still hovering, and said in a firm and commanding voice, the voice of a prince, 'The blood has been spilled, the shadow has lifted and we are all in the light. And so the world must now change.'

The General Secretary looked at him, his face expressionless for an instant. Then that thin half-smile broke over his features, lightening them all at once. 'Yes, Your Royal Highness. Indeed it must.' He looked at me. 'Indeed it must,' he repeated, and nodded at me in a way that wasn't exactly warm or friendly, but was full of something else, something worth even more. And that something was respect.

So history was made in that moment and the pain of a hundred years had begun to roll back. And though I knew it would take time, a great deal of time for us all to trust each other again, for the opposing forces to co-exist once again, it was still a start. One we would never regret.

Thirty-Eight

The Count, his son and Bastien were hauled away for questioning, while my friends and I reunited with a good deal of joy, laughter and exclamation. On the way back to the city we sat all together in the same carriage. Olga told me how she, Tomi and Max – or rather, Ash – had cobbled together what she called a 'compass spell' out of my locket and our bits of hair she'd forgotten to throw away, to try and find out where I had gone after Dremda.

'Our first spell, and a little crooked, I think, because it did not bring us straight to where you were but instead to Andel.'

Andel laughed heartily. 'I could take offence if I did not know what you meant, dear Miss Ironheart.'

'Well, you say you do not believe in magic,' she said crossly, 'so when it bring us to you I am sure there must be mistake.'

'Not a mistake,' piped up Tomi, eagerly, 'because it was Andel's barge that brought us to Faustina after all.'

'So it did but slow. And he not let us try any other spell either to hurry it along,' grumbled Olga. But the glance she shot at Andel quite belied her cross tone, and knowing that, he grinned.

'Magic may be all very well in its place but that is most definitely not on *Wanderer*,' he said firmly.

'Oho, Andel, so now you are converted you will be no doubt writing to the author of *The Laws of Magic* to set him straight on its existence?' I said.

'Hmm,' he said, looking a little sheepish, 'I'm actually thinking of writing my own book – on how the laws of magic might actually work . . . at least sometimes.'

Olga snorted and Ash, laughing, said, 'Good luck with that, then,' and added, with a sidelong glance at me, 'At least you'll have expert advice to call on.'

I blushed. 'I'm no expert, not at all, not in the least, I'm just . . .'

But he stopped me with a look that made me tingle from the top of my head to the tip of my toes. He lifted my hand to his lips and kissed it, saying, 'Are you ready, then, Selena?'

I nodded, rather nervously. For we were off to the palace to see his father and mother – the Emperor and Empress.

'Good,' he said, 'because I know it will be just wonderful.'

I must have looked a little cynical because he smiled and said, 'Not only will they be glad to meet you but I know that my mother especially will be happy knowing that a new chapter is beginning in the story of the empire.'

He told us then that his mother had long believed that something should be done about the situation with magic.

'Being from Ruvenya herself, she simply does not share the official line, though she'd never say so in public,' he said. 'I suppose it was partly her influence that made me think about it in a different way, as well as reading about our history, and the ideas I was exposed to at university.'

'Like *The Laws of Magic*,' Andel said, mischievously, and Ash laughed.

'True enough. That forced me to think, what exactly is magic? What do we want from it? And why do we in charge of this empire try to control it so tightly, when other countries seem to manage to muddle along with it?'

'Dangerous thoughts indeed,' I said, echoing something the General Secretary had said to us just before he had left with his men and their prisoners. 'Perhaps the plot against the Prince had not just been about ambition and power,' he'd said. 'Winds of change have cautiously begun to blow and some people are afraid of it. The old guard, you understand, who think nothing should ever change and dangerous thoughts should be crushed like walnuts.' He'd given me a meaningful look and I understood by it that he'd meant people like Bastien. But not himself.

I had made a strange ally but one that I knew would be steadfast, even if he did not share all or even most of my ideas, or Ash's. He wanted the Mancers to turn the page, too. He knew it had to happen. And he was glad it had begun.

We called in first at the Hotel Bella, for there was something I needed to get before we went on to our final destination.

I must have looked quite a sight as I dashed in through the servants' entrance, but never mind. Back in the room, I unlocked the desk and saw that, though the casket of pearls and the documents were just as they had been when I left, the twig had changed. It was covered not only in leaves but in flowers too, and from them came a scent so fragrant that it made my senses swim. I touched the twig to my forehead, my heart and my hands, and I whispered, 'Thank you. Thank you. I will always try to be worthy of your trust.'

Then I remembered the pretty dress and coat hanging in the closet. Where I was going, you were expected to look the part and right now the only part I looked in my dishevelled state and stained, rumpled grey dress was that of a servant. The servant girl, disowned by all, crouching in the kitchen amongst the ashes of the fireplace – hardly a fit bride for a prince. But even as the thought flashed into my head, I laughed and pushed it away. The time for parts and roles was over and my friends were waiting. Taking the twig with me, I left the room, went down the stairs and out through the main entrance. I had nothing to hide, not any more and not ever again.

Ash had been right. I'd had no cause for concern at all. The Emperor and Empress received us with great joy and relief. While the Emperor was still unwell and bedridden, the Empress told us she was sure he would be on the mend soon.

'The General Secretary thinks a spell was cast over him by that treacherous Mancer to make him ill,' she said, 'but

I believe it went deeper than that. I believe that deep inside he was uneasy, and that unease was caused by the fact that something was wrong, really wrong.'

She turned to Ash. 'We both felt it; we both felt that something must have happened to you in Ashberg, my darling son,' she said, hugging him, 'for we could not understand your sudden coldness and indifference; it felt almost as though we were dealing with a stranger. I was even beginning to suspect someone might have put you under a spell. Not that I ever guessed the truth, of course.'

'I'm so sorry, Mother,' said Ash, hanging his head.

'Bah, what's past is past,' she shrugged, 'and now you are back with us. And though I do not approve of what you did, because of it you have seen and understood more of our people, and that can only be good for a future emperor. But best of all,' and here she looked at me, smiling, 'you have brought back not only a lovely girl to be your bride, but one who has the true measure of your heart and soul. How can any mother not be glad of that?'

I tried to kiss her hand but she drew me up and kissed me on both cheeks instead, and said, 'I know those stuffy old Faustinian courtiers would be shocked by my lack of ceremony, but I am Ruvenyan and we are an emotional people and I'm blowed if I'm going to put a steel rod up my spine even in private. I hope you feel the same, my dear, because otherwise we may not get along.'

'Oh, yes, I do! I do,' I said, fervently. 'Very much so. I don't have a steel rod up my spine nor ever could, even if my life depended on it. I'm much too prickly and twisted, so I've been told.'

She roared with laughter and gave me another kiss on the cheek and from that moment I became firm friends with Ash's mother, and though she could never replace mine, still I think my mother would be glad to know that her daughter was welcome in another woman's home.

Thirty-Nine

So much has happened since then. The Emperor took action at once: old laws were thrown out, blanking was completely outlawed, and all sorts of people who'd been in prison for magical offences were let out. And he took our advice for a new system of laws relating to magic. A new Magic Registration Office was set up to regulate the practice of magic, but in a fair way. Shapeshifters were no longer considered illegal aliens. Moon-sisters were outlaws no more. Mancers were less secretive, thus less feared, and their membership open to more people.

A new wind of freedom and hope began to blow throughout the land. This extended to the government of provinces like Ashberg, who were to be given more independence, with local elected parliaments set up again as they had once been in the distant past. That part was Ash's doing. He was also adamant that when the time came for him to be Emperor, I was to rule jointly with him. (I hope that won't be for a long, long time – I have grown to like his parents very much.)

Meanwhile, the Count, his son and Bastien were tried and stripped of their rank, privileges and lands, banished from the empire for life. They were fortunate to escape execution and life imprisonment; and it was only due to the merciful heart of my Ash who saved them, for both the General Secretary and the Emperor were disposed to be harsh.

We heard later that the three traitors had boarded ship for the other end of the world, that the ship had been wrecked, and that only Maximilian von Gildenstein had survived, washed up on the shores of a far distant land where he disappeared. I know that Ash hopes that the treacherous man who was once his childhood friend might be redeemed one day. Unlike me, Ash has never hated anyone in his life, for he has a sweetness of soul as genuine as it is rare. I doubt von Gildenstein is really capable of such a transformation, but doubt is not the enemy of hope, only its cynical friend. And so I say nothing about it. How can I? The transformation of the empire, even in these short eighteen months since the true Prince's safe return, is more than even the most dizzily optimistic prophet could have predicted for a lifetime. So who is to say that even the hollow and envious heart of Maximilian von Gildenstein cannot be made anew?

A few days after the events at the hunting lodge, my father died, with me at his bedside. Happiness had made me, if not forgiving, at least willing to see him again one last time, if only for the sake of my mother who had so greatly loved him. When I turned up at his door in one of the imperial carriages, the panic of my stepmother and stepsisters can be imagined. Scared stiff that in my new ascendancy I would take my revenge on them, they had no idea what to do and were torn between falsely confident smiles and cringing obsequiousness. I did not care what they thought or how they behaved. I only wanted to see my father on my own. And though I knew they were probably listening at the door, I did not care about that either.

He was unconscious still and only opened his eyes once, towards the end. He looked at me then. 'Selena,' he whispered, and that was all. Not 'Forgive me' or 'I'm sorry', or even 'I didn't mean to do it, they made me'. It was just that, just my name – *Selena* – but the way he said it and the look in his eyes made a lump come into my throat quite unexpectedly. If he had asked for my forgiveness or had made excuses, I would have stayed cold as duty, hard as stone. If he had said that he had loved me in his way, I would have turned my back on him. But he didn't say any of those things. And that made all the difference, so that I took his hand and I held it until he drew his last breath. Then I sat there a moment with him, thinking sadly that it had all been too little too late, for the love that should have been there between us had withered long ago. And yet, somehow, I was glad I'd been there with him at the last. And I hoped that he would rest in peace, for there was only compassion in my heart for him now. Then I got up and left that house behind.

After that, Grizelda wrote to me a couple of times, and then Odette, but I did not answer. Then a note came from Babette, and that I did answer, because unlike her mother and sister she did not try to worm her way into my graces by false expressions of regret or pathetic appeals to non-existent family sentiment. She just wrote, 'I hope you will be happy. Sincerely, B.'

My note was just as brief, saying, 'Thank you.'

It was sincerely meant too. I'd been caught completely by surprise for she was the last one I'd have thought had it in her to think of someone beside herself. And I'd frightened her badly with my trick with the spider. But people were surprising – even, I had to remind myself, people like my step-family. And Babette's note was one small, unexpected bright spot where none at all had existed.

They sold my father's house in Ashberg and went to live in Almain, where Grizelda, ever on the lookout for a good match, apparently met and married an admiral. I have not heard directly from them again and I have not tried to find out what has become of them. Time has passed, and with it any lingering bitterness. I do not wish them any ill in their lives; I have made my peace with the past and moved on with my life. That is all.

As for little Tomi, his overawed parents came from Ashberg to collect him a couple of days after the events at the hunting lodge, but Olga and Andel stayed in Faustina for a while before setting off to Ruvenya. They all came back, of course, for our wedding a few weeks later. Little Tomi was a very proud pageboy, and my dear friend, Maria, came with her daughter, and Sister Claudia came too.

Olga and my mother-in-law, Empress Alexandra, have become great friends too, and chatter away in Ruvenyan. She was the one who persuaded Olga that there was no good reason why she shouldn't accept Andel's offer of marriage.

'There's no reason,' she had said, 'that a barge-dwelling philosopher and a footloose werewolf couldn't live together perfectly happily, wandering up and down the rivers and lakes of the empire and Ruvenya and Almain, or any other place they happen to choose. And who would not envy such a life?'

While my mother-in-law is a great romantic – my father-in-law is not so much. An anxious man, he was a little stiff and hard to know at first, because he'd been brought up so formally, unlike his wife. But once I got past the stern facade, I came to learn that he is a man who tries hard to live up to his duty but who is also kind and a little shy. My darling Ash's character is a blend of those things – his mother's warmth and his father's determination to do the right thing – with a whole magical element of his own.

Ash and I don't stay at court the whole time. I couldn't stand that, and neither could he, not any more. Since our wedding a year ago, we've spent as much time as we can in Ashberg, not in the castle but in a house we bought on St Hilda's Square – one of those charming houses whose sight used to cheer me in my sad past. We have a small staff and we try to live as normally as possible, going for long walks every day. Our neighbours were deferential and overawed at first, but we made it clear we did not stand on pomp and ceremony, but were there because Ashberg is my home and I love it.

You can imagine the consternation at the Angel, when they discovered that the girl they'd snubbed was now the Crown Princess! The bowing and scraping that went on the day I swept in there would have been disgusting if I hadn't found it amusing. And when I calmly declined their cakes and tea, and revealed that I had only come to take their scullery maid Maria away to give her a job, the look of disbelief on their faces was so comical that I *did* burst out laughing! They'd have been even more dismayed, I suppose, when they saw the 'job' we'd given Maria: her very own business – a beautiful dressmaker's shop which has already become the talk of Ashberg, and is giving Madame Paulina a run for her money. Oh, and Maria's daughter Rosa got married last year, wearing a new, magnificent creation of her mother's. Ash and I went to the wedding, and though at first the country people were very shy, they soon forgot who we were and Ash said it was the best party he'd ever been to, much better than anything at court.

We went back to the forest lands a few months ago and saw that things had started to change. Game had returned to the woods, crops were growing again, the animals thriving, and there was hope throughout the land – even in Smutny. It was funny to see that grouchy old headman, not exactly a bright ray of sunshine (that would have been a little too much to ask) but looking much less like he'd been sucking on a lemon. He told us a brother of his whom he'd not seen in years had unexpectedly come to visit – and there he was – my brave bank teller! He recognised me, of course, though he made out that he did not. Not because he was afraid, but because the old headman was so proud of boasting to his brother that he had 'met the Crown Prince and Princess when they were on their uppers' that clearly his brother did not have the heart to upstage him. (I might add that I had made sure that the money he had 'borrowed' for me was returned discreetly, no questions asked.)

We went to a ceremony at Dremda on a beautiful night of full moon. The waterfall was flowing again, if not yet to its full volume; the muddy water had cleared and the trees had grown new leaves. It was no longer an empty place, for the moon-sisters had emerged, from all corners of the land, out of hiding and had come to gather. The old ones who had never dreamed this day would ever come; the middle-aged ones who no longer had to keep their secret; the young ones who had only recently learned of their heritage – all had new hope in their eyes as they clustered around us with soft exclamations and garlands of roses and hazel leaves. The oldest of them all solemnly presented us with *The Book of Thalia*, and as Ash and I turned the page together, these words appeared:

The protection of Dremda will always be with you and evermore will your names be spoken with love and honour.

Then everyone cheered and we were led to a bower garlanded with flowers, by the side of the pool. We were given dishes of honey and cream, and soon the solemnity of the occasion dissolved in the sweetness of the meal, and the happy chatter and laughter of the moon-sisters.

There remains just one more thing to tell. We planted the hazel twig in the palace gardens the day after those tumultuous events and it has flourished there ever since. It has become a hazel tree of great beauty and every so often, when I'm at court, I go to sit under it and think – about my mother, about Ash, about the past and the present, and the future. I have plucked no leaves from it since that day, for I know in my heart that is not what it is for, now. One day, I may need the magic again, and I know it will not fail me. But right now the hazel is there as a living reminder of the greatest enchantment of them all: the true and enduring magic of love.

Three Wishes

Isabelle Merlin

Careful what you wish for . . .

When Rose creates a blog for an English assignment, she doesn't realise it will change her life. An elegant stranger arrives to announce that Rose has an aristocratic French grandfather who would like to meet her.

Rose arrives in France to find that her grandfather lives in a magnificent castle. Utterly enchanted, she grows to love her new life – and Charlie, a charming boy who is equally besotted with Rose.

But as Rose begins to delve deeper into her family's past, her fairytale turns into a nightmare. Who is friend? Who is foe? Someone wants her dead. And she must find out who before their wish comes true!

Available at all good retailers

Read on for the first chapter

Careful what you wish for

*C*areful what you wish for. That's always the message in those old stories where someone gets given three wishes. Careful – don't say the first thing that pops into your head . . .

In my mind, it all starts with the blog. I know in many ways that's not really true. It started a long time before that, years ago in fact, even before I was born. But in my mind, it doesn't feel like that. It feels like somehow, before the blog, my life was the same as it had been for the last eight years, since I first went to live with Aunt Jenny after my parents died in the crash. And it seems like, after the blog, things began to get weird . . .

The blog began as an English assignment. Our teacher, Ms Bryce, told us that she thought it would be interesting for us to use 'cutting-edge new media' alongside 'conventional essays and stories'. But she wanted it to be a proper blog, not just the add-on diary kind you have on MySpace or Bebo. It was supposed to have a theme and she was very excited about the project.

Not so most of the class. My best friends – Portia Warren, Alice Taylor and Maddy Fox – groaned and moaned about it. I pretended to moan too. But secretly

I didn't mind at all. I never mind writing, as long as it's creative stuff. I really want to be a writer. A really good, best-selling kind of writer. But I don't like ordinary English assignments much. You know the kind I mean – ones where you have to write about the meanings and messages in books. I can do it okay, but I just don't like it. It spoils good books and makes boring ones even more boring.

I didn't want to set my blog around a serious theme, like some of the ideas Ms Bryce had put up on the board: 'Famous Writers', 'Issues of History', 'Great Journeys' and stuff like that. Or even the humdrum sorts of ideas, like 'My Holidays', or 'My Family History' (that was hardly something I could write about back then anyway, as I knew practically nothing about it). I wanted to do something fun and a bit out there. So I decided I'd do it around the theme of three wishes, you know, the kind given by fairies.

When I was a little kid, I totally believed in fairies. I was sure that by squinting my eyes a bit and looking really, really hard, I would actually see them. I read fairy books and I looked at fairy pictures and I thought and thought about what I would ask for if a fairy popped up beside me one day and declared she'd come to grant me three wishes. I wrote down wishes on little bits of paper and left them under my pillow or under trees or anywhere I thought a fairy might find them. One year, I actually got the wish I'd asked for: a beautiful fairy-princess doll all dressed up in this gorgeous sky-blue dress and bright silver shoes, with gauzy wings and a crown. I knew fairies existed then, because you couldn't find anything like her in the shops. She was special. She was unique. She was fairy magic come to me. Her name was Celestine and I loved her to bits.

But the next year, everything changed. I was at school one day when the principal came into my classroom. She looked very pale. She took me to her office and told me that Mum and Dad had been in a terrible head-on smash with a truck on the highway and that they had died – Dad instantly and Mum on the way to hospital. They'd had no chance, she said, no chance at all. I can still remember how she began to stutter as she spoke and her face looked all crumpled, and how she kept saying, 'Oh, you poor little thing, Rosie! You poor little thing!' and trying to hug me. I remember a fly buzzing around that hot room, and alighting once on the principal's nose. But I don't remember how I really felt. They said afterwards I was in shock.

Aunt Jenny came very soon after and she took me home – to her home, that is. I knew her already quite well because she and my mum Annie, the younger of the two, were very close and always popping round to see each other. It wasn't far, anyway – Aunt Jenny lived in the next street. She looked after me, comforted me and tried hard over the next few years to be both father and mother to me, though it was hard for her. She missed my parents almost as much as I did and she didn't have much money.

My parents hadn't left any money, either. They had good jobs, but they had never been able to save. They loved to enjoy themselves and do fun, extravagant things, like hiring a Rolls Royce to drive to the beach, where we'd have a magnificent picnic, served by a waiter in a tuxedo. Or they might get a joy-flight over the mountains – Dad had his pilot's licence – or buy beautiful clothes or gorgeous toys for me. So they would max out their credit card and just do whatever they felt like, and I loved it. Anything, it seemed, could happen with them. Come to think of it, maybe that's why it was so easy for me to believe in fairies and things like that. My parents sprinkled fairy dust over everything. And it wasn't just to do with spending money, either. They loved each other, and me, really, really dearly, and they weren't afraid to show it and to tell me, over and over again.

So when they died, for me the fairies died too. I couldn't believe in magic wishes any more, because the only thing I wanted during that terrible time was for the accident never to have happened and Mum and Dad and I to live happily together back in our own home. And though I wished it ever so many times, it never came true, of course. Eventually, I settled down to life with Aunt Jenny, and though I missed my parents terribly, as the years passed the ache of their absence grew softer. That was partly time passing, and partly it was because of Aunt Jenny. She's much more anxious than my mum and dad were and sometimes she fussed and flapped, but she was also very kind and loving and I couldn't have asked for a better guardian. The only thing that was a real problem was money. Aunt Jenny worried about that constantly.

Aunt Jenny's a dressmaker, a really good one, but she's a hopeless businesswoman. She's too nice. A soft touch, some people say. She gives discounts to people who could really afford to pay full price. And she makes excuses for people who don't pay on time and who make out they're too skint to pay straightaway. And so money's always tight.

She worked from home, in the back room of our flat, which she'd set up as a workroom. It's a rather nice room, actually, big and full of light, with a couple of tall old-fashioned mirrors on stands, and two tailor's dummies, and beautiful black and white framed photographs of film stars on the walls. Aunt Jenny loves the glamorous actresses of the past, like Grace Kelly, Audrey Hepburn and Marilyn Monroe. There are shelves for the materials, a filing cabinet for the patterns, a table for the sewing-machine and comfy chairs for the customers to sit on when they're ordering stuff. And there's a CD player for the music Aunt Jenny likes to play when she's sewing. It's nearly always from the same era as those film stars – jazz, mostly. I think she'd have liked to live in a world like that, a dreamworld of elegant ease and effortless sophistication. She'd like to have had a design studio catering to those glamorous beauties.

Aunt Jenny makes all kinds of clothes, but she specialises in evening dresses. She's really, really good at those. Slinky satin or full-skirted organza, the latest thing or vintage style, she'd make something gorgeous, with beadwork and sequins and lace and stuff sewn on by hand. She'd love to make mostly the kinds of clothes worn by those classic film stars, and sometimes she can persuade people that's what they should want. But not often. People mostly want things they see in gossip mags, the clothes they see celery-stick-thin modern celebrities wearing. Aunt Jenny gets disappointed – she thinks a lot of modern fashion simply doesn't suit most normal body shapes – but she has to do what the customer wants. And she always makes it beautifully, no matter what she thinks.

When I was little, Aunt Jenny would sometimes use the scraps from some splendid evening dress to make me fabulous costumes for school plays or fancy dress parties or Book Week parades, all those sorts of things. And, as I learned later, it was she, of course, who had made me my Celestine doll . . .

Anyway – getting back to my blog, I'd decided I'd go back to my childhood obsession and write about three wishes. Don't ask me why I returned to something I thought I'd left behind. It just seemed like a good idea at the time. Now I think it's kind of spooky.

The internet's such a weird place. Sometimes it feels to me like a fairytale kind of country. There are trolls and wizards and zombies and people hiding out under false names and others who transform themselves into what they're not. There are all kinds of nasties waiting to trap the unwary and then there are good fairies who make amazing things happen. You can have invisible friends – people you've never met in the flesh. All sorts of odd magic, good and bad, seems to hover there. It was back to the old wishes under a pillow kind of thing – except this time on the web. Maybe that's why calling my blog Three Wishes seemed like a good fit.

When I'd finished setting it up, I thought it looked pretty cool. Ms Bryce did too. She gave me full marks for it. But seeing it up there, in that smart and professional-looking format, made my heart beat faster. What if – you never knew – what if the blog attracted attention from people other than my friends? What about if a publisher saw it, and thought, *Hey, this girl can write, maybe I'll ask her to do a book!* I'd heard of that happening before, that bloggers were discovered by publishers, and their dream of writing a real book came true. I didn't think about it too much, because I knew it was unlikely. But it was at the back of my mind, some of the time at least.

Okay, you might be thinking, what about those three wishes then? What did you write? Well, you can go and have a look at my blog for the full deal – it's at http://fairychild3wishes.blogspot.com. But basically they were:

1. To win a lot of money in the lottery so Aunt Jenny doesn't have to scrimp and save (we occasionally get lottery tickets but have never won anything).
2. A pair of silver shoes like Celestine's, except in my size.
3. For something exciting to happen to me, because I want to be a really good and popular writer and how can you be that if you just live an ordinary, humdrum kind of life?

In my first post, I'd written, very solemnly, about how you had to be careful what you wished for. ✿⊱ (Don't forget that whenever I've included this rose, it means you can go and look at my blog, http://fairychild3wishes. blogspot.com, to see what I wrote.) I wrote about the people who made stupid wishes and what happened to them. I wrote about people who didn't think things through. I thought I was safe from that because I had really thought about those three wishes. I didn't want to ask for impossible things. No time-travel or supernatural powers or what have you, just things that might come true. Portia, Alice and Maddy wrote down their own wishes in the comments boxes and I thought their wishes were a good deal more unrealistic than mine. Alice even asked for a magic wand! (Mind you, I used to try out that one on the fairies when I was a little kid – I thought you could then trick them into giving you unlimited wishes.) I believed I'd taken my own advice really rather well, and heeded the warning message of those old stories. What I didn't realise back then was that 'careful what you wish for' isn't really just advice or even a warning. *It is a threat.*

Pop Princess

Isabelle Merlin

A ticket to a millionaire lifestyle . . .
or a one-way trip to the underworld?

It's a simple twist of fate that catapults Australian teenager Lucie Rees from her ordinary life in an ordinary town to a strange, exciting job in Paris as friend to ultra-famous but troubled young pop star Arizona Kingdom. But it is more than a simple twist of fate that will see Lucie entangled in mysterious happenings that soon put her in terrible danger.

Who can she trust? Will the holiday of a lifetime in Paris turn into her last days on earth?

Available at all good retailers

Cupid's Arrow

Isabelle Merlin

Love at first sight has never been so terrifying.

It's been a while since 16-year-old Fleur Griffon has had one of the weird and scary dreams that used to plague her childhood. So she's really creeped out when she starts dreaming of being hunted through a dark forest by an unseen, sinister archer.

But when her bookseller mother unexpectedly inherits the magnificent library of a famous French author, Fleur forgets all about her fears. Excitedly, mother and daughter travel to Bellerive Manor, near the ancient French town of Avallon, reputedly the last resting place of the 'real' King Arthur. And it is there, in the magical green forest near Bellerive, that Fleur meets a handsome, mysterious boy called Remy Gomert. It seems to be love at first sight, beautiful as a dream.

But Fleur's nightmare is just about to begin . . .

Available at all good retailers

Bright Angel

Isabelle Merlin

Sylvie is in the wrong place at the wrong time . . .

When Sylvie and her older sister Claire survive a horrific encounter with a gunman, they're sent to stay with their aunt in the south of France for a change of scene. There, Sylvie meets a charming, enigmatic little boy called Gabriel, who tells her he can see an angel sitting on her shoulder. Not so charming is Gabriel's fiercely protective older brother, Daniel, who's just plain rude. But it's love at second sight when Sylvie gets to know Daniel better – until Gabriel disappears and Sylvie starts to wonder if Daniel is telling the whole truth about his family. And then there's Mick, the geeky guy who has a major crush on Sylvie . . .

Why does life have to be so complicated? And how can such a beautiful village hide such dark and dangerous secrets? Sylvie will need all her courage, the skills of the mysterious Houdini – and the blessing of the angels – to see her friends and family again.

Available at all good retailers